IT'S HIS SAVAGE LOVE FOR ME

A Romance Collection

DANI LITTLEPAGE
TINA MARIE

It's His Savage Love For Me

Copyright © 2020 by Dani Littlepage & Tina Marie

All rights reserved.

Published in the United States of America.

All rights reserved. No part of this publication may be reproduced, distributed, or transmitted in any form or by any means, including photocopying, recording, or other electronic or mechanical methods, without the prior written permission of the publisher, except in the case of brief quotations embodied in critical reviews and certain other noncommercial uses permitted by copyright law. For permission requests, please contact: www.colehartsignature.com

This is a work of fiction. Names, characters, places, and incidents either are the products of the author's imagination or are used fictitiously. Any resemblance of actual persons, living or dead, businesses, companies, events, or locales is entirely coincidental. The publisher does not have any control and does not assume any responsibility for author or third-party websites or their content.

The unauthorized reproduction or distribution of this copyrighted work is a crime punishable by law. No part of the book may be scanned, uploaded to or downloaded from file sharing sites, or distributed in any other way via the Internet or any other means, electronic, or print, without the publisher's permission. Criminal copyright infringement, including infringement without monetary gain, is investigated by the FBI and is punishable by up to five years in federal prison and a fine of $250,000 (www.fbi.gov/ipr/).

This book is licensed for your personal enjoyment only. Thank you for respecting the author's work.

Published by Cole Hart Signature, LLC.

Mailing List

To stay up to date on new releases, plus get information on contests, sneak peeks, and more,

Go To The Website Below...

www.colehartsignature.com

IT'S HIS SAVAGE LOVE FOR ME

The Atlanta Edition

DANI LITTLEPAGE

1

"We've been debating about this for ten minutes now." Darrin chuckled. "Are we going to dine in tonight, or are you gonna let me take you somewhere nice this evening?"

"Darrin, we just went out for dinner over the weekend," Sybil protested. "We had a delicious seafood dinner at McCormick & Schmick's, and you wanna go out for dinner again?"

"See? That's the thing about eating. It's a daily thing, shawty."

"Shut up." She laughed. "Fine. We can go out for dinner tonight, but we're gonna have to limit our dinner dates to twice a week. There are other things we can do together besides eat, Darrin," Sybil stated.

"You're right. So is seven p.m. cool?"

. . .

"Yes, that's fine."

"A'ight. See ya later, shawty."

"Lata."

Placing her phone face down on her desk, Sybil was all smiles as she thought about the man, she'd been dating for the past three months. Out of all the men that she'd come in contact with over the past year, Darrin was a gift from God to Sybil. He had his own trucking company, made good money, knew how to treat a lady, and had his own everything, and what she loved most about him was that Darrin was a man of his word. She also loved the fact that he was consistent. Sybil didn't have to guess if he was interested in her or what he wanted. He let it be known for the jump that he wanted her to be his lady. She never thought that a late-night trip to the gas station could change her life, but Sybil was grateful she gave him the time of day.

After daydreaming for a few seconds, the voice of the receptionist came through on the intercom, letting her know that her next appointment had arrived. Granting her permission to let them in, Sybil looked for a patient's file in the small pile of folders on the left-hand side of her desk. When a sixteen-year-old girl entered her office with her mother, Sybil could tell by the expressions on their faces that neither of them were happy to be there. Standing to her feet to greet them, she shook their hands before they all sat down. After explaining why they were called in, Sybil informed them that the young girl was pregnant. Instantly, the mother became irate while tears rolled down the child's face. It took her a few moments to calm the mother

IT'S HIS SAVAGE LOVE FOR ME

down, and when she did, she informed them of the options they could choose to handle the situation they were faced with. Agreeing to go through with the pregnancy, Sybil prescribed prenatal vitamins for the child and scheduled her next appointment. Once she handed the mother her card, she told them that they could call her if they had any questions before they left the office.

THROUGHOUT HER WORKDAY, SHE HAD KIDS BETWEEN THE ages of twelve to eighteen coming in her office for pregnancy and STI testing. A few people came in for regular checkups, but those were the bulk. Working as a family nurse practitioner at Planned Parenthood allowed her to see people from all walks of life from the young to the elderly. The teenagers that came in reminded Sybil of her twenty-year-old son that was attending Lincoln University in Pennsylvania, which was her and her son's father alma mater. Since learning that he lost his virginity at fifteen, she worried about him getting an STI or getting some little hot ass girl pregnant. Every time she talked to him, she reminded him to use condoms and not to give her any grandchildren until after he graduated. Thanks to her son living with his father since he was ten, he managed to stay on the right track so far. His freshman year was going to be over soon, and she was so proud of the grades he was pulling in and the man he was growing into.

AFTER A LONG DAY OF WORK, SYBIL SAID HER GOODBYES TO the staff as she headed out the door. Popping the locks to her 2019 atomic-silver Lexus ES, she tossed her Chanel purse in the passenger's seat before getting comfortable behind the wheel. After she put the key in the ignition, she revved the engine, put the car in drive, pulled out the lot, and headed to her home in Sandy Springs, GA. At age thirty-five, Sybil was a remarkably successful and independent woman. She had a successful career, she made six figures, and her house, along with her car, was paid off. She paid her bills on time and had the financial freedom to do anything under sun.

ALTHOUGH SYBIL GOT KNOCKED UP AT THE AGE OF FOURTEEN, she was determined to make something of herself. With the help of her grandmother, she and her baby father were able to graduate from high school and college. After receiving a degree in nursing, Sybil was torn between continuing her education and raising her child. Once her baby's father, James Bennett, convinced her that he could raise their child on his own, she moved to Winston-Salem, NC to attend the state university where she received her master's and doctoral degrees. When she completed her college education, a couple of her sorority sisters informed her of the many job opportunities they had in Georgia. After spending a few months with her son in Philly, Sybil moved in with one of her friends and began her nursing career at the age of twenty-eight.

BEING AWAY FROM HER SON, WYATT, WAS VERY DIFFICULT FOR her to deal with. Although she tried to call him daily and went to visit him whenever she could, Sybil felt like a failure as a parent. She felt like she put her education over her child, but she knew that wasn't the case. Everything she'd accomplished was for her and her son. Sybil made sure Wyatt knew that, no matter how many times she had to remind him.

THIRTY-FIVE MINUTES LATER, SHE PULLED INTO THE DRIVEWAY of her five-bedroom and five-and-a-half-bathroom home. Killing the engine, Sybil snatched up her purse, slammed the door shut, and let herself in the house with her key. Heading in the living room, she flopped down the couch, kicking off her Christian Louboutin pumps. The silence in her home was something she'd grown comfortable with. It was her gift and curse. Some days, Sybil wanted someone there with her, but other days, she wanted to be alone. She wanted someone there that day. As she continued to relax on her couch, her ringing phone interrupted that. Removing her phone from her purse, she smiled when she saw it was her son calling.

"Wassup, Mom," Wyatt cheerfully greeted.

"Hello, my son," she sang. "How are you doing?"

"I'm good. I passed my math and history exam I took last week."

"Way to go, baby," she boasted. "See what happens when you don't try to study all the material in one night?"

"Yeah." He chuckled. "I studied throughout the week and went over the notes I took before my history exam. It was a cakewalk."

"That's my boy. I'm so proud of you, Wyatt," Sybil squealed.

"Thanks, Mom."

. . .

"So what's on your agenda for summer? I'm already making plans to be in Philly for a month so we can spend time together."

"That's what I wanted to talk to you about. I wanna come stay with you for the summer."

"Seriously?" She gasped in shock.

"Yeah. Every holiday and summer, you come to Philly to see me. I feel like I should come see you this time. See how you're living down there in the A," Wyatt replied.

"Oh my God! I would love that!"

"I knew you would." He laughed. "I have finals for the next two weeks. As soon I'm done, I'm gonna be on my way down there."

"That's fine with me. Are you coming by yourself, or are you bringing someone with you?"

"I don't know yet, but I'll let you know soon."

"A'ight."

. . .

"Is there anything I need to know before I get down there?"

"Like what, son?" Sybil asked, confused.

"Are you living with or dating anybody?"

"Well, I am dating someone," she responded shyly. "You'll meet him when you get down here."

"Tell me about him."

Giving her son the rundown on Darrin, she made sure not to leave out the important details like how respectful he was to her and how she enjoyed spending time with him. After informing him of his two kids, she knew that Wyatt was looking forward to meeting Darrin, even if was just to interrogate him. Ending the call a few minutes later, Sybil excitedly danced through her living room and up the stairs to her master bedroom, where she began looking for an outfit for her date. She couldn't believe that her son wanted to spend the summer with her. Sybil was looking forward to performing her motherly duties for him. Even though he was grown, he was still her baby, and she couldn't wait to spend the summer bonding with her son.

2

As Jace sat in his last class of the semester, he was pissed that he received low C's on his last three exams. With finals starting that upcoming week, that meant he had to get a B+ or better on his final exams to maintain his B average. Since he received low scores on his exams, he was going to do the mature thing and study instead of partying. Just the thought of studying irritated Jace. All he wanted to do that weekend was pack, spend time with his homies, and fuck his bitches one last time before they left for summer break. If he wasn't on academic probation, due to a horrible first semester of his sophomore year, he wouldn't have been so hard on himself. Taking full responsibility for his fuck-ups, Jace was determined to get off academic probation and keep his promise to his mom and his homie's dad.

When his class was over, he turned on his Beats wireless headphones before heading out. With 50 Cent's *Get Rich or Die Tryin'* album playing, Jace walked through the campus, saying wassup to a few familiar faces as he headed to his dorm. As he jogged up the stairs to his room, he removed his key, letting himself in. When he saw his roommate and right-hand man, he turned his music off.

"Wassup, Dub Beezy?" he greeted glumly, giving him a handshake.

"Ain't shit, man. Why you looking like that?" Wyatt asked with a shirt in his hand.

"I can't go to the party tomorrow night. I gotta study for finals." Jace tossed his backpack on his bed. "I got low C's on my last three exams. So now I gotta ace these finals in order to pass my classes."

"Damn, JC," Wyatt solemnly responded. "Well, look at this way, you still passed, and as far as studying, when you're finished, I'll quiz you on the material."

"A'ight." Jace cheered up a little."

"And lucky for you, my nigga, that party has been moved to tonight. So we can party hard tonight and start studying tomorrow." Wyatt grinned.

"Bet!" He clapped his hands together, no longer worried about his test. "So what's ya plans for the summer? I know you ya pops got something planned."

"Actually, I'm spending the summer in Atlanta with my mom." He grinned. "I told her about it the other day, and she was hype as fuck that I wanted to spend the summer with her."

"Damn, man. Them bitches in the A bad as fuck. I know you gonna act a fool down there." Jace joked.

"You know I am, but I ain't just gonna be slanging dick all summer." He laughed. "My pops told me that I gotta get a job while I'm down there so I can have some money in the bank when I return for school. He thinks my mom is gonna spoil me by giving me anything I want because she doesn't see me that often." Wyatt shook his head.

"I can understand why she would want to. You've been living with ya pops since you were ten. You told me that the only time you've seen your mom was holidays, your birthday, and a month during the summer. She probably feels a little guilty about not being able to spend that much time with you over the years." He flopped down on his bed.

"I know she does, but I told her that I understood why she was away and that I wasn't mad at her. My mom spent like eight years in school so she could have a career, and she has that now. She worked hard to be an example for me, and because of that, she's successful in life. She has no reason to feel guilty," Wyatt honestly answered. "I love my mom."

"Yeah, I know. Every time I turn around, ya ass always on the phone with her." He laughed.

"Fuck you, JC." Wyatt flipped him the bird.

"Man, I wish I was going with you to Atlanta. I'm gonna be bored as fuck this summer without you."

"How about you roll with me?"

"Word?"

"Yeah, man. My mom has a five-bedroom crib with five and a half bathrooms. She showed me my room, and I can't wait to get there." He widely grinned. "We even got a pool, my nigga."

"Count me the fuck in!" Jace excitedly jumped to his feet. "I can't wait to meet ya mom."

"I just hope we'll still be cool when the summer is over." Wyatt sighed.

"Why wouldn't we be?" Jace asked, confused.

"You'll see when we get there."

Shrugging off his homie's comment, Jace began packing his things as they continued talking about all of the things they wanted to do in Atlanta and how he was going to ask his mom, Hazel, if he could go away from the summer. Hazel, like all mothers, was overprotective of Jace. Besides the stereotypes society had against men of color, due to his older brother getting locked up for attempted murder, his mother was trying to make sure he didn't go down the wrong road. Although she put a lot of pressure on him to do well in school, Jace understood why she did. For that reason, he was trying his best not to let her down.

After the duo packed away most of their things, Wyatt dipped out to meet up with one of his chicks while Jace picked out his drip for the night. Copping a squat at his desk, Jace

IT'S HIS SAVAGE LOVE FOR ME

smirked as he read the text from one of his chicks, telling him that she was on her way over to do some freaky shit to him. Cleaning up a little bit, Jace lit an incense to make the room smell good. As he waited for his sex buddy to arrive, he couldn't help but think about the conversation he and Wyatt had earlier. He couldn't understand why they wouldn't be cool at the end of the summer. Since meeting him at the freshman mix and mingle, he and Wyatt had been inseparable. Even though their family dynamics was different, they had a lot of things in common. He was the one that helped him get back on track with his grades. Jace had nothing but the utmost respect for his right hand. So, he couldn't understand why he would say some shit like that, but he was curious to find out why he did.

3

After spending the past two weeks moving his things to his dad's crib and taking finals, Wyatt couldn't wait to get to Atlanta. All he did was brag about all the things he and his mom were going to do while he was there. Instead of flying down like he wanted to, his father insisted on driving him down there. His dad claimed he wanted to spend some time with him before he went away, but Wyatt believed that his dad just wanted an excuse to see Sybil and how she was living. When he learned that the drive was twelve and half hours, he had his doubts about spending that much time in the car with his old man. With interesting conversation, music, and his dad letting him drive, the road trip went better than expected.

With only an hour left of their drive, Wyatt gazed at the window at the six lanes of traffic on the expressway. Although he was hype about spending the summer with his mom, he was having second thoughts about inviting Jace to come with him. He was afraid that his homie would try to hit on his mom like his friends in the past did. Whenever his mom would come to his school for a conference or ceremony, they always thought that Sybil was his sister or friend instead of his mom. For Sybil to be fourteen years older than him, she looked very young for her age. She reminded him of the actress Nia Long when she played in *Friday*. He thought back to all the arguments and fistfights he'd gotten into with friends and strangers for saying disrespectful shit out their face about his mom. He lost a lot of friends because of his mom's attractiveness, and Wyatt was afraid that the same thing was going to happen with Jace.

"Aye, son." James tapped his shoulder. "What you thinking about over there?"

"Just having doubts about Jace coming down." Wyatt sighed. "I got a feeling that he's gonna try to hit on my mom like the rest of my friends did in the past."

"I was wondering when you were gonna say something about that. When you told me that you invited him down here with you, I thought you forgot about the promise you made to never bring ya friends around your mom again." He chuckled.

"Nah. I ain't forget about that. I guess I invited him so I wouldn't be alone while mom was at work and spending time with her nigga." Wyatt shrugged.

"Ya mom is seeing someone now?" his dad asked in shock.

"Yeah. His name is Darrin." He glanced over at James. "He's gonna be at the crib along with his two kids."

"When I talked to Sybil the other day, she didn't tell me that she was dating."

"Did you tell her that you've been married for almost three years?"

"You got a point there."

"I didn't think you and mom talked about things other than me."

"Son, I've known ya mom for two decades, and just because we haven't been together in years doesn't mean we're not friends. Believe it not, I still care about ya mom a great deal. If I wouldn't have made the foolish mistake of cheating on her and getting ya stepmom pregnant while we were in college, I woulda married Sybil right after graduation," James admitted.

The car fell silent for a moment.

"So what are you gonna do about Jace? You know he's flying down with his mom tomorrow."

"I'ma give my homie the benefit of the doubt. He's looking forward to being down here for the summer, and I don't wanna fuck up his summer. Plus, if he does hit on her, I'm sure Mom will set his ass straight," Wyatt reassured him. "You think my mom and Ms. Hazel are gonna get along? You know she's a little on the ghetto side."

"A little?" He scoffed. "But nah, I'm not worried. Ya mom knows how to hold her own against any-damn-body. For her to only be five-six, she got more heart than most men."

As they chopped it up the rest of the way to his mom's crib, Wyatt's worries faded away for the moment. Instead of thinking about the negative, he decided to remain positive. Pulling into the driveway a half hour later, his mouth dropped at the sight of the beautiful home and the Lexus and BMW that was parked in the driveway. Honking the horn, the duo waited for Sybil to come out to greet them.

"Damn!" James gasped. "I knew Sybil was doing good in life, but I didn't know she was living like this. Look at this crib."

"I know, right! This shit dope as fuck!"

"Hold up. I know that ain't Sybil," James asked in disbelief.

"Yeah. That's her." Wyatt chuckled, watching his mom come out the house.

"Daammmnnn! She's finer than she was when we were younger!"

"Dad, get yaself together, man." He laughed.

"A'ight. I'm cool. Here we go."

༻✹༺

"Hey, Mom." Wyatt greeted her with a smile.

"Ahhh!" Sybil screeched. "My baby is here!" She tossed her arms around his neck.

Hugging her tightly, he lifted her off her feet.

"I missed you so much."

"I missed you too." He chuckled.

"Wassup, Sybil." James tried to keep his eyes on her face.

"Hey, James. It's good to see you," Sybil spoke when she was back on her feet.

"Same here. I see all of your years of school done paid off."

"Yes, it has." She nodded proudly. "Will you be joining us for brunch, James, or are you heading out?"

"If it's a'ight with you, I'd like to stick around for a lil' bit."

"Okay. Come on in. Y'all can meet my friend and his kids." She grinned widely.

With James and Wyatt following behind her, Sybil led the way to the kitchen, where Darrin and his children were.

"Darrin, kids, I'd like y'all to meet my son, Wyatt, and his dad, James. Wyatt and James, I'd like for y'all to meet my friend, Darrin, his daughter, Ivanna, and his son, DJ."

The men shook hands while Ivanna stood off to the side and waved. As the men conversed with each other, Sybil and Ivanna gathered the platters of food, carrying them to the dining room table.

"You have a very handsome son, Ms. Sybil." Ivanna shyly grinned, placing the platter of French toast on the table.

"Thank you, Ivanna." She smirked as she placed the bacon and fried chicken in the middle of the table.

"Do you think he'd like to hang out with me and a friend when his friend arrives?"

"I'm not sure," Sybil honestly answered. "You'll have to ask him."

"You wouldn't mind us hanging out together?" Ivanna asked, surprised.

"Not at all. I mean, you know all the party spots, and I'm sure Wyatt and Jace are gonna want to experience nightlife in Atlanta." She nodded.

"Thanks, Ms. Sybil." Ivanna smiled. "And I know how mothers are about their sons. I give you my word that I won't get Wyatt and Jace into any trouble."

"I'm holding you to that because Wyatt is my only child." Sybil pointed at her. "You get what I'm driving at?"

"Yes, ma'am."

"Hey, bae, we brought in the rest of the food from the kitchen," Darrin announced, entering the dining room.

"I got the juice, Mom," Wyatt held up the pitcher of mimosa.

"Thank you. Son, where's ya dad?"

"I think he's giving himself a tour of ya crib." He chuckled.

"Oh hell no he ain't," she stormed off to find him.

Before Sybil could march up the stairs, James came walking down them with a paper towel in his hands.

"Wassup?" He chuckled.

"I thought you were roaming around my house. You were point five seconds from getting cussed out," she warned.

He smirked. "I'm not roaming through ya crib, Sybil. I just needed to use the restroom before I hit the road." James reached the bottom of the stairs.

"You're leaving already?"

"Yeah." He sighed. "I just wanted to spend time with Wyatt and check out ya living arrangements. You're doing better than I expected," James admitted.

"And what did you expect?" Sybil placed a hand on her hip.

"It doesn't matter." He shook his head. "Tell our son I'll holla at him later."

Frozen in place, she watched her ex walk out the front door. Sybil was confused by his last statement and wanted to know what he meant, but she didn't want to press the issue. Her son was there, and nothing was going to kill her vibe. Pushing their conversation to the back of her mind, she strolled back to the dining room, where everyone had begun eating without her.

"Y'all must've been hungry." She smirked at them.

"I'm sorry, Mom, but it's been a while since I had a home-cooked breakfast." Wyatt stuffed his face.

"Don't they have eggs and stuff at Lincoln?" Ivanna asked.

"They do, but I don't eat their cooked breakfast. I don't trust it. All I eat is cereal and Hot Pockets for breakfast."

"Spoken like a true college student." Darrin joked, making everyone laugh.

"Well, I can't make any promises, but I'm gonna try to make as many home-cooked meals for you as I can, son." Sybil smiled.

"I'm looking forward to it." He chewed his food with a smile.

As they reminisced about their college days and Wyatt's summer plans, Sybil was happy with how well her male friend and son were getting along. Wyatt's opinion of Darrin and his family were especially important to her. Even though they still weren't official, she still wanted the two men in her life to get along.

After an hour and a half of bonding, Sybil, Wyatt, Ivanna, and DJ cleared off the table while Darrin went out back to take a phone call. Once the dishes were in the dishwasher, she escorted her son down to the finished basement, where he and his friend were going to be sleeping. The finished basement had a fifty-five-inch TV with a sound bar. The PS4 and Xbox One had all the latest games and instantly grabbed Wyatt's attention. The kitchenette, full bathroom, two separate bedrooms, and the fact that the basement had its own separate entrance earned Sybil some major cool points with her son. She watched in delight as her son examined every inch of his new living space.

"Well, son, how did I do?" she nervously asked.

"Mom, this house is dope, but this right here," he pointed to his surroundings, "you outdid yaself with this here. I love this, and my homie, JC, and his mom are gonna flip out once they see all this," he claimed with excitement.

"I'm glad that you're happy with the accommodations, son." Sybil smiled. "So is there anything I need to know about JC and his mom? It's been a long time since I met a parent of a friend of yours."

"Well, Ma, the only thing you need to know is that he and his mom are very... hood," Wyatt hesitantly answered.

"You mean they're ghetto?"

"Very." He laughed. "My homie grew up in southwest Philly, and his mom grew up in north Philly. All they know are the streets. Ms. Hazel is a hard-working single mom, and she's very overprotective of Jace. When you meet her, don't be offended if she asks you if you're some type of queenpin. They think that only ballers, entertainers, and drug lords live this good." Wyatt smirked.

"I used to think the same thing. So I do understand. Don't forget now, I'm a Philly native myself. Just because I'm living my best life doesn't mean I forgot where I came from." Sybil smirked.

"I heard that." He nodded his head in approval. "Are we finished with the tour, Ma? I wanna hop on the game for a minute."

"I have one more thing to show you, and I believe that once you see this, you're gonna forget all about that game." Sybil smiled. "Follow me."

Heading out the basement entrance, the duo made their way to the three-door garage in the front of the house. As they stood in front of the second garage door, Sybil opened the garage with the push of a button, revealing a blue 2018 BMW M3. Unable to hold his composure, she laughed as she watched her son race over to the car, jumping inside.

"Ma, is this really my car?" he asked excitedly.

"It sure is. I already got the title changed and added you to my insurance. All of the paperwork is in the glove compartment." Sybil walked over to the car.

"I can't believe you gave me a car! This is so dope! Thanks, Ma!" He jumped out, hugging her tightly.

"You're welcome, son." She giggled. "You can't live down here without a car, and since you're gonna be working and partying, you need your own whip." Sybil handed him the key.

"Wait 'til I tell pops and JC about this!" He took off running toward the basement.

"I see you gave him the news about the car." Darrin grinned on his way out the front door.

"You saw that, huh?" She chuckled, closing the garage with the remote.

"I really enjoyed meeting yo' son, bae." He met her in the middle of the driveway. "He's a real stand-up guy, and my daughter definitely has her eyes on him."

"She told me that she wanted them to hang out, and I told her that it was okay. I just warned her not to get my boy into any trouble." She wrapped her hands around his neck.

"I see your motherly instincts are kicking in."

"They never left. Just because my son was raised by his father doesn't mean I stopped being a mother. I worked damn hard to provide a better life for me and my son. I'm just glad he's here to enjoy all of this with me."

"I can see that my time with you is gonna be limited now that your son is here," Darrin spoke in a low tone.

"Just because Wyatt is here doesn't mean anything is gonna change between us, Darrin. We're still gonna have our date nights and alone time like usual," she assured him.

Kissing her lips passionately, Sybil melted in his arms as their tongues danced in each other's mouths. When Ivanna and DJ came rushing out the house, they broke their kiss before Darrin informed her that he was going to be out of town for about a week. One of his drivers were away on vacation, and he had to fill in. Upset by the news, Sybil pouted as she watched him hop in his truck and drive away. That was the third time since they met that Darrin had to fill in for one of his drivers. Although he needed to leave for work-related purposes, she felt like he was being called away for other reasons. This was one of the reasons why Sybil hadn't made things official yet. As she made her way back into the house, she went upstairs to her bedroom, where she flopped down on her bed. Snatching up her phone, Sybil confirmed her dinner date for the upcoming week with her sorority sisters. With Darrin gone for the week, it gave her a chance to brag to her friends about her handsome son spending the summer with her.

4

"Oh my God!" Hazel placed her hand over her chest. "I never thought I'd be soooo happy to be back on the ground." She took a few deep breaths.

"Since we're back on the ground, can you let go of my arm now." Jace tried to control his laughter.

"Don't be laughing at me, boy. You know I have a fear of flying." She released his arm.

"I know that, Ma, but do you have to be so dramatic? The flight was cool the whole time, but you still held on to me like the plane was about to crash." He shook his head.

"I wasn't being dramatic, Jace," Hazel pointed out. "I was holding on to you just in case something happened."

"If you say so, Ma." He smirked.

As the duo made their way off the plane, Jace was so excited to be in Atlanta that he walked ahead of his mom all the way to the car rental counter.

"I see ya ass is ready to get rid of me quick, huh?" Hazel rolled her eyes, standing next to him in line.

"I'm not tryna get rid of you, Ma. I'm just ready to see what the A has to offer. You know this is a turn up city, and I'm ready to see what this city is all about," Jace voiced with a grin.

"Yeah, well, all I know is you better not get none of these bitches down here pregnant. I'm not tryna be a grandma until I'm in my fifties, and I'm only forty-two."

"You ain't gotta worry about that," he confirmed. "I just wanna have fun and enjoy myself."

"And ya ass better get a job like you told me. You need to learn to be responsible and make ya own money. I don't mind helping you out, but ya ass is old enough to do some shit on ya own now."

"I know, Ma," Jace replied, annoyed. "You've been telling me this shit for the past two weeks."

"You better watch ya tone when you're talking to me." Hazel gripped him up by his shirt, drawing attention to them. "I will knock ya ass out in front of all these people if you take that tone with me again."

Nodding his head in understanding, she released Jace before taking her place at the counter. Once they had their car, Jace tossed their duffel bags in the back seat, then hopped in the passenger's seat. After typing in the address into the GPS on Hazel's phone, he handed her phone back to her as she pulled out of the lot. Finding a radio station, Jace stared out the window as he nodded his head to Lil Baby's *Drip Too Hard*. He admired the variety of cars that were on the expressway, and he was surprised at the amount of luxury cars that were on the road. He was impressed by the Porches, Ferraris, Bentleys, Benzes, BMWs, and Cadillacs he saw. The only people he knew that drove cars like that were street pharmacists, rappers, and athletes. Jace knew that being down south was quite different from up north living. The six-lane expressway and fancy cars were just a couple of them.

Twenty-five minutes later, they pulled into the driveway of the beautiful home with a three-car garage, and Jace and Hazel were lost for words. The Lexus and BMW that were parked in the driveway proved that Wyatt wasn't bullshitting about his summer living accommodations.

"Are you sure we're at the right house?" Hazel nervously asked. "I don't want to get arrested for trespassing."

"Ma, will you chill out? This is the right address. My homie told me that his mom pushes a Lexus and she gave him a BMW to roll in while he's down here. Plus, the address is right there above the door." He pointed.

"Wyatt's mama must be fucking a kingpin or some type of celebrity. I know for a fact that she can't afford this shit on her own," Hazel stated matter-of-factly.

"Please don't say that shit to her," Jace pleaded. "Please don't embarrass me."

"Boy, ain't nobody gonna embarrass you."

When Jace spotted Wyatt coming up the driveway, he jumped out, making his way over to him.

"Maaannnn, this crib is everything!" Jace exclaimed.

"I told you it was." Wyatt gave Jace a quick hug. "Wassup, Ms. Hazel?" He waved.

"Boy, you better get ya ass over here and give me a hug." She extended her arms.

"Sorry." He chuckled, hugging her tightly.

"So where's ya mom?"

"Here I am." A thick, curvy woman emerged from the house.

"JC, Ms. Hazel, this is my mom, Sybil Bailey. Mom, this is my homie, Jace, and his mom, Hazel," Wyatt introduced everyone.

Jace's and Hazel's mouths gaped in disbelief. After a few seconds of staring, Hazel erupted in laughter.

"Boy, if you don't stop playing with me." She playfully hit Wyatt's arm. "This child is not ya mama. Now stop messing around and go get ya mama please."

"I'm not playing, Ms. Hazel. This is *really* my mom," he expressed in a serious tone.

"Ma, I think he's serious." Jace continued to stare at the brown-skinned beauty.

"She looks young enough to be ya sister, Wyatt." Hazel gasped. "How old are you?"

"I'm thirty-five."

"Get the fuck outta here!" She looked her up and down. "And this is your house?"

"Yes."

"You own this, or are you renting?"

"I own everything you see out here." Sybil smirked.

"Bitch, stop!" Hazel shouted in disbelief.

Sybil couldn't help but laugh.

"Wyatt, take Jace and show him around or something. I need to talk to ya mama for a little bit."

"Okay," Wyatt replied, confused.

As the two women made their way into the house, Jace's eyes were glued to Sybil's round, fat ass until they disappeared inside. When he realized he was staring, he quickly got himself together before his homie could notice.

"Ya mom is wild, man." Wyatt chuckled.

"Tell me about it." Jace shook his head.

"Come on and let me show you where our rooms are."

Looking back at the front door, his mind drifted to Sybil and what they were talking about before following Wyatt down the driveway to the amazingly finished basement. A wide grin appeared on his face as his eyes landed on the game systems, the huge smart TV, and the kitchenette, but what he loved the most was the room he was staying in. The queen-sized bed was better than the twin-sized beds at school and his full-sized bed at home. Besides the dresser and mirror, the room was bare, but he planned on making it his own.

"So what do you think, man?" Wyatt grinned.

"This crib is way better than you described, Dub Beezy." He grinned. "Our summer is off to a great start already, and we ain't even do shit yet." Jace closed the door to his bedroom.

"I told you this crib was everything, JC. You haven't even seen the upstairs yet. Come on so I can give you a tour." He headed toward the stairs.

"Let's chill for a minute. I'll go upstairs once my mom

leaves." Jace shook his head. "I know she's probably asking ya mom all types of shit about her life. She's so extra sometimes."

"Don't worry. I already warned my mom. She knows how to handle herself." Wyatt chuckled, heading over to one of the two recliner chairs.

"Speaking of your mom, she seems nice." He tried to keep a straight face as he sat in the other recliner chair.

As he waited for Wyatt to respond, he knew by the expression on his homie's face that he struck a nerve.

"Let's cut the shit, man. What you really wanted to say is that my mom is she bad as fuck, right?"

"What?"

"Come on, man. Ya ass ain't blind. I know you see how attractive she is. So go 'head and say it." He sighed, annoyed.

"Why would I sit here and talk about ya mom like that, man?" Jace asked, confused.

"You don't know how many friends I've lost because they tried to hit om my mom or said some disrespectful shit about her in front of me. That's why I said I hope we're still cool after the summer. I thought you were gonna try to hit on my mom, too," Wyatt confessed.

"I know how you feel, man. I had a few homies that said they wanted to fuck my mom too when I was younger," Jace admitted. "But you don't have to worry about me doing that, Dub Beezy."

Giving his right-hand man a handshake, he was glad that he was able to put Wyatt's worried mind at ease. After getting that situation understood, they duo spent the next two hours playing *Call of Duty 4*. They were caught up in the game that they didn't hear their mothers enter the basement.

"I'm glad I'm making Jace's ass get a job because if I didn't, he'll be playing this damn game all summer," Hazel snidely replied.

"Wyatt played this game all night. He fell asleep with the controller in his hand," Sybil added.

"Y'all not gonna keep talking about us like we ain't sitting right here." Jace glanced back at them.

"And what you gonna do if we don't?" His mom stood in front of him.

"Come on, Ma. Move out the way." He tried to see around her.

Unable to see, Jace instantly died, and soon after, so did Wyatt.

"See, Ma? You made us die," he huffed.

"Boy, you got all summer to play that damn game. Now get up and give me a hug. Sybil is about to take me to my hotel. I need a nap."

Doing as he was told, Jace stood to his feet, hugging his mother tightly. He locked eyes with Sybil who was standing a few feet away, watching them with a smile. The light-denim Bermuda shorts and white tank she wore had her body on full display, even though it was mostly covered. Closing his eyes, he tried to push his thoughts of best friend's mom to the back of his mind and think about something else.

"I'm gonna miss you, son." Hazel kissed his cheek. "And you better call me a few times a week."

"I will, Ma, and I'm gonna miss you too." He kissed her cheek before releasing her.

"I'm gonna let you keep the rental car too. After talking with Sybil, I want you to have ya own vehicle to get around in. I know Dub Beezy ain't gonna mind taking you wherever you wanna go, but just in case y'all work schedules are different or you just wanna venture out on your own, you need ya own whip."

"Bet! Thanks, Mom!"

"You're welcome."

"Dub Beezy?" Sybil eyed her son, confused.

"It's just a nickname, Ma." Wyatt laughed.

"It's cute. I like it." She held her hand out for a pound, and he dapped her.

"Come outside with us so you can get ya bag out the trunk."

As Jace followed the women up the basement stairs, he shouted for Wyatt to put on *NBA 2K20*. Making their way outside, he admired how beautiful the main level of the house was on his way out the front door. When Hazel popped the locks to the car, he listened to the two women make plans for the evening and wondered how he and Wyatt were going to spend his first night in the city known for partying. Removing the bags from the backseat, Jace placed his mom's bag in the back seat of Sybil's Lexus. He hugged his mom once more before they got in the car and drove off.

Heading back in the house, he locked the door behind him, then strolled back to the basement. Ready to shout his return to his homie, Jace stopped himself when he saw that Wyatt was on the phone. He tossed his bag in his room before flopping down in his chair. As he picked the team he wanted to play with, he overheard Wyatt ask the person he was talking to about a party and what their friend looked like. After he confirmed the details, his homie ended the call, sporting a huge grin.

"I hope you're ready to party tonight, my nigga. We've just been invited to one of the hottest clubs in the city," Wyatt excitedly informed him.

"You've been down here for a day, and you already got invited out somewhere?" Jace asked, surprised. "My man," he quoted Denzel Washington from *American Gangster*.

He gave Wyatt a handshake, giving him his props.

"Who'd the invite come from?"

"Ivanna. She's the daughter of this nigga my mom is dating named Darrin. I met them yesterday, and shorty is bad as fuck, man."

"Word?"

"Hell yeah. She's thick as fuck, and I could be wrong, but I think she's got a thing for the kid," Wyatt boasted.

"Check you out." He smirked. "The young grasshopper has finally learned something from the master," Jace teased.

"Fuck you, man." Wyatt playfully swung at his friend.

"Well, don't make any decisions yet because once these hoes down here get a load of me, you won't be nothing but an afterthought."

5

It had only been a week that Wyatt and Jace had been staying with her, and Sybil was enjoying their company. The silence that she'd grown accustomed to was replaced with good vibes, conversations, and laughter. Every morning, she woke up an hour and half early to fix the boys breakfast before she went to work, and she cooked dinner for them as soon as she came home. Besides talking to Darrin on FaceTime three times a day while he was out of town, the highlight of her day was having dinner with the boys and hearing about their job search and the women that they came across. Although both boys were equally handsome, they were complete opposites. Both standing over six feet with muscular builds, Wyatt and Jace were like day and night. Her son was a cinnamon complexion, had a fade full of waves, cat-like eyes, and a charming smile. Jace, on the other hand, was the complexion of a Hershey's bar with a bleached high-top fade, dark-brown eyes, a bright smile, and a diamond stud in his right ear. While Wyatt was more of the romantic type, Jace didn't seem to know the meaning of the word. To Sybil, his ass was rude and conceited. Aside from his looks, she didn't understand what girls saw in him.

After another week of pregnant teens, STI tests, and counseling sessions, Sybil was more than ready to unwind with her girls that evening. She hadn't seen her sorority sisters in a month, and they had a month's worth of updates to catch up on. As soon as four o'clock hit, she snatched up her purse, said her goodbyes, and rushed out the door. Hopping into her car, Sybil drove through the crowded expressway to the Publix not too far from her house. She went food shopping for the house and made sure she got the boys specific snacks and sports drinks. Once she paid for her groceries, a few men offered to help Sybil with her bags, but she declined. As flattered as she was, they didn't compare to the man that currently had her attention. Pulling into the driveway of her home, she popped the truck before entering the house.

"Wyatt! Jace! Come get the groceries out the car!" she shouted down the basement.

"Okay!" they responded in unison.

A few seconds later, the boys came up the stairs, kissed her cheek, then went outside to get the bags. Placing her purse on the counter, Sybil took off her Jimmy Choo pumps before removing her phone from her purse, sitting on one of the barstools. As she checked her emails, the boys came in with their hands full of bags.

"How was y'all's day? Any luck with the job search?" she asked, placing her phone on the counter.

"Yeah. We received calls today telling us we're hired," Jace announced.

"That's great! So where will y'all be working?"

"At the Cumberland Mall." Wyatt began putting the groceries away. "I'll be working at Foot Locker."

"And I'll be working at Jimmy Jazz. I gotta call my mom and tell her the news." Jace grinned.

"Congratulations, boys." She smiled. "When do y'all start?"

"Monday," they replied in unison.

"Cool. So what do y'all want for dinner?"

"No need to cook for us tonight, Ms. Sybil. Me and Dub

Beezy have dinner dates tonight with two girls we met at the mall this week."

"Oh really?" she asked, surprised.

"Yup, and dig this, Ma. We ain't gotta pay for nothing. They're treating us to dinner." Wyatt did a little dance.

"Damn." Sybil chuckled. "Well, all of us will be out of the house tonight."

"Where you going?" her son asked in an authoritative tone.

"If you must know, I'm having dinner with a couple of my sorority sisters. It's something we do every month."

"I never knew you were in a sorority, Ma."

"Oh yeah. I'm about that life." She did one of her sorority poses. "You know ya dad is in a fraternity."

"I know. He wants me to join his frat." Wyatt sighed. "I don't think the whole pledging thing is me."

"Do some research on it, and just think about it, Dub Beezy." Sybil smirked.

Grabbing her phone off the counter, she made her way upstairs to her room, where she picked out an outfit for the evening. When she was finished, she removed her clothes before soaking in the tub for nearly an hour. After completing her body and skin care regimen, Sybil got dressed in a white knee-length sleeveless dress with a pair of royal-blue tassel heels and a royal-blue blazer. Finishing her look with diamond hoops, necklace and bracelet, she fixed her short bob before checking herself out in the mirror. Snatching up her phone, she snapped a couple of photos with her blazer on and off before sending them to Darrin. Ready to head out, she filled her white Dolce and Gabbana purse with what she needed then headed downstairs.

Heading to the kitchen to get something out of her other purse, Sybil heard the sliding doors opening and turned around to see Jace walking in.

"Hey, Jace. I don't want you and Wyatt staying out too late tonight. I know y'all think y'all grown and everything, but I still

33

would like for y'all to be home at a decent hour, and don't have any of those fast ass girls in my house."

Finding what she was looking for, she turned around to face Jace, who was eyeing her strangely. The ways his eyes scanned her body made Sybil a little uncomfortable, but she couldn't look away. His eyes were speaking to her, but she was unsure what they were saying.

"Jace?"

"Huh?" He snapped out of his trance

"Did you hear what I said?"

"Yeah. Yeah. You don't want us out too late and don't have no hoes in the house." His eyes remained trained on hers.

"Right. Have fun on y'all's date."

Turning to leave, Sybil felt that his eyes were still on her, and she switched out the door as quickly as she could, unaware that her ass was jiggling all the way out the door. Popping the locks to her car, she tossed her purse in the passenger's seat, slid behind the wheel, revved the engine, and pulled out of the driveway. As she headed to downtown Atlanta, her mind drifted back to the way Jace was staring at her in the kitchen. Sybil couldn't help but wonder why he was staring at her like that and if she should confront him about it. Deciding not to give it any more thought, she pushed it to the back of her mind and turned up Mary J Blige's *Just Fine* on her radio.

A half hour later, she arrived *Ruth's Chris,* an expensive restaurant and pulled up to the valet. When one of the valets opened her door, she warned him not to fuck up her car before heading inside. Giving the name of her party, the hostess escorted her to the table where her two friends were waiting for her. All smiles, her besties and line sisters, Leah and Dominique, stood to their feet to greet her. After hugging her friends, Sybil removed her blazer before sitting down at the table.

"I know it's only been a month since we've last seen each other, but it feels like it's been longer than that," Dominique, the beautiful redbone, stated.

"Yesss," Leah, the brown-sugar beauty, chimed in. "I don't care how busy we get. From now on, we gotta keep our monthly outings."

"I agree," Sybil added. "So what's new with y'all?"

"Girl, work has been kicking my ass for the past few weeks, and I almost ran away from my husband and kids." Dominique shook her head.

"Why?"

"What happened?"

"Y'all, I would get home from work, and my house would look like a tornado had hit it. Book bags in the middle of the floor, dishes piled high in the sink, and trash cans overflowing. In my bedroom, Glenn's clothes are all over the place, candy wrappers and soda cans all over the nightstand. Then, my husband expects me to cook in all this mess and help the kids with their homework. He gets home from work like two hours before me, but he wants me to do everything," she ranted. "So one day, I couldn't take it anymore. I cussed my kids and husband out so bad that I had them speechless. Then I left the house and went driving around the city until like two in the morning, and when I got home, my house was spotless." She grinned. "And it's been like that ever since."

"Damn, Dom!" Leah gasped in shock. "I hated that your family pushed you to that point, but you did what needed to be done to get results."

"Yes I did because they were testing my gangsta." She joked.

They all laughed, and the waiter approached their table a couple of seconds later. After ordering appetizers, entrées, and a bottle of wine, the waiter left their table with a smile to put their order in.

"So what's new with you, Leah?" Sybil asked, anticipating the answer.

"Nothing but this." She extended her left hand, exposing a diamond ring.

"Oh my goodness! Dominique screeched. "Are you and Levi engaged now?"

"Yes!" Leah beamed. "And y'all already know that I want y'all in my wedding."

"Congratulations, sis!" Sybil hugged her bestie. "And thank you for wanting us in your wedding."

As the trio discussed the details of Leah's wedding, the waiter brought them their appetizers and wine. After he got finished filling their glasses, the waiter took off, leaving them alone to eat. The crab cakes, barbeque shrimp, and stuffed mushrooms that were placed in front of them looked and smelled delicious. After taking a moment to bless the food, the trio dug in.

"So Sybil, don't think you're just gonna stuff yo' face with mushrooms and not give yo' girls an update on your relationship with Darrin." Leah pointed her fork at her.

"Mm-hmm," Dominique hummed. "Spill it."

"Okay." She laughed. "Me and Darrin are good. We're almost at the four-month mark, but we're still not official yet."

"What?"

"Why not?"

"I don't know..." she dragged out the word. "I guess I'm a little nervous about being in a relationship, and I have a feeling that Darrin isn't being honest about everything he's doing when he goes out of town," Sybil admitted.

"Has he given you a reason to feel like this?" Dominique asked, concerned.

"Not really," she answered honestly. "He called me every day he was away. When he can't talk, he texts. He's always wining and dining me." Sybil blushed. "Darrin is a really good man, and my son likes him too. I guess I'm just tryna find a reason to sabotage this."

"Girl, don't do that." Leah pointed at her. "Don't push away the best man you met after all the fools you've dealt with."

"That's right, Syb. You deserve to be happy, and if Wyatt

likes him, I call that a win in my book." Dominique shoved a shrimp into her mouth.

"So do I. So let that man love you and stop tripping," Leah encouraged.

"Okay. Okay," Sybil agreed.

"How are things going with yo' son and his friend?" Dominique questioned.

"It's going fine." She beamed. "I love having him down here with me. I'm gonna be in my feelings when it's time for him to leave."

"We're gonna have to stop by and see Mr. Wyatt. We haven't seen him since we graduated from Lincoln."

"Do you have a picture of your son and his friend? I wanna see them."

Removing her phone from her purse, Sybil went to her son's Instagram page and tapped on a photo of Wyatt and Jace they took that evening before going on their date. She handed her phone to Leah and watched her expression.

"Oh, Sybil! Wyatt has grown up to be a handsome young man, and his friend is handsome too!" Leah exclaimed, handing Dominique the phone.

"Girl! I know you got yo' hands full with these two." Dominique passed the phone back to Sybil. "I just know they got these young Atlanta heffas going crazy."

"From what they've told me so far, they do." She shook her head.

"I always wondered what it would be like to mess with a younger man." Leah smirked.

"You actually thought about that?" Sybil asked in disbelief.

"Hell yeah. The only reason I haven't is because of the stories I heard from the chicks who have."

"What stories?" The duo eyed her suspiciously.

"I heard that messing with a young boy in their twenties is a dangerous thing. They dick you down so good that these chicks were buying them any and everything they wanted. They ruined their relationships to be with these boys, only for them to leave them high and dry a few months later," Leah informed them. "Some of these chicks are still chasing what they had with their lil' tenderoni. Fucking with a young nigga can really fuck yo' life up."

After briefly discussing how good the young bucks were looking, the waiter returned with their entrées and refilled their glasses. The trio continued to laugh and talk the rest of the evening.

Nearly an hour later, they were putting their food in boxes. Finishing their wine, they paid the tab and left the restaurant. Once she gave her ticket to the valet, they waited for them to bring their cars. Hugging her besties goodbye, they got in their vehicles and drove home.

When she made it to her house, she wasn't surprised when she saw that Wyatt's car was still gone. Making her way in the house, Sybil sauntered upstairs and kicked off her shoes. After changing her clothes, she grabbed her phone from her purse before climbing into bed. Ready to call Darrin, she smiled when she saw that he was calling her on FaceTime. Answering the call, Sybil greeted him with a huge smile, and they talked until she dozed off to sleep.

6

After a month of being in Georgia, Wyatt had grown to love everything about Atlanta. The candy-painted cars with the rims, the nightclubs, and especially the girls. Since he arrived, he'd met over twenty Georgia peaches, but none of them stuck around no longer than a week. He tried to do the right thing by treating them with respect. He tried not to fuck them too soon and offered to take them out on dates, but they didn't want the gentleman treatment. The Georgia peaches he came across wanted to be treated like thots. Fast-food restaurants and forty dollars here and there. Wyatt couldn't understand why all the females that crossed his path played him to the left. After overhearing Ivanna's friend call him too nice, a pretty boy, and soft, the confidence he had in himself faded a little.

After working the day before, he was glad to have the next two days off. Although he loved his job at Foot Locker, Wyatt enjoyed having the house to himself on the weekdays he had off. If he wasn't in the house playing the game, he would go cruising around Georgia, checking out the different cities. On the weekends, he and Jace were at the hottest nightclubs, partying into the wee hours of the morning. After the club, they would hit up the Waffle House to eat with a couple females from the club before they went back to their places to bang their backs out. They had more than a few one-night stands since they touched down in the A, but Wyatt wanted something more than that. He wasn't looking for a relationship. Just a friend with benefits for the remainder of his time there, but now that his ego was bruised, he was deep in his feelings.

WAKING UP AT SEVEN THAT MORNING, HE DID A QUICK workout before hopping in the shower. With *Motivation* by T.I. coming through his Beats Pill speaker, Wyatt rapped the lyrics as he washed his body from head to toe. After lingering in the shower for a few more minutes, he stepped out, wrapped a towel around his waist, washed his face, and brushed his teeth. Taking a few moments to clean up behind himself, he headed back to his room and got dressed. A white tee, a pair of gray Nike sweatpants, Nike socks and slides is what he decided to lounge in for the day. Once he brushed his head, Wyatt snatched up his phone, then headed upstairs to the kitchen to eat breakfast. He appreciated how his mom went out of her way to prepare breakfast for him and Jace every morning and cooked dinner for them every night. Even though they didn't spend any one-on-one time together, he believed that their bond was getting stronger every night they spent together.

GRABBING A PLATE AND A GLASS FROM THE CABINET, HE PUT strawberry pancakes, sausage links, grits with cheese, and eggs on his plate before filling his glass with orange juice. As his phone began to ring, he placed his food and drink on the counter, then reached in his pocket for his phone. When he saw that it was Ivanna's friend, Rory, the one that called him soft, calling, he declined her call. Ready to dig into his food, his phone started ringing again. Taking a deep breath, he answered.

"Wassup?" he dryly greeted.

"Damn, Wyatt. That's how you greet me now? What happened to gorgeous and beautiful?"

"What you want, Rory?"
"I left my earrings and bracelet over there when I came to the cookout last week. Can I come by and get it?"

"Yeah. Ya shit gonna be in the mailbox."

"In the mailbox?" she asked, feeling some type of way. "I was hoping I could come in and chill with you for a little bit or something."

"I don't think so."

"And why the fuck not?" Rory became angry.

"'Cause I got something, or should I say someone, to do in a few hours." He lied with a smirk. "So like I said, ya shit will be waiting for you in the mailbox."

. . .

When she didn't reply, Wyatt hung up and began eating his food. Rory called him a few more times after that, but he didn't answer. He didn't decline the call or silence the ringing. He just laughed as he shook his head. Hearing footsteps downstairs, he knew that Jace was awake and ready to eat.

"Wassup, nigga," Jace grumbled.

"Ain't shit, man." Wyatt gave his boy a handshake. "How was the party last night?"

"Maaannn, that shit was litty like a motherfucka." He grinned, removing a plate and glass from the cabinet. "They had a twerk contest, and that shit got crazy. I ain't never seen twerking like that before. The shit they did should only be allowed that strip club, my nigga." Jace bragged as he fixed his plate. "The top three bitches that won had niggas all over 'em. The bouncers had to escort them to their cars when they left."

"Damn." He chuckled.

"A few bitches asked about you last night too." Jace filled his glass with juice.

"Oh yeah?"

"Yeah. Lisa, Asia, and Kim." He sat on the stool next to him.

IT'S HIS SAVAGE LOVE FOR ME

. . .

Wyatt nodded his head, not showing any interest. When he didn't respond, Jace spoke again.

"I heard you on the phone a little while ago. You were kinda cold to whoever you were talking to, Dub Beezy," Jace stated. "You straight, man?"

"I overheard Rory, Ivanna and the bitch they brought over here last week talking about me. She told them that I was soft, JC." Wyatt finished off his food. "I treated all of these females with respect. Texted and even called them, and they all played me to the left."

"I told ya ass before that these hoes don't want a nice nigga, man. They want savages. Niggas that's gonna make them chase 'em. You gotta be a lil' rude to these hoes to show 'em you ain't no pushover. Just like females make us work for them, we gotta make them work for us. Stop making shit too easy for 'em, man," he lectured. "Just like they think they're the prize, we're a prize too. Every bitch don't deserve *good morning* texts, dates, gifts, and their pussy ate."

"No the fuck they don't." Wyatt laughed.

"I'm glad you finally put that nice guy shit to the side and showed that you could be a little coldhearted. Now that you did that, Rory ain't gonna leave ya ass alone. Don't be surprised if she popped up over here tripping."

. . .

"She's supposed to be stopping by to pick up her earrings and shit. I told her it was gonna be waiting for her in the mailbox."

"Put that shit in there. That's only gonna piss her off more. I'm telling you, man. You're gonna see a different side of shorty," Jace reassured him.

Laughing at his friend, Wyatt headed over to the sink with his dishes in his hand. After washing them, he snatched up Rory's jewelry that was on the table next to the front door. He jogged to the mailbox, placed the items inside, and jogged back inside. Wyatt stayed in the kitchen talking with Jace until he was finished eating. When his plate was free of food, they washed all of the breakfast dishes before they headed back down to the basement to play the game. They discussed the activities that they wanted to do when they arrived back at Lincoln for their junior year. When Jace mentioned joining a fraternity and told him what it was about, Wyatt made a mental note to do some research on his own.

After an hour of game playing with Jace, he continued playing the game by himself while his boy got ready for work. As he continued to kick ass in *Tekken 7*, his focus was broken when someone began pounding on his door.

"Who the fuck is that?" Jace asked, angrily.

. . .

"Wyatt, open this fucking door right now!" a female yelled from the other side.

"That's Rory." Wyatt laughed.

"What I tell you, Dub Beezy?" He chuckled. "I'ma go out the front, but let me know how this turns out." Jace jogged up the stairs by twos.

"Wyatt, you better open this fucking door before I knock it down!"

Calming down his laughter, he took a deep breath before opening the door.

"Who the fuck you got up in here, huh? Where that bitch at?" She stormed past him.

He watched her go from room to room, looking for a bitch that wasn't even there. It was taking everything in him not to laugh at her ass, but it was difficult to do. When she got ready to go upstairs, he grabbed her by the arm, stopping her.

"Let me the fuck go," Rory shouted, pulling away.

"You better calm the fuck down, shorty," Wyatt shouted with bass in his voice. "Who the fuck you think you is coming up in here like you run shit? You done bumped ya head, man."

. . .

"You really put my shit in the mailbox and thought I wasn't gonna confront yo' ass?"

"You can't confront me about shit. You ain't my bitch. So just get ya shit and leave, Rory. We ain't got shit else to talk about." He released her arm.

"Why are you treating me like this, Wyatt?" Rory spoke in a soft voice. "I thought we were feeling each other, then yo' ass switched up on me. What happened?"

"I thought we were too, but then I realized I ain't ya type. You said I was too nice and soft, right? That's what you told Ivanna and Chante. So if I'm all that, just leave me the fuck alone,"

Wyatt harshly stated, turning his back on her.

Walking back to his reclining chair, he picked up the controller and continued playing the game. A few minutes later, she stood in front of the TV, making him pause the game.

"Wyatt, I didn't mean what I said, okay? The only reason I said that is because Chante was about to make her move on you. So I said what she wanted to hear to get her to back off," Rory admitted. "No nigga I've dealt with has treated me with the respect that you have. The *good morning* texts and the dinner dates we went on are special to me. When you fell back, I really felt some type of way. Shit, I still do."

"SO WHAT YOU SAYING?" HE STOOD TO HIS FEET.

"WHAT I'M SAYING IS... I FUCKS WITH YOU, WYATT, AND I wanna get to know you better." She stepped closer to him. "And I'm sorry for what I said."

"COME SHOW ME HOW SORRY YOU ARE."

FORCING HER TONGUE IN HIS MOUTH, WYATT DIDN'T HESITATE to grab her fat, round ass as they slobbed each other down. Lifting her pink sleeveless mini dress, his dick became hard as a rock when Wyatt noticed that she wasn't wearing any panties. Ready to get down to business, he ended their lip locking and bent her over. With her hands planted firmly on the arms of the chair, she looked back at him. His long, thick dick made Rory's mouth water, and she made a mental note to suck it before she left. Once he placed the condom on, he entered her wet pussy forcefully, causing her to moan. As he pounded her pussy from the back, Wyatt loved the way her ass jiggled with each stroke.

"YEEESSS, WYATT! FUCK THIS PUSSY, BOY!" SHE HISSED.

GRABBING BOTH OF HER WRISTS, HE PULLED RORY INTO HIM, forcing his dick to go deeper. Her moans and screams grew louder causing him to go harder.

. . .

"Oooo... shit! I'm 'bout to cum!"

Releasing her wrists, Wyatt placed his hands on her waist as she threw her ass back while shouting to the high heavens, letting him know that she'd came. Still dicking her down, he exploded inside of the condom. Taking a moment to get himself together, Wyatt slid out of her, throwing the condom in a nearby trash can. As he pulled his boxers and sweatpants up, he smirked at an exhausted Rory, who was pulling down her dress. Walking over to her, he gently grabbed her by the throat.

"I don't care what bitch try to shoot their shot with me. I better not ever hear you disrespect my character again. You hear me?"

"Yes," Rory replied seductively.

"Now take ya ass in my room and wait for me. I'll be in there in a minute."

Pecking her lips, he smacked her ass as she walked away, doing what she was told. As he sat down in his recliner chair, he removed his phone from his pocket and went to his text messages.

Wyatt: JC, you ain't gonna believe this shit, man.

7

After clocking out after another fun-filled day at Jimmy Jazz, Jace gave his male co-workers a handshake and gave a quick hug to his female co-worker before heading out the store. As he made his way out of the mall, he ignored the lustful stares of the chicks that he passed on his way out of the building. Normally, he would try to get at least one female's number, but he wasn't feeling like himself. He even turned down a dick suck from one of the six chicks he was talking to. Jace had another woman on his mind. An older woman, and her name was Sybil Bailey.

Since the night he saw her in that white dress and blue blazer, she occupied his thoughts eighty percent of the time. Whenever he was fucking some chick or jacking off, Sybil would enter his thoughts. He imagined himself rubbing, smacking, and squeezing her ass while she rode his dick in the reverse cowgirl position. Jace wanted her bad, but he knew he couldn't have her. She was his best friend's mom, and now that her and that nigga made their relationship official, Sybil was off the market.

Popping the locks to the Chevy Impala his mom rented for him, he jumped inside and got comfortable behind the wheel. As he pulled out of the lot, his phone began to ring. Knowing that it was his mom from the tone, he answered.

"Boy, ya ass is getting a lil' too comfortable with not calling ya mother," Hazel spoke with anger. "I haven't heard from you in like two weeks. I had to text Sybil just to see how you're doing. Wassup with that?"

"I'm sorry, Ma, and from now on, I'll call or text you every day," Jace assured her as he drove onto the expressway.

"You better," she warned. "So what's new with you? I see that your savings account is growing."

"Yup," he happily answered. "I love my job, Ma. You won't believe how many numbers I've gotten so far."

"I can only imagine. All I know is you better be using protection 'cause if you get one of them hoes pregnant, we're gonna have a problem," she threatened.

"I keep telling you that I'm not gonna get anyone pregnant. I'm not tryna have any kids right now."

"Good. Well, I'm gonna let you go. I just wanted to hear ya voice."

"Ma, before you go, I got a question to ask you."

"Okay."

"How would you feel if I started dating an older woman?"

"An older woman? How old are we talking?"

"Thirty-six."

"I don't know how I'd feel about you dating a woman that's sixteen years older than you, Jace," Hazel honestly answered. "Older women are mature and more settled. They don't do things that twenty-something-year-olds do. They don't do clubs and shit like that. Young bucks like yaself, like to play games and have fun. Older women are looking for serious relationships which is something you're not ready for. I know I can't tell you who to date, but I strongly suggest that you don't get involved with an older chick. Stick with girls ya own age, a'ight?"

"A'ight, Ma." Jace chuckled. "Thanks for the advice."

"Anytime, son. I love you, and you better call me before the week is out."

"I love you too, and I will."

Ending the call, he drove the rest of the way home in deep thought. He weighed the pros and cons of trying to pursue Sybil and whether it was worth losing his best friend. Jace never thought about her rejecting his young ass. That wasn't a concern of his. He tried to figure out what it was about her that had him wanting her so bad and came up with a few things. Aside from her youthful face and curvaceous body, Jace liked that she was a go-getter, completely independent, and successful. She was the true definition of a hard worker, and he admired her. Never in his life had he been attracted to an older woman. Especially not any of his friends' moms. Jace always bagged every chick he set out to get, and Sybil was next on his list.

Twenty minutes later, he pulled into the driveway and noticed two cars he didn't recognize. When he saw that Wyatt's car was gone, he scooped up the phone and hit his line.

"Yo, JC. Wassup?"

"I just got home from work. Ya mom got company or something?"

"Yeah. My aunt Dom and my aunt Lee. They're her sorority sisters. They came through to have dinner with us, but I already made plans to take Rory to Dave and Buster's."

"Oh, a'ight. Are you coming back home, or you spending the night at her crib?"

"I'll be home my usual time."

"Bet. See ya later."

"A'ight, man."

Ending the call, Jace tucked the phone in his pocket before parking his car in his usual spot and killing the engine. He secured the locks of his car with the remote as he headed toward the front door. As he entered the house, he heard laughter and singing coming from the kitchen. Heading in that direction, he stood in the opening, watching the women rap and dance to Lil'

Kim's *No Time*. With a smile plastered on his face, Jace got a kick out of watching Sybil act a fool with her friends. When she noticed him standing there, she quickly turned the music down and straightened up.

"How long were you standing there, boy?" she asked with a smirk.

"I ain't been standing here that long, Ms. Sybil." He chuckled. "So this is how you act when you get with your girls, huh?"

"Hell yeah," she replied. "Every time we link up, it's a party."

"You damn right," a pretty redbone agreed.

"Jace, these are my best friends and sorors, Dominique and Leah." Sybil pointed to each of them.

"Nice to meet you, young man," they replied in unison.

"Same here." He smiled.

"Dinner will be ready in like thirty minutes. I'll let you know when it's done." Sybil walked over to the stove.

"Okay."

As he headed toward the basement, Jace quickly scanned her body with his eyes. His dick jumped in his pants as he examined her curves. Closing the door to the basement, he made his way down the stairs, heading straight for the bathroom. In need of shower, he ran the water, got undressed, and hopped in. With his dick standing at attention, Jace grabbed the soap, lathered his hands, and started jacking off. He closed his eyes and thought about Sybil's bright smile and the way her ass looked in the leggings she was wearing. Fantasizing about sucking her titties while he was fucking her, Jace came all over the shower wall in the matter of seconds. After cleaning himself and the wall up, he wrapped a towel around his waist, snatched up clothes, and went to his room to get dressed.

"Aye, Jace?" Sybil called, "Come eat, honey."

"Okay! I'll be up in a minute!" he shouted back

After putting on his socks and slides, Jace headed upstairs. Opening the door, he heard the ladies having a conversation about Sybil and Darrin and decided to listen in.

"Wait a minute, Sybil? You mean to tell me that made things official with this man without giving that D a test drive first?"

"I hate to admit it, but yes. I did, and now, I'm stuck with a man that can't sexually satisfy me."

"Is he really that bad?"

"Leah, the man is a nice size, but he cums quick. I guess the pussy is too wet for him because after ten minutes, he's howling like a damn wolf in the night."

The ladies erupted into laughter.

"Can he at least eat it?"

"Dom, don't get me started on the man's head game, okay? I mean, I heard that men can't do both. It's either one or the other, but my man can't do either. I wanna call his baby mama and ask her how the fuck she had two kids by this nigga," Sybil vented.

"Well, Sybil, don't throw the man away because he can't sexually please you. You can always teach him what to do."

"And if that doesn't work, make sure you always got batteries for yo' vibrator."

"Leah!" She laughed.

"Aye, I'm just being honest."

"Syb, Darrin is a good man, okay? Just talk to him about this and see if he's willing to fix it."

"A'ight. I'm gonna try, but you know that telling a man that his sex is trash is only gonna bruise his ego."

"If it does, then so be it. You gotta be honest."

Taking a moment for his smile to fade, Jace took a few deep breaths before entering the kitchen, getting the women's attention.

"There you are." Sybil picked up his plate, handing it to him. "I figured you didn't wanna stay up here with us for dinner. So I made your plate."

"Ahhh. Y'all didn't want me to be a part of y'all girl talk, huh?" His eyes shifted between the three women.

"Maybe next time." Leah chuckled.

"Okay. Enjoy the rest of y'all night."

Smirking on his way down the stairs, Jace was beyond pleased with what he heard that night. As he sat in the recliner chair eating his dinner, he thought long and hard about whether he should make his move on Sybil or not. Wyatt was his boy, and he valued their friendship, but his desire to have his mom was something he couldn't deny. She had a want, and Jace had a need. He just needed to convince Sybil to see things his way.

8

Sitting at her desk, Sybil stared at the text message from Darrin asking to see her that night. She knew that the evening was possibly going to end with sex, which was something she wasn't looking forward to. Instead of responding, she left the message on read as she prepared for her next patient. As she continued to work, her thoughts kept drifting to Darrin and their problem. Sybil couldn't understand for the life of her how a man as fine and successful as Darrin couldn't perform sexually. The more she thought about it, the more frustrated she became.

After years of not having sex, she was ready and willing to give the pussy to Darrin whenever he asked for it. They had sex four times since they made their relationship official three weeks ago, and each time was just like the last—short and unsatisfying. Since having dinner with her friends, Sybil tried to find a way to tell Darrin that she was sexually unfulfilled, but she didn't have the courage to tell her man that his sex was wack as fuck.

When 12:30 p.m. rolled around, she grabbed her purse and phone on her way out of the building. She had a lunch date with her son at a soul food restaurant nearby. Sybil was shocked when he met her in the kitchen early that morning and offered to treat her to lunch. Always wanting to spend time with Wyatt, she immediately accepted. Popping the locks to her car, Sybil hopped in and headed to the restaurant. After a short drive, she found a parking spot on the street, directly across the street in the restaurant. With her Gucci tote bag hanging on her wrist, she got out of the car, secured the locks, then jogged across the street with her heels clicking against the concrete. Entering the restaurant, Sybil spotted her son sitting at a table near the back of the restaurant. She grinned as she made her way over to Wyatt, catching the eye of the handful of men that were in there.

"Everywhere you go, you got niggas staring at you, Ma." Wyatt greeted his mom with a grin and extended arms.

"You have an attractive mother, Wyatt. The sooner you accept that, the better off you'll be." She chuckled, hugging her son.

"If you say so, Ma." Wyatt shook his head, helping Sybil with her chair.

"Look at you being a gentleman," she teased.

"I always try to be a gentleman." He sat down across from her. "But I don't treat all women like this. Just you and Rory, but she likes the savage side of me more than the gentleman side." He smirked.

"Ya savage side? What savage side?" she asked with a raised eyebrow.

"She likes when I'm aggressive, takes charge, and how I check her when she gets outta line. I can't be nice to her all the time."

"Ohhh, so it's something like being a gangsta and a gentleman?"

"Exactly."

Sybil couldn't control her laughter.

When the waiter approached their table, Wyatt took the liberty of ordering for both of them. She was impressed with the selection of food and the drink he'd chosen for her, which made her smile. Once the waitress took off, she continued their conversation.

"So are you and Rory serious?"

"We're just friends with benefits right now, but my feelings are growing for her. I had to fall back from her a little bit because I feel like we're getting too attached to each other," Wyatt explained.

"Friends with benefits? That means y'all fucking with no strings attached, right?"

"Yeah, Ma." He nodded his head.

"Okay. I just had to make sure." Sybil gave a small smile. "There's nothing wrong with taking some time away from your significant other. Just don't spend too much time away from her. I'm glad that you found a girl you like spending most of your time with, but I'm confused about how you ended up with Rory. I thought you and Ivanna liked each other."

"We did, but since you're dating her dad, it felt like I was talking to my sister or something. So we decided to just be friends, but she does have a thing for Jace though."

"Oh really?"

"Yeah. She wants to get with him, but she's too scared to shoot her shot."

When the waitress brought them their food and drinks a few minutes later, Sybil said a short prayer before they dug in. The salmon, greens, and candied yams Wyatt ordered for her was delicious. She ate all that she could before pushing her plate to the side.

"That was sooo good, son. I'm gonna have to box this up and take it with me." She wiped her mouth with a napkin.

"I'm glad you enjoyed it, Ma." Wyatt smiled. "I'm glad you were able to have lunch with me. I've been wanting to spend some one-on-one time with you for a while now. I just didn't know how to go about telling you."

"Boy, whenever you wanna spend time with me, just say the

word. I will stop time if I have to just to spend five seconds with my son." Sybil grabbed his hands

"I know you will, Ma. I'm glad I decided to come down here for the summer. I love being down here with you. I love it so much that... I'm thinking about transferring schools and moving down here for good," Wyatt expressed.

"Oh, son, I would love that." She beamed. "The colleges and universities are great here. I just want you to carefully think about this before making your final decision, and if you still wanna move down here, you'll have to see if it's cool with ya dad, okay?"

"A'ight, Ma."

"I gotta get back to work, son. I'll see you when I get home."

Standing to their feet, Sybil hugged and kissed Wyatt before instructing him to box up her food. As she made her way out of the restaurant with her keys in hand, she looked both ways before jogging over to her car, popping the locks. Once she was inside, she slammed the door shut, revved the engine, and pulled off down the street, making it back to her job five minutes early. After spending the rest of her day counseling pregnant teenagers and families, Sybil was more than ready to call it a day. Besides the wonderful lunch date with Wyatt, she still had to make a decision about seeing Darrin that night. Waving bye to her co-workers, Sybil got in her Lexus and drove home in silence.

When she pulled into the driveway, Sybil sighed when she saw Darrin standing in front of his black 2019 Yukon Denali with shopping bags in his hand. Parking in front of the garage, she grabbed her bag and got out of the car. As she walked toward him, Sybil put a fake smile on her face as hugged him tightly.

"Hey, baby. I wasn't expecting to see you here."

"I know, but when you didn't respond to my text, I figured I'd just stop by." He released her.

"What's this?" Sybil pointed to the bags in his hand.

"I bought you a few things so you won't be mad at me for what I'm about to say."

"And what is that?" she asked, becoming upset.

"I have to go out of town for two weeks, and I'm leaving tonight," Darrin nervously spoke.

"I have to personally deliver some materials to a store in Florida, and the following week I have a conference to go to."

Hearing that he was going to be out of town for two weeks struck a nerve. Already bothered with his poor bedroom performance, it was time for her to express how she really felt.

"I feel like you're lying to me," Sybil angrily blurted out.

"What?"

"I feel like you're not being completely honest with me about the things you be doing when you go out of town, Darrin. I understand that sometimes you have to fill in for your employees here and there, but now it's happening too often."

"Where the fuck is this coming from, Sybil?" he asked, confused. "What? You think I'm cheating on you when I go outta town or some shit?" Darrin became angry.

"I hope not because if you fucking her the same way you fuck me, trust me, she's fucking someone else," Sybil spat with no remorse.

"So you mean to tell me that every time we fucked, you weren't pleased?"

"How could I be pleased when you only last ten minutes, Darrin? I've been trying to figure out a way to tell you this in a nicer manner, but I'm tired of holding this shit in," she confessed.

"So what are you saying? You don't wanna be with me now?"

"I didn't say that. I thought by telling you this that you would want to fix the problem. I like and care about you a lot. I don't want us to break up over this. This issue can be fixed, and I want us to fix this, but if you don't, there's nothing else I can say."

Tossing the bags at her feet, Darrin didn't say a word as he got in his truck and drove away. When he was out of sight, Sybil picked up the bags and headed toward the front door. Letting herself in, she went straight upstairs to her room, changing out of her work clothes and into a pair of pajama shorts and a tee shirt. After placing the shopping bags in the closet, she removed her phone from her purse, then strolled downstairs to the kitchen. Heading straight for the cabinet, Sybil removed a large wine glass and bottle of pink Moscato. She filled her glass to the brim, took a huge gulp, and filled it again. With her glass in hand, she looked through the freezer for something to cook for dinner. As she removed the steak, she heard the basement door open and quickly snatched her knife off the counter ready to attack.

"Whoa, Ms. Sybil! It's me!" Jace shouted with his hands up.

"Boy! You scared the shit outta me! I wasn't expecting you to be here." She placed the knife on the counter.

"I went in early today so I got off early. I didn't mean to scare you," he answered. "Sorry I startled you."

"It's okay. How was work?"

"It was cool. I'm glad to be home though."

"And why is that?"

"I get to spend time with you." Jace seductively bit his bottom lip.

Staring at each other for a moment, Sybil couldn't stop the smirk that spread across her lips. For the past week and some change, Jace had been flirting with her. At first, she ignored his comments of how good she looked in her work clothes and how nice her hair looked, but when he met her in the kitchen early one morning, expressing his feelings for her, Sybil was speechless. She was flattered that a boy as young as Jace found her sexually attractive, but she immediately shut him down. The thought of her being involved with her son's best friend was something she couldn't wrap her mind around. Although Sybil rejected his sexual advances, it didn't stop her from entertaining the thought. Her views of him being cocky and rude no longer irritated her. It was somehow sexy to her now.

"Jace, I done already told you that I can't be sexually involved with you." She chuckled.

"So you're gonna have to find some type of way to get rid of these feelings you have for me."

"I know you don't mean that, Ms. Sybil." He stepped closer to her.

"And how do you know that?"

"Because I noticed that since I told you that I was interested in you, you've been wearing those tight ass leggings with no panties and you stopped wearing bras with your tee shirts. Whenever you catch me staring at you, you smile at me, letting me know you wore that shit for me," he replied in a deep voice, towering over her. "Why else would you be down here in these lil' ass shorts if you weren't expecting me to see you in them?"

Guilty of everything he was saying, Sybil was at a loss for words. Taking in the smell of his cologne, her pussy began to throb as he began leaning down to kiss her.

"Jace, I can admit that I was teasing you, but I was just having fun. I have a man now, and I don't wanna cheat on him." She moved away from him.

"A man that can't sexually satisfy you?"

Sybil shifted her weight from one foot to the other.

"You just said that you did all that shit just to tease me. If you weren't thinking about us being involved with each other, you wouldn't have even done all that." He walked over to her. "So stop fighting this shit and let me make you feel how ya man can't."

Towering over her again, Sybil didn't have a chance to protest. Jace forced his tongue in her mouth, placing his hands on her waist. The electric shock that flowed through her body sent her hormones into overdrive. Her pussy was so wet that her shorts were soaked. Backing up into the kitchen table, he lifted her up, placing her on the edge. With their tongues still dancing each other's mouth, Jace lifted her shirt and began fondling her breasts.

"Jace, wait." She broke their kiss. "I can't do this. We... We can't do this." Her voice trembled as he rubbed her nipples with his thumbs.

Kissing her lips again, Jace leaned her back on the table, spreading her legs with his. Moans escaped her lips as she ran her fingers through his hair. Moving from her mouth to her breasts, Jace licked and sucked her right nipple as he played with the left one.

"Fuucck," she hissed, looking down at him.

Moving over to the left nipple, Jace gently grinded it between his teeth as he used his free hand to move her shorts to the side.

"Damn. I got you wet like that? Ya shorts are soaked, ma." He chuckled.

He inserted two fingers deep inside her and removed them. His fingers were covered with her juices. Licking one of his fingers clean, Jace put the other one in her mouth, and Sybil did the same, staring him in his eyes. As she bit her bottom lip, he ripped her shorts, exposing her shaved, wet pussy. Watching him lick his lips as he admired her body turned her on even more. She debated with herself about going all the way through with this or not, but once she saw his long, thick, curved shaft, Sybil had made up her mind.

Once he put the condom on, Jace placed himself at her center. They stared at each other for a moment before he thrust deep inside her wetness, causing her to moan loudly. Grabbing her ankles, he held them in the air and deep stroked her pussy. The pain and pleasure that she felt in her stomach had her running. Sybil was trying her best to take the pounding he was giving her, but she couldn't. Placing her legs around his waist, Jace placed his hands on the table, leaning over her.

"For you to be a grown ass woman, you don't take dick very well," Jace whispered in her ear. "My young bitches take dick better than this."

Pissed off by his words, Sybil locked her legs together and grinded her hips against him, matching his rhythm.

"Mm-hmm. That's right. Fuck this dick."

Staring him in his eyes, Sybil moaned, groaned, and screamed his name as he fucked her on the kitchen table. At the moment, she didn't give a fuck about them getting caught or any of the consequences of their actions. She was enjoying herself, and the dick was amazing. With her legs shaking, Sybil felt her orgasm building. Jace began fucking her harder as she dug her nails into his arms.

"Oh my God! Jace! I'm... I'm..."

Screaming at the top of her lungs, Sybil squirted all over his dick while he exploded inside the condom. Taking a moment to catch their breaths, Jace kissed her lips before helping her off the table.

"Damn, boy. That shit was amazing." Sybil tried to keep her balance. "I wasn't expecting it to be like that."

"Neither was I. It was better than I imagined."

"So... what now?"

"We're gonna get cleaned up, and you're gonna make dinner like usual, and when Wyatt goes to sleep, I'ma have ya ass for dessert."

Smiling seductively, Sybil snatched her ripped shorts off the floor before leaving the kitchen. Jace slapped her ass as she walked away, causing her to look back at him. When reached the master bathroom, she ran the water for the shower, then got in. As she thought about her sex session with Jace, Sybil wasn't sure what she was getting herself in to. She thought about the stories Leah told her about the women that messed around with young niggas and became nervous. How was she going to stop herself from getting attached when the sex was so good? She knew that messing around with Jace was a risk. If they got caught, she could lose the one person that mattered to her the most—her son. Not ready to give up the best sex she had in years, Sybil was going to try her best not to mess up their arrangement.

9

When Wyatt arrived at work that morning, his normal happy disposition was replaced with a solemn one. Since his lunch date with his mom nearly a week ago, the only thing that was on his mind was if he should stay in Philly with his dad or move to Sandy Springs with his mom. Although he was born and raised in the city of brotherly love, he felt that moving to Georgia would be a better option for him. After spending nearly two months in the peach state, Wyatt didn't want to leave. He already researched the colleges he wanted to transfer to, but that was all he did. He didn't want to take any steps in the transfer process until he spoke with his dad.

After helping customers all morning, Wyatt clocked out for his lunch break. As headed out of the store, he felt his phone vibrating in his pocket. Removing it, he took a deep breath before answering the call from his dad.

"Aye, Dad. Wassup with you?" he cheerfully greeted.

"You know me. Working hard every day, son, and judging from ya bank account, I see you've been working hard too."

"Yup. I haven't missed a day of work since I started. I even pick up extra hours here and there."

"I'm glad you're working hard, Wyatt. I just knew that ya

mom was gonna be giving you money left and right," James confessed.

"Nah. Mom hasn't given me a dime, and I didn't ask her for anything. Everything I have, I got on my own. Except the BMW." He chuckled.

"Yeah. That is a nice ass car. So you only got a few weeks left down there. What day do you wanna come back?"

"Yeah.. . about that. I wanna stay down here and transfer schools," Wyatt sternly stated.

"You what?"

"After spending time down here with Mom, I wanna live down here with her."

The phone was silent for a few seconds.

"No."

"Huh?"

"If you can huh, you can hear. I said no," James responded angrily.

"Why not, Dad?" Wyatt asked, becoming upset.

"I let you go down there to spend the summer with ya mom, not for you to get comfortable and wanna stay down there for good. Did ya mom put you up to this?"

"No, she didn't. I made this decision on my own. I talked to her about it, and she's cool with me living down here. She told me I had to talk to you first."

"Why do you wanna live down there, Wyatt? Is it because of a girl or something?"

"I wanna live down here because I haven't lived in the same state as my mom since I was ten. I'm tired of the long-distance relationship I have with her. I miss my mom, and I know that if I return to Lincoln, I'm just gonna find a way to be down here with her. I know you weren't expecting this. Shit, I wasn't either, but I gave this a lot of thought, Dad."

"I had a feeling that one day you were gonna leave me to be with your mom." James sighed.

"I guess that time is now. I'm gonna miss you, son."

"I'm gonna miss you too, Dad, but nothing's gonna change. We're still gonna talk every day, and I'll still come visit. How about you come down here and turn up with me for my birthday?"

"Hell yeah. I like the sound of that," James replied in an upbeat tone.

"Cool. I'll hit up later on in the week. I'm on lunch, and I need to eat."

"A'ight, son. Talk to you later."

Tucking his phone in his pocket, Wyatt smiled to himself as he stood in the Chick-fil-A line for his food. He thought he was going to have to fight harder for his dad's approval. He was both nervous and excited about moving to Georgia with his mom. Even though his plan was to stay on campus, he was looking forward to popping up at his mom's house every now and then for a home-cooked meal. After getting his chicken sandwich, mac and cheese, and lemonade, he removed his phone from his pocket before taking a seat at the nearest table. He sent a text to his mom, letting her know that he was here to stay. Noticing he had a text from Rory, he opened the thread.

Rory: Aye, Dub Beezy. We need to talk ASAP. I'll be waiting for you at yo' crib when I get off work.

Wyatt: What do we need to talk about?

Rory: It can wait. See you later.

Wyatt: A'ight.

Placing his phone on the table, he realized he only had fifteen minutes left of his thirty-minute break. Not in a rush, he took his time eating his food until everything was gone. Taking a moment to let his food digest, he tucked his phone back in his pocket, disposed of his trash, and made it back to work just in time for his co-worker to take her break. For the rest of his shift, he thought about Rory and what she wanted to talk about. Wyatt knew for a fact that she wasn't pregnant by him. So whatever they needed to discuss had to be about the sudden distance between them and what caused it.

Since they fucked in his basement, he and Rory had been on multiple dates, and if they weren't getting down at his house, they were in her Atlanta apartment, causing a major disturbance. His strong like for her was slowly turning into more, and Wyatt didn't know if he could handle them being anything more than what they were. He thought that dicking down and being with other chicks would take his mind off Rory, but that only made him think about her more. Unlike the other chicks, she didn't work hard to impress him. She kept it real with him about everything. Although they didn't dig deep into each other's lives, they shared parts of their lives that no one knew about. Not even their parents. Neither of them had ever been involved in a serious relationship. No matter how much Wyatt tried to convince himself that he wasn't falling for her, she proved him otherwise. Rory's caramel-colored skin, Coke bottle frame, big brown eyes, and pretty smile knocked him down every time he saw her. She was the best sex partner he'd ever had, and his mom liked her. She was the perfect match for him, but his fear of commitment stood in the way.

When 5:30 p.m. rolled around, Wyatt strolled out of the mall and over to his car, popping his locks on the way. Bringing the car to life, he pulled out of the lot and headed home. As he pulled into his driveway, he saw Rory's silver 2018 Nissan Altima parked in the driveway, along with his mom's and Jace's cars. For the past week, his homie had been beating him home. When he asked Jace about it, he said one of his co-workers asked him to switch shifts with him, and he did. Wyatt admired how his homie helped someone out other than him. Jace only helped people that he fucked with, so for him to help someone else was a big deal.

Parking in his normal spot, he jumped out the car, entering the house through the front door. When he heard Rory and his mom talking and laughing in the kitchen, he headed in that direction. Watching the two women in his life cooking in the kitchen put a smile on his face. He never brought chicks to his dad's crib because he didn't like any female that much, and he didn't want them bonding with his stepmom. Even though he didn't have a problem with her, Wyatt wanted to experience certain things with his mom and that was one of them. Turning her head in his direction, Rory's smile grew wider.

"Hey, Wyatt," she greeted with her eyes focused on his.

"Hey. What y'all in here laughing about?" His eyes shifted back and forth between them.

"Oh, your mom was just telling me about how overprotective you were of her when you were little." Rory chuckled.

"How was I overprotective?" Wyatt stepped into the kitchen.

"Sometime when ya dad would hug or kiss me, you would get in between us and push him back," Sybil replied. "I don't know why you did that, but it was very cute." She walked over to him, kissing his cheek.

"You were a mama's boy, Dub Beezy?" Rory teased.

"I wouldn't say that I was a mama's boy, but I definitely do love my mom." He winked at her.

"I know that's right." Sybil grinned. "Go 'head and change ya clothes. Dinner will be ready in a minute."

"A'ight."

Heading down to the basement, Wyatt gave Jace a handshake before dipping into his room to change his clothes.

"Aye, Dub Beezy?

"Wassup?" He shouted back, removing his uniform.

"Why is Rory tryna hook me up with Ivanna?"

"What's wrong with that? I thought y'all were vibing?" He removed a pair of ball shorts from his drawer.

"We are, but Chante has been tryna get with me too, and I can't choose which one I want, man."

"You never told me that Chante was tryna get with you." Wyatt stepped out of his room.

"Yeah. She's been coming to my job on my lunch break tryna suck me off in the bathroom and shit."

"Did you let her?"

"Surprisingly, no. I know I don't have any ties to shorty, but since Ivanna is the chick I'm talking to, it's only right that I stick with her," Jace honestly answered.

"Damn, man. You used to run through best friends like it was nothing. I never thought you would be the one to calm down and stick with one chick." He chuckled.

"I'm tryna be a one-woman man like you, my nigga." Jace joked.

"Whatever, nigga."

They laughed.

When they heard footsteps coming down the stairs, they turned their heads in that direction and saw it was Rory.

"Ms. Sybil said come up and eat, but Wyatt, I need to talk to you right quick."

Taking his cue to leave, Jace paused the game and headed upstairs. Once they heard the basement door shut, she spoke.

"First, I just wanna say I'm not pregnant, but I'm sure you knew that already. I wanted to talk to you about our situationship."

"What about it?"

"For the past few weeks, we've been kinda distant. At first, I had a problem with it because we were having a lot of fun together, but then I found myself getting attached to you. So after doing some serious thinking, I decided that we need to end things between us now," Rory answered with a straight face.

"What?" Wyatt stood to his feet, walking over to her.

"Yo' ass is gonna be going back to school soon, and I don't want it to be hard on either one of us."

"So what I'm hearing is you wanna end things because you starting to fall in love with a nigga and it's gonna hurt you to see a nigga leave?" He smirked, towering over her.

"No, no, no." She shook her head. "That's not true at all." Rory blushed.

"You ain't gotta admit it. We both know the truth."

Leaning down to kiss her, she wrapped her arms around his neck as he placed his hands on her waist.

"Aye! Knock it off you two and get y'all asses up here and eat!" Sybil yelled down to them, making them laugh.

"I am starting to fall for you, Wyatt, and I'm really gonna be in my feelings when you leave."

"Look, let's not worry about that right now. Let's just enjoy the time we have left, a'ight?"

"Okay."

Giving her a quick kiss, the duo headed upstairs where they sat down and had a nice dinner. As they chowed down on lobster alfredo and asparagus, Wyatt noticed that his mom was spending a lot of time on her phone, which was something she never did at the dinner table. He knew she wasn't talking to Darrin, because she informed him of their breakup a few days after it happened. With his curiosity getting the best of him, Wyatt needed to know who she was texting.

"Mom, you're never on the phone during dinner. Who you texting over there?"

"Believe it or not, ya dad." Sybil rolled her eyes.

"Oh yeah? What y'all talking about?"

"If you must know, I'm asking him about his three-year marriage."

"How you find out about that?"

"Ya aunt Dom told me today. He's been texting me all summer for updates about you and asking me about my relationship with Darrin, and not once did he mention that he was a married man." Sybil shook her head.

"Maybe he didn't tell you because he married the girl he cheated on you with?" Wyatt replied absentmindedly, causing Jace to kick him under the table.

"He what!"

Everyone stared at her with wide eyes. Without saying another word, Sybil turned her phone over and continued eating her food. As the three of them continued to talk, Wyatt kept a close eye on his mom. Although she seemed to be fine, he knew that a silent woman was a dangerous one. As they made plans to go to Six Flags the upcoming weekend, Sybil got up from the table, placing her plate in the sink.

"Wyatt, Jace. Can y'all clean the dishes and put the food away please?" she asked with her phone in hand.

"No problem," Jace replied

"Yeah. We got this, Mom."

"Rory, it was nice having you over for dinner." She smiled.

"Thanks for having me, Ms. Sybil." Rory returned the smile.

"Enjoy the rest of y'all's night."

After they finished their dinner, Wyatt and Jace cleaned the dishes while Rory put the rest of the alfredo in a container. With Rory letting it be known that she was ready to be fucked, he gave Jace a handshake goodbye before they headed toward the door. When they heard Sybil shouting at someone on the phone, he told Rory to wait for him in the car as he went up the stairs by twos. Standing in the doorway of his mom's room, he watched as his mother paced the floor as she talked on the phone. After telling his dad to go to hell, she tossed her phone on the bed, letting out a sigh of frustration.

"Ma?"

"Yes, son."

"I haven't heard you cuss like that since I've been down here."

"Yeah, well, ya dad tends to bring this side out of me." Sybil chuckled, still pacing. "When we were together, he used to keep things from me all the time, thinking that he was sparing my feelings. Him keeping shit from me only made shit worse. After all these years, he's still doing the same shit, and I don't understand why. We haven't been together since our junior year of college, and James is still doing the same shit." She shook her head. "I don't even know why the hell I care or why it's bugging me so much."

"Maybe it bothers you for the same way it bothered him when I told him you were dating Darrin." He walked over to her.

"What?"

"I know I'm breaking the guy code by telling you this, but when my dad saw you the first day I came down here, he couldn't control himself. He said you looked good and was impressed with ya accomplishments."

"He did?" she asked in disbelief.

"Yeah. He regrets the day he cheated on you. I think he misses you, a lot," he spoke sincerely. "And call me crazy, but I think you might have some leftover feelings for him too."

"Boy, please. I don't want ya lying ass daddy. Now get outta my room. Tryna play matchmaker and shit." She laughed.

"Bye, mom." He kissed her cheek.

Bouncing down the stairs, Wyatt strolled out the front door locking it behind him. Hopping in the passenger's side of Rory's car, he reclined back in his chair as she drove out of the driveway. With her right hand massaging his dick through his ball shorts, he closed his eyes and thought about his mom and dad. Thinking back to how his mom had cussed out his dad, he knew she still had feelings for the man, even though she denied it. Wyatt already knew how James felt, but he needed to get them to realize that. With the wheels of his mind spinning, he had to come up with a master plan to get his parents back together.

10

"Yeeesss, Jaccee," Sybil moaned, bent over the bathroom sink. "Fuck this pussy."

Biting his bottom lip, Jace gripped her hips tighter as he thrust his dick deep inside her. Since the first time they fucked in the kitchen, they'd been going at it like rabbits. Every morning and every night for the past two weeks, they jumped each other's bones. With each time being better than the last, Jace couldn't get enough of Sybil. The way her body reacted to his touch and the things she did when she rode his dick had his young ass mesmerized. Hands down, she was the best he ever had. Even though he tried to convince himself he wasn't sprung, Jace knew that he was just lying to himself.

With their bodies, moans, and groans making music of their own, he kept his eyes trained on Sybil through the mirror. Her sex faces and the way she moaned his name caused his strokes to get more forceful and deeper. When she dropped her head, Jace pulled her by the hair, lifting it back up.

"Didn't I tell you I wanted to see ya face the entire time? Huh?" he whispered in her head.

"Yes." She gasped.

"So why you drop ya head?"

"You... you're... fucking me too gooooddd," she moaned.

With a handful of her hair, he put a deeper arch in her back and continued punishing her pussy. Sucking on her neck, causing her legs to shake, Jace knew she was at her breaking point. As she twerked on his dick, he watched the way her ass bounced and jiggled and tried not to cum, but he couldn't stop it. With her juices covering his dick, Jace filled the condom with his sperm. Once their breathing was back to normal, he slid out of Sybil and flushed the condom down the toilet. Pulling up his boxers, he smirked as he watched Sybil pull her nightshirt down. She was still bent over the sink with her eyes closed, unable to move.

"What's wrong, baby?" He stood behind her, lifting her up.

"Mmmm. I'm sleepy, and my legs are sore," Sybil whined.

"Come on. Let me help you to the bed." Jace chuckled.

Slowly walking into the bedroom, Sybil climbed into her king-sized bed, pulling the covers over her. Kissing her lips, he tried to walk away but she grabbed the back of his shirt.

"You're not gonna lay with me for a minute?"

"I would, but that last time I did that, Wyatt almost caught us," he spoke in a low tone.

"Will I see you later?"

"I don't know yet, but I'll let you know."

"Okay."

Kissing her cheek, Jace left her room, closing the door behind him. Making his way back to the basement, he headed to the bathroom to take a quick shower. When he was finished, he wrapped a towel around his waist, then headed to his room where Jace put on a new Polo undershirt and boxers. Flopping down on the bed, he checked his phone and saw that he had a few texts from Ivanna. They were texting each other before he went to give Sybil her morning dose of vitamin D. When he read that she was excited about going to Six Flags that day, Jace didn't feel the same way. He'd rather stay behind and spend time with his sexy ass cougar.

After he almost got caught coming from Sybil's room last week, she suggested that they slowed things down. Although he assured her that he was going to be more careful, she told Jace that he shouldn't switch up his routine too much so they wouldn't get caught. Once he realized that she was right, he decided to finally give Ivanna a chance. She'd been trying to get close to him for nearly two months, but he never gave into any of her advances. To him, she was a little on the aggressive side. She didn't wait for him to come at her, and she tried to call all the shots. Ivanna was acting like the man instead of the bad bitch that she was. When she changed her approach and showed him that she could be feminine, she had his attention. Even though things were going good between them, that didn't stop Jace from thinking about Sybil.

Dozing off for a couple of hours, his alarm woke him up at 8:30 a.m. Not ready to wake up, he silenced the alarm and pulled the covers over his head. A couple of minutes later, there was a knock on his door, and he knew it was Wyatt.

"Aye, JC? Get ya ass up, nigga. It's time to get this money."

"Give me like five more minutes, man."

"A'ight, but if you ain't out in five minutes, I'ma come in there and pour water on ya ass like I did when we were in school." Wyatt laughed.

Laughing as well, Jace tossed the covers off him and got out of bed. Once he opened the blinds, he removed his uniform from his closet along with a pair of new sneakers. Placing his uniform on the bed, he headed to the bathroom to wash his face and brush his teeth. When he was finished, he went back to his room and got dressed. After putting on his G-Shock watch, Jace moisturized his hair, tucked his phone and wallet in his pocket, and left the room. Sitting in his recliner chair, he watched Wyatt finish his game of *Madden*.

"We're gonna have to go to work hungry this morning. Ma upstairs knocked the fuck out,"

Wyatt spoke with his glued to the TV.

"For real?" He acted surprised. "Since we've been down here, she's cooked breakfast for us every morning."

"I know. I don't even be hungry all the time, but after fucking Rory until five something this morning, a nigga need a good breakfast to get my strength back up."

"I know how that can be." Jace chuckled. "What did she have to talk to you about a couple of days ago?"

"She basically tried to push me away. She's catching feelings for ya boy, and she didn't want to go through the trouble of missing me when I left," he replied. "But I told her we'll cross that bridge when we get to it."

"I heard that." Jace nodded his head, "But we're leaving in a few weeks, man. You think it's gonna be easy to leave shorty behind? I know ya ass caught feelings for her too."

"Yeah, I did, but I don't plan on leaving her behind."

"She's coming back to Philly with us?" he asked in shock.

"Nah... I'm staying down here."

"You what?"

"I'm staying in Georgia, JC." Wyatt turned the game off.

"Nigga, when did you decide all this? Did you talk to ya dad about this?" Jace became upset.

"I talked to my mom about this almost a week ago, and she said yeah. I talked to my dad about it the day Rory came over. He wasn't too happy about it at first, but he said it was cool for me to stay down here too. On Monday, I'm gonna apply to one of the universities down here and get my credits transferred."

"Did you tell Rory about this?"

"Not yet. I'm gonna surprise her."

"Damn, man." Jace shook his head. "I knew you liked spending time with ya mom and the nightlife of the A, but I didn't think you'd like it to the point you wanted to move down here."

"Shit, neither did I, man," Wyatt confirmed. "Ain't tryna sound like a punk, but I miss my mom, man. I've had both my mom and dad for the first ten years of my life, but when my mom left for school, an important part of me was missing. Seeing my mom on holidays and birthdays ain't cutting it for me no more. I wanna be able to see and spend time with her when I want to. So I made the decision to stay here."

"I feel you, my nigga. I'ma miss you, man."

"Yeah. Me too, but you can always come down and visit me, and just because I'm moving don't mean we still can't be friends."

Giving his boy a handshake, the duo stood to their feet and left for work. Since they worked the same shift that day, Jace rode with Wyatt to work. When they arrived at the mall, Wyatt informed him that Rory and Ivanna were going to stop by during their lunch break to chill with them before they went into their stores. After clocking in, Jace assisted the few customers that were already in the store. As he performed his duties with a smile, he was lowkey feeling some type of way about the news his friend laid on him that morning. Although he understood why Wyatt wanted to stay, he felt like his friend was leaving him behind. Since their freshman year, they considered themselves to be the dynamic duo. Whenever one needed the other, they were always there. Now that his right-hand man was transferring schools, who was going to be there for him?

Aside from losing his friend, Jace thought about his situation with Sybil and what was going to become of it. In all reality, he knew that he couldn't do anything for Sybil besides give her some good D. He was a college student that didn't own shit but the clothes on his back and sneakers on his feet. Even though their relationship was only sexual, Jace fucked with her the long way. She opened her home to him and treated him with kindness. She didn't judge him or talk shit about his ghetto ass mama. With his bedroom skills already being A1, fucking Sybil made him better. She taught him how to make love and all the right things to say. She told him that she loved when he was in savage mode, but not all women and girls wanted their pussy pounded all the time. The nights they would lay in bed, they talked about whatever came to mind. Jace never pillow talked or cuddled with any girl, and the fact that he experienced that with an older woman made it that much special. He hated that he was going to have to give that up, but he knew it wasn't going to last forever.

※

AFTER A LONG DAY OF WORK, JACE AND WYATT LEFT THE mall with news outfits to wear for their date that night. When they arrived home, they informed Sybil that they wouldn't be home for dinner, and when she told them she wasn't cooking, the duo was surprised. Learning that she had plans of her own made Jace feel some type of way, but he didn't let it show. After taking a quick shower, he popped the tag of his new royal-blue Nike shirt before pulling up his black denim True Religion jeans. Lacing up his black and royal-blue retro Jordans, he put on his gold link chain and gold watch. After checking himself out in the mirror, Jace went upstairs looking for Sybil. When he saw her sneaking out the front door, he followed behind her.

"And where you think you going?" he angrily asked, eyeing the short denim shorts, teal-colored tank top, and sandals she was wearing.

"If you must know," she turned around to face him, "I'm going over to Dominique's. They're having a cookout for her husband's birthday."

"Dressed in these lil' ass shorts?" Jace pointed.

"These shorts ain't lil', Jace. Now go back in the house before my son hear you talking to me like this." Sybil dismissed him with a wave of her hand.

"Not until you give me a kiss."

"What?"

"You heard me."

Making sure the coast was clear, he pulled her close to him, kissing her lips passionately. When they ended their kiss, they both stared at each other for a moment. Every time they kissed, Sybil gave him a seductive look, letting him know that she was ready to fuck, but not that time. The look she gave him was different. Her eyes weren't just telling Jace that she wanted him. They were telling him that she cared about him. Kissing her again, he opened the car door for her.

"You better be good," he warned in a low tone.

"You too." She returned the warning.

"If you make it back before me, let me know."

"I will." Sybil winked at him.

Closing the door, he watched Sybil drive off before going to his car to search for his hair pick.

"Aye," Wyatt called, coming out the front door. "You ready to go?"

"Yup." Jace tossed his pick back in the car.

"Did you see my mom before she left?" Wyatt asked as they got inside his car.

"Yeah. She said she's going to Dominique's for her husband's birthday. I checked her about the shorts she was wearing, but she dismissed me." Jace shook his head as Wyatt pulled out of the driveway.

"I be having to talk to her sometimes about some of the clothes she wears myself." He chuckled. "Her work clothes are clothes, but some of her dresses and shorts be a lil' too short for my liking." Wyatt expressed, heading toward the highway. "I'm glad you spoke up, man."

"No problem, Dub Beezy. You're like my brother. So ya mom is my mom too. Shit, I would expect you to speak up or step up on my mom's behalf." He half lied.

"Yeah, but ya mom will cuss my ass out though."

They laughed.

"You ain't never lied."

"I wanna thank you, man."

"For what?" Jace curiously asked.

"For keeping ya word and not hitting on my mom. I really thought that you were gonna go behind my back and betray me, but you never did, man. I knew that we were tight before, but now, I consider you family. You said we were *like* brothers, but you're my brother *for real*."

Giving his boy a handshake, Jace instantly felt like shit after hearing Wyatt's views on their friendship. He was glad that his friend viewed him as family, but it was based on a lie. If Wyatt knew that he was fucking his mom every chance he got, Jace knew that their friendship would be no more and his relationship with Sybil would be destroyed. As they headed to their destination, his mind raced as he thought about how he should handle things with Sybil. He knew that his friendship was more important than pussy, and if it was just about sex, Jace would've ended it in a heartbeat. There were feelings involved that weren't easy to ignore, which made his decision that more difficult to make.

When they arrived at Six Flags, Wyatt found a parking spot in the crowded lot before they met Rory and Ivanna at the entrance. Giving them hugs, the men paid for their dates' tickets, strolling inside. As they stood in the long line, Jace held her from behind as they expressed how much they enjoyed their lunch date earlier that day. Inching their way to the front of the line, Ivanna whispered in his ear what she wanted to do to him when they left as she squeezed his dick. Even though he told her that he couldn't wait, Jace wasn't looking forward to fucking her.

After riding every roller coaster in the park, the couples got something to eat. As they chowed down on their food, he checked his phone and saw that he had a Facebook message from Sybil. He tried to keep a straight face as read how much she'd rather be with him than with her friends. Noticing the irritated expression on Ivanna's face, Jace tucked his phone back in his pocket. When they were finished with their hot dogs, curly fries, and nachos, they played games, and the girls were pissed they lost to the boys. Instead of rubbing it in their faces, they let them choose a prize that they wanted before heading to the gift shop. Buying a few things for his mom, Sybil, and Ivanna, the four of them made their way towards the exit. As

they headed over to Ivanna's car, held onto her hand the entire time.
"Man, I haven't had that much fun in a while." Jace grinned.
"We gotta do this again before we leave," Jace expressed
"I agree," Wyatt added.
"Please don't bring that up right now." Rory sighed. "I'm not ready to have that discussion yet."
"Neither am I," Ivanna chimed in. "We just started talking for real, and I'm not ready for you to leave yet, JC."
"Changing the subject then. What y'all wanna do now?" Wyatt asked.
"I don't know about y'all, but we're about to go back to Wyatt's crib and fuck," Rory responded bluntly.
"Damn. bitch." Ivanna laughed. "Well, go 'head 'cause me and Jace have plans of our own."
"Cool. See, y'all later."
Giving his boy a handshake, Ivanna hugged Rory before they headed over to Wyatt's car. When she unlocked the door to her 2019 Toyota Corolla, they got in, slamming the doors shut. As she pulled out of the lot, Jace removed his phone and responded to Sybil's messages. When she told them that they needed to talk to him about something important, he assumed that it was about something bad. Tucking his phone back in his pocket, he glanced over at Ivanna, who looked upset.
"Aye. Why you look like that?"
"Because you're rude as fuck, Jace! That's the second time you've been on yo' phone. Do you gotta respond to them hoes right now?"
"First of all, I wasn't talking to no hoes. I was responding to my mom. It's fucked up that you think I would disrespect you like that?" He pretended to be upset. "And even if I was, you shouldn't be worrying about them. I'm here with you."
"Whatever, nigga." Ivanna sucked her teeth.
After a short ride to her apartment in Mableton, she parked her car in the nearest spot before hopping out the car, slamming

her door shut. As she walked ahead of Jace, he shook his head as he followed her to her apartment. When they were inside, Ivanna tossed her keys on the glass coffee table. Tired of her attitude, he hugged from behind and sucked on her neck. Trying to fight him off, Jace began fondling her breasts through her shirt.

"Jace, let me go." She struggled to get away. "You ignored me for two months and then when I finally do get you, I still don't have ya full attention," she complained. "Let me go!"

"You really want me to let you go?" he asked, biting her neck gently.

She didn't respond.

"I asked you a question." He pulled her hair.

"No," she moaned.

"Take ya fucking clothes off," Jace ordered, releasing her.

Turning around to face him, he watched Ivanna strip out of her fitted pink Polo tee shirt and denim skirt, revealing her Savage X Fenty bra and panty set. As he removed his jeans and boxers, the sight of his dick made Ivanna drop to her knees. Jace watched as she made his dick disappear in her mouth and grabbed a fistful of her hair. He groaned, moaned, and cussed as she tried to suck the skin off his dick. With his entire shaft in her mouth, he watched in awe as Ivaana stuck out her tongue, licking his balls. As his nut began to build, Jace announced that he was about to cum. Sucking his manhood a few seconds more, he watched as she removed his dick from her mouth and stroked it until Jace exploded all over her chest.

After taking a moment to clean herself off, she removed her bra and panties before climbing on the bed in doggy style position. As he rolled the condom on his dick, Jace smirked as he watched the way she twerked with her ass in the air. Standing behind her, he slammed his dick inside her, causing her to scream. As he pounded her from the back, Jace grabbed her hips, thrusting deeper inside her.

"Shhiiittt," Ivanna hissed, throwing her ass back.

"You like that?"

"Yeessss, Jamar!"

Stopping instantly, Jace pulled out of her without saying a word.

"What the fuck are you doing?" She got off the bed.

"Bitch, you just called me another nigga's name. You think I'ma finish fucking you after that?"

"No, I didn't call you another nigga's name, Jamar."

With her eyes growing wide, Ivanna realized her mistake and tried to clean it up, but it was too late. After disposing his condom, he put his clothes back on and left. Once he was outside, he ordered an Uber. Jace rode home in silence, and he couldn't help but laugh to himself. After all the trouble she went through to get his attention, she ended up losing him for good because she couldn't keep her names straight. Even though they weren't official, Jace wasn't going to deal with being called another man's name. He could get pussy from any chick, and to him, Ivanna's wasn't that good. When he made it home, he saw Wyatt's car parked in the driveway. Instead of going inside, he hopped in his car and went to the nearest hotel, where he and Sybil spent the rest of the night tangled up in each other.

11

"Sybil, did you season the meat already, or do I need to?" Dominique shouted from the kitchen.

"Nah, they seasoned already and ready to go on the grill," Sybil confirmed.

"Cool. Let me get started then." She carried the tin pan outside.

"Girl, I can't believe you have a twenty-one-year-old son now." Leah shook her head. "How do you feel, Syb?"

"To be honest, I don't even know. I mean, I wanna say I feel old, but look at me." She spun around. "I look good for my age."

"Yes, you do, sis," Dom agreed from outside.

"I can't believe you agreed to let James come down for Wyatt's birthday gathering. I thought you were mad at him for not telling you about his marriage?" Leah spoke, heading outside with three wine glasses.

"I was at first." Sybil carried two bottles of wine outside. "But after I realized I had no right to be mad, I let it go." She shrugged, placing the bottles on the table.

When Dominique and Leah erupted in a fit of laughter, she looked at them in confusion.

"What is so damn funny?"

"Syb, you're our girl, and you know we know you better than that. The reason why you were pissed is because you still have feelings for that man," Leah stated matter-of-factly.

"That's right. I don't care how long y'all have been apart. You still have a soft spot for that man." Dom pointed at her.

"Both of y'all sound like my son. He said the same thing." Sybil chuckled. "But James and I have been talking a couple days out of the week since then. We're working on being friends again, and I'm gonna leave it at that."

"Every great relationship starts with a friendship," Dominique added from the grill. "I'm all for the friendship, but I think y'all are gonna be something more."

"So do I." Leah filled their glasses with wine. "When I told my fiancé James was coming down, he was too hype."

"So was my husband. Y'all know these men are gonna act a fool when they get here." Dominique laughed.

"Don't I know it. They haven't seen each other in years. I got a feeling that once James sees them, he's gonna want to move down here," Sybil stated.

"That won't be so bad now that Wyatt is staying down here." Leah sipped her wine.

"Mmm," she hummed. "Leah, girl, thank you for getting my son into Clark Atlanta at the last minute. I owe you big time."

"Girl, you know I will do anything for that boy, but if you really wanna thank me, I'll take a brand-new Louis Vuitton bag."

"Girl, I'll get you three if I need to. You came through in the clutch." They clanked glasses.

"We're back," Wyatt announced with Jace and James with bags in their hands.

As she sipped her wine, she watched as James greeted her friends with hugs and kisses. For some reason, he looked different from the last time she'd seen him. He was rocking one of his many fraternity shirts with a pair of light denim True Religion jeans and a pair of wheat-colored Timbs. His cinnamon complexion was the same as their son's, and their eyes were identical. His fade was full of waves like Wyatt's, but James had a full beard and mustache. Wyatt was his dads' twin, but she hadn't realized it until then. She couldn't believe that he still had the same charm and swag that made her fall in love with him when they were younger.

With her wine glass in hand, Sybil switched past James and the boys. Placing her glass on the counter, she removed two tin pans from the fridge that were filled with seafood and potato salad. When she heard the sliding door open and shut, she knew by the Burberry cologne that James was in the kitchen with her.

"Damn. So you're just gonna walk by me without speaking, huh?" he spoke.

"You were taking your time getting to me. So I came in the house to get the sides." Sybil smirked.

"You always gotta be difficult, Sybil?"

"I'm just fucking with you." She walked around the counter with her arms extended.

Embracing each other tightly, he moaned in her ear, causing her to smirk.

"It feels so good having you in my arms again." James kissed her neck.

"You need to slow your roll, James." She pushed him away. "This ain't that type of party. We're working on rebuilding our friendship, and that's it for right now. Let's not forget that you're still a married man." Sybil walked back over to the counter.

"You're right. My bad. Is it out of line for me to say that you're sexier than motherfucka?" He seductively licked his lips.

"Nah. You don't look too bad yourself. Now take one of these pans."

Sharing a seductive stare, he picked one of the pans up, carrying it outside, and she did the same. As she and Leah covered the table with a tablecloth, they placed paper plates, cups, napkins, plastic cutlery, food, and alcohol on top. With ice, soda, and beer in the cooler, everyone sat around, bobbing their head to the tunes that Wyatt was playing. As she chopped it up with James about their plans after the pregame party they were having, Sybil wasn't too pleased that he was taking their son and Jace to the strip club. She didn't want her secret lover and son wasting their money on strippers, but since they were going with James, she didn't protest. It was hard for her not to look at Jace or in his direction out of fear that someone might figure them out. All that ran through her mind was the amazing sex they had that morning and the conversation that followed.

With her back pressed against her truck that was parked in the garage, Sybil tried her best not to moan. Jace had her by her ass cheeks, filling her with all nine inches of his hooked shaft. Her nails sunk into his back as she grinded against him, matching his rhythm. Sinking his teeth into her neck, she cussed in a whispered tone as she tightly closed her eyes. The pain and pleasure made her wetter with each stroke. Pressing his lips against her ear, Sybil let out a few light gasps and low moans so he could hear her. She knew that was what he wanted. They knew it was a bold move to be fucking each other with Wyatt at the house, but she didn't care. He was leaving the next day and needed her last fix before he left.

When they met at the hotel a week ago, she asked him if he thought about moving to Georgia, and when Jace informed her that he expressed interest in it, Sybil smiled. Suggesting that he move down there and transfer schools, she offered to pay for his apartment. Jace told her that he'd think about it. As they cuddled the night away, she fell asleep without a care in the world. She never thought that doing something so wrong could feel so right. As much as Sybil tried to convince herself that she wasn't catching feelings for the young boy, her actions said otherwise. She found herself online shopping for expensive things on Jace's behalf that she never purchased. Sybil wanted to buy him designer everything. She even thought about buying him a car. She had fallen victim to his savage lovemaking and ways, and she felt like she needed to reward him for his amazing performance throughout the summer.

As his departure day neared, Sybil asked him every day if he made his decision to stay, and he told her no every time. The fact that he was taking so long to give her an answer gave her time to do some serious thinking. After weeks of lying to herself, Sybil finally admitted that she had fallen in love with Jace. He made her feel things, sexually and emotionally, that no man her age had. He listened to her when she talked. He made her laugh, and she learned that it wasn't just her looks that he was attracted to. The thought of having a relationship with Jace crossed her mind a few times, but Sybil knew it would never work. He had his whole life ahead of him, and she wanted more than just a sexual relationship. As much as she didn't want to, she had to let him go.

As he dug deeper into her pussy, Sybil's legs began to shake. Trying to keep her orgasm at bay, she wanted the moment to last as long as it could. No longer able to control it, she wrapped her legs tighter around him as she rode out her wave of ecstasy. After a few more strokes, Jace exploded in the condom he was wearing. Placing Sybil on her feet, her arms remained around his neck. They were silent for a moment as their breathing went back to normal. Seconds later, she broke the ice.

"Jace, uh, I know... why you haven't given me an answer about moving down here."

"And why is that?"

"Because you don't want to." She moved to the front of the garage where the light was.

He sighed as he positioned himself back in front of her.

"I ain't gonna lie, Sybil. Our lil' situationship was fun as hell. I love spending time with you and being inside you, but you and I both know that we can't be anything more than this. I'm still wanna live life and have fun, and you deserve a man that's gonna give you more than a good fuck." Jace lifted her chin so she could look at him. "You know what I'm saying is the truth."

"I know." Sybil sighed. "I'm gonna miss you, young bul."

"I'ma miss you too, old head."

They laughed.

Kissing her lips, they embraced each other one last time before they left out of the garage. She made sure the door was shut as Jace headed to the basement entrance. Entering the house through the front door, Sybil went upstairs to her room, climbed in bed, and dozed off.

Around five that evening, Dominique's husband, Glenn, and Leah's fiancé, Levi, arrived along with Rory and Chante. When the hot dogs were finished, Dominique placed them on the table while the men excitedly greeted each other. Sybil smiled as they wished Wyatt a happy twenty-first birthday. As she continued admiring her son and his father, she locked eyes with Jace. Unable to look at him without showing any emotion, she broke their intense stare down. Tuning back into the conversation she was having with Leah, Dominique, Rory, and Chante, James began passing out shot glasses. The women had vodka and the men had Henny. With everyone standing to their feet, Wyatt turned the music down as James stood in the middle ready to make a toast.

"First, I wanna start by saying happy birthday to my son, Dub Beezy."

Everyone said celebratory cheers.

"I'm proud of the man you've grown into, and I pray that the life lessons and morals don't fade now that Georgia is your new home."

Raising their shot glasses, they downed their drinks, then turned the music back up. As the women made plates for the men, Sybil was about to pass a plate to her son, but Rory was on it, and Chante made a place for Jace. A little disappointed that her son and secret lover had girls taking care of them, she just smiled and gave James the plate she made. With drinks and good vibes flowing throughout the party, Dominique, Leah, and Sybil jumped to their feet when Crime Mob's *Knuck If You Buck* came through the speaker. Getting in line, they did their sorority stroll to the beat. When Rory joined the stroll line, the girls were shocked to discover that she was a part of their sisterhood. When they were finished, the men pushed their plates to the side and showed the women how it was done, doing their stroll to *Wipe Me Down*. The women whooped and hollered as they did their thang. With his eyes trained on her, Sybil seductively eyed her ex. When they were in school, she loved watching her man stroll and step with his frat brothers. She was shocked that it still had that effect on her.

After spending the evening having a good time, the party came to an end a little after ten. James was ready to take the boys out for the night. When Leah and Dominique agreed to let their men go to the strip club, the girls decided to turn the party into a sleepover. Ready to go swimming, the women snatched up their purses, heading inside to change. As Sybil jogged up the stairs, she went over to her dresser and removed one of her bikinis. Tossing it on the bed, she jumped when she saw James standing in the doorway. Without warning, he walked over to Sybil, placed his hands on the sides of her face and kissed her lips. Placing her hands on his arms, her tenseness faded as she got into it. When he pulled away, they stared at each other for a moment before she spoke.

"Wh... What was that?"

"I've been wanting to do that since the first time I saw you again. I thought ya man was gonna be here, but Wyatt told me that y'all ended. So, I decided to make my move," he replied.

"James, I already told you—"

"I know what you told me, Sybil, and I know that I'm married, but that doesn't mean I'm happy. Kira was the only one that put up with all my bullshit. She cared about me, and we had a child together. I was getting older, and I was tired of being alone. So I married her, but that's not where I wanna be. My heart has always been yours, Sybil," James sincerely replied.

"Wow... I.... I don't know what to say."

"Say that you'll think about giving me a real chance. I don't mind us starting over. As long as it leads to us being together."

Taking a few seconds to think, the knocks on the door interrupted their moment.

"Aye, Dad, you rolling with us or you staying here?" Wyatt asked with a goofy look on his face.

"Here I come, son," James answered. "My flight doesn't leave until one. Maybe I can take you to breakfast or something and you can give me your answer then."

"Okay." She smiled.

Kissing her again, Wyatt kissed her cheek before following his dad out the room. As she sat on the edge of her bed, Sybil thought of everything that James had just expressed to her. There was no doubt in her mind that she still had feelings for him. She needed to take a moment to sort through her feelings. Although she and Jace decided to end things, Sybil wasn't over him yet. She was comparing the two of them in her mind already just by the way they kissed, and they were a tie. Knowing she couldn't base her decision on that alone, Sybil knew that she needed to give James a chance and get to know him again. It was going to be difficult to push her memories and feelings for Jace to the back of her mind, but she was going to try.

12

TWO MONTHS LATER...

After a two-hour meeting with a couple of prospective donors, James and his partners had gained over a million dollars in donations for his alma mater. Shaking hands with the men and women, they escorted their guests out of the office. As they went their separate ways into their offices, he closed the door behind him and sat behind his desk. Removing his phone from his pocket, James checked his email to see if his gifts arrived at Sybil's job. When his phone began to ring, he smiled when he saw that it was Sybil calling.

"Hey, sugarfoot. What's going on?" he answered the FaceTime call.

"Mr. Bennett, you are showing off with these surprises." She beamed. "First, it was the surprise visit last month. The jewelry from Tiffany's. The new Christian Louboutin pumps I wanted. Now, you brought me a new Gucci purse with the matching belt and sneakers. Not to mention this big ass edible arrangement. You got me ready to leave my job right now and get on an earlier flight out of here."

"I'm glad you like the gifts, sexy." James seductively licked his lips. "I can't wait to see you tonight."

"Neither can I." She tilted her head to the side, blushing. "I know you told me to just focus on us and not mention ya wife, but I feel a lil' strange creeping around with a married man, James. Even if the man is my son's father."

"I know and appreciate your patience, boo. I have a few more things I need to do before I break the news to Kira. Shit, I wouldn't be surprised if she tells me she wants a divorce. We haven't been in a good place since May."

"May?"

"The day after I dropped Wyatt off down there, I called out your name when she was giving me head." He shook his head.

"Stop lying!"

"I'm very serious. She almost bit my shit off. When I came down for Wyatt's birthday, Kira got mad when I told her that she couldn't come with me. We've been sleeping in separate rooms since I got back. Things are so tense between us, and now, it's starting to affect my baby girl."

"Damn, James. Are you sure you really wanna leave Kira? I know she's the chick you cheated on me with in college, but she's still your wife. Maybe you should try to work things out with her," she expressed sincerely.

"I appreciate ya concern, Sybil, but my mind is made up. If I woulda done right by you the first time, there would be no Kira. This is the happiest I've been in the past two months, and I wouldn't change a thing about it." James smiled.

"When did you become such a smooth talker?"

"I had a lot of practice."

"I remember when we were younger, your way of telling me I looked nice was saying 'don't get fucked up around here'." Sybil imitated him.

They both laughed.

"You were a straight savage back then. You never told me shit straight out, and you never expressed your feelings. If it wasn't for your actions, I wouldn't even know that you loved me."

"So how did you know a nigga loved you?"

"Well, when we were kids, you always brought me my favorite chocolate whenever it was that time of the month. You never left my side when I was pregnant. You used to watch what I ate while I was pregnant." She laughed. "When we were in college, you walked me to my classes, even though it made you late for yours. Every time I passed an exam, you rewarded me with head because you never did it any other time." Sybil bit her bottom lip

"I damn sure didn't. That wasn't my thing back then." He chuckled.

"That's why I made sure I passed every exam I took." She giggled.

"Damn, I didn't think you still remembered all of that. I guess actions really do speak louder than words."

"Yeah, they do."

"Well, since I never told you before, I'm gonna tell you now. I love you, Sybil Bailey."

Her eyes grew wide.

"Oh my God." She gasped. "That sounded so sexy."

James laughed.

"I love you too, James Bennett. My next appointment is coming in. I'll let you know when I'm on my way to the airport."

"A'ight, love."

Ending the call, James placed his phone on the table. With a smile on his face, James gathered the files for his next meeting before heading out of his office. As he sat in his meeting, he thought about how he was going to handle things with Kira. There was no doubt in his mind that Sybil was the woman he wanted to be with. He just didn't know how to break the news gently to his wife.

Aside from ending things with Kira, he thought about his next move after the divorce. He thought about moving to

Georgia to be closer to Sybil and Wyatt. He thought about his daughter, Jasmine, and how she would handle the news. James recalled when he and Sybil broke up and Wyatt's reaction. His son didn't talk to him for a month after he confessed what he did. He could only imagine how twelve-year-old daughter was going to take the news.

After his last meeting of the day, James gathered his things and headed out of the building. He waved to a few of the students as he strolled through the parking lot. Working at his alma mater for the past ten year as a college alumni and development officer definitely had its perks, and James loved seeing the improvements of the university, thanks to the donations they received. That weekend was homecoming weekend, and he couldn't wait to show Sybil all of the changes that were made. Popping the locks to his black 2019 Jaguar XF, he tossed his briefcase in the passenger's seat before taking his place behind the wheel. Once the door was closed, James brought his car to life, pulled out of the lot and drove to the four-bedroom, three-bathroom home he owned.

Arriving at his house fifteen minutes later, James pulled into the driveway, next to an unfamiliar car. When he noticed a man in the driver's seat, he killed the engine and jumped out. Tapping on the window, the man rolled down his window.

"Can I help you, my man?"

"Nah. I'm just waiting for Kira." The stranger looked him over.

"And who are you?" James tried to control his anger.

"I'ma friend of hers."

"Yeah. I know what that means."

Backing away from the car, he turned around and strolled calmly to the front door. When he got inside, he heard Jasmine and Kira arguing upstairs. Jogging up the stairs by twos, James stormed down the hall to his room where the commotion was coming from. With her hand raised in the air, he pulled Jasmine back before Kira could hit their child.

"What the hell is going on here?" He roared.

"I don't know. When I got home, mom told me to pack up my things. I asked her why, and she went off on me!" She explained.

"Go wait in your room while I talk to your mom, Jazzy."

Eyeing them suspiciously, she left the room. When he heard the door shut, Kira spoke.

"As you can see, I'm packing my shit and leaving. I'm not gonna sit around and watch you disrespect me any longer, James." She filled her duffel bag with clothes. "I know you wanna be with Sybil. So go 'head and be with her. My man is waiting for me outside."

"I don't mind you leaving, but what I do mind is you bringing that nigga to my crib. What the fuck is wrong with you?"

"Hmph. If you must know, that nigga has been all up and through this house while you're at work and while you were in Georgia last month," Kira snidely replied.

James let out an angry sigh.

"And as far as Jasmine, I'm taking her with me. He has a nice house in Chester in a better school district. You can see her whenever you want."

"No, I'm not." Jasmine spoke from the doorway. "I wanna stay here with my dad. I'm not living in a house with a man I don't know who has two teenage sons." She crossed her arms over her chest.

"I told you that nothing is gonna happen to you!" Kira shouted.

"You don't know that, and I don't feel comfortable around that man. At least I know I'll be safe with my dad."

"What you mean you don't feel comfortable around him?" James turned in her direction.

"When you were out of town visiting Wyatt, mom invited him over for dinner. When she left to go to the bathroom, he kept telling me how pretty I was and looking at me all weird. He looks at me like that all the time. I don't like it, and I'm not going." Jasmine fought back tears.

Looking at Kira, he waited for her to respond, but she didn't.

"You ain't got shit to say about that?"

"Look, Vince isn't that kinda guy, a'ight? She's probably just overthinking." Kira shook her head, packing the rest of her things.

"Like I said. I don't mind you leaving. Our marriage has been over for a while now, but Jasmine is staying here. *You* can see her whenever you want to, but you better not have her around that nigga," James warned.

"Fine. I'll be here to pick her up next weekend."

Zipping up her duffel bags, Kira stormed past them without saying another word. As he embraced his daughter, the front door slammed shut.

"Dad, are you mad at mom?"

"Honestly, I'm not. I haven't felt the same about your mom since I bumped into an old flame a few months back. So our marriage was going to end eventually," he replied.

"Do you still love mom?"

"I will always have love for ya mom. She gave me you."

Looking down at his daughter, James kissed her forehead, making her smile. Once his daughter felt a little better, he offered to take her to the mall, which really cheered her up. After sending her to change her clothes, he stripped out of his suit and tie. Grabbing a pair of light-denim Balmain jeans, a white Polo shirt, and his fraternity varsity jacket, James put his clothes on before stuffing his feet into his black Nike boots. Before leaving the walk-in closet, he checked his shoe boxes that were on the top self of the closet to make sure his money was still there, and it was. Kira didn't know about the bank rolls he kept in the Nike shoeboxes. Since she revealed that she had a nigga all up and through his crib, James wasn't sure if they discovered his secret stash. Although he had plenty of money in the bank, he still liked to keep a few stacks tucked away in shoeboxes. It reminded him of his days in the streets and what he overcame. It also reminded him to always stay humble and appreciate what he had.

Leaving his room, he met Jasmine in the hall, showing off her outfit to her dad. With his wallet, money clip, and phone in his pockets, the duo headed out the door, locking the door behind him. Opening the door for his daughter, James closed the door for her before taking his place behind the wheel. As he brought the car to life, he removed his phone from his back pocket when he felt it vibrate. When he saw the text message from Sybil saying that she was on her way to the airport, he smiled. Pulling out of the driveway, James allowed Jasmine to sync her phone to the car so she could play her playlist. They already had an understanding of the type of music she was allowed to listen to, so he didn't mind.

After listening to songs by Monica, Fantasia, Mary J. Blige, Teyana Taylor, and Ella Mai, he was happy when they arrived at the Christiana Mall thirty-five minutes later. Hand and hand, they strolled through the mall until they reached Abercrombie & Fitch, which was one of her favorite stores. He followed Jasmine around the store as she picked out all the clothes she wanted. He noticed a few boys checking her out while she shopped, but when they saw James mean mugging them, they backed off. Although she was only twelve, her height and the way she was built made her look a little older. After trying on her clothes, he paid for her things, then they headed to the next store.

After an hour of shopping at multiple stores, James found the nearest bench and copped a squat while his daughter went into the Pink section of Victoria's Secret. Removing his phone from his pocket, he scrolled through Facebook until he saw a post that Sybil made about going to Lincoln weekend for homecoming weekend. Reading the comments, he chuckled when he read Wyatt's comment. *Have fun mom. Make sure you, Aunt Dom, and Aunt Lee don't get in no trouble.* After responding to his son, he continued scrolling down his timeline until he heard a familiar

IT'S HIS SAVAGE LOVE FOR ME

voice. Looking up, he saw Jace leaning on the rail a few feet away from him, talking on the phone. With his phone in hand, James stood to his feet, heading in his direction. Ready to tap him on the shoulder, he stopped when Jace said Sybil's name. When he heard him ask if he could bend her over like he did over the summer, his heart dropped to his feet and blood pressure went up. Tapping him on the shoulder, Jace turned around. With a shocked expression on his face, he told Sybil that he'd call her back.

"Lil' nigga, did I hear you right? Did I just hear you say you fucked Sybil over the summer?" James asked in a low tone.

Dropping his head, he lifted it back up with confidence.

"Yeah, Mr. JB. Me and Sybil got down over the summer," he replied.

"I'm assuming my son doesn't know about this?"

"Nah. He doesn't."

"Wyatt was just telling me how you kept his word to him and never tried to hit on his mom. I saluted you for being a man of ya word and putting friendship over pussy. Damn was I wrong." He shook his head. "Have you and Sybil been talking all this time?"

"Nah. The last time I saw or talked to her was at Wyatt's party. Wyatt told me that she was coming up for homecoming. So I hit her up through Facebook Messenger."

The men stared at each other for a moment before Jace spoke again.

"So I'm guessing you're gonna tell Wyatt now."

"I don't know yet. You've been a pretty solid dude until now, but I don't think I'd be able to live with myself keeping a secret like this from my son," James responded.

"Daddy!" Jasmine called him.

"I gotta go."

Walking away to join his daughter, he managed to remain calm for the sake of his daughter. He didn't know who he was more furious with—Jace for betraying his son, or Sybil for giving

99

her pussy to a young buck and betraying their son. He thought back to the party to see if he noticed anything strange between the two of them, but he didn't. Not once did he notice either of them staring at each other. They didn't even go near each other. They played that shit so smooth that nobody would've guessed that they were sleeping around. Now that James knew their secret, he didn't know how to feel about Sybil. He didn't even know if he was going to tell his son.

Pushing the situation to the back of his mind, he put his focus back on his daughter and enjoyed the rest of their outing.

13

The fun-filled weekend went by too fast for Sybil and her friends. Being back on campus brought back a lot of memories for the trio. They were glad to see the updates their alma mater had made over the years. It felt good seeing the rest of their line sisters, as well as the other alumnus that was there to partake in the festivities. Sybil was having so much fun with her friends that she was no longer upset about James's last-minute cancelation. When she called him to let her know that she arrived at her hotel, he explained to her about what happened between him and Kira. After he told her that he was spending time with his daughter, Sybil made him promise that he would come see her before she left. After the call ended, she noticed that his tone was different. The smooth, deep voice he usually used was replaced with a tone of annoyance and borderline anger. Even though they had only been reunited for a couple of months, she still remembered his tones and moods.

Waking up Sunday morning with a hangover, Sybil dragged herself to the bathroom to brush her teeth and wash her face. As she dried her face with a towel, the ringing of her room phone caused her head to throb. With a hand on her forehead, she made her way over to the nightstand to answer it.

"Hello?"

"Hey, girl. It's Leah. I woulda called your cell, but I can't find my phone."

"Wassup."

"We ordered you some food from room service, so come on up to Dom's room."

"A'ight. I'll be up in a minute."

Placing the phone back on the receiver, Sybil searched for a pair of leggings in her MCM duffel bag. Slowly putting on her pants, she slid her feet into her Gucci slides before grabbing her room key. As she searched for her phone, the pounding on the door made her migraine worse. Walking to the door as fast as she could, she snatched it open ready to cuss out the person on the other side, but when she saw it was James, she stopped herself. Before she could say anything, he brushed past her causing Sybil to stumble.

"What the fuck is wrong with you this morning?" she asked, letting door slam shut.

"So that's what you do now, Sybil? You just go around fucking ya son's friends?" he huffed, standing in the middle of the floor.

"I don't know what the fuck you're talking about." She lied with a straight face.

"How the fuck are you standing in my face lying to me right now!" he shouted. "I know that you were fucking Jace over the summer!"

Hearing James reveal her secret made her heart rate increase. The angry expression on James's face, along with his flaring nostrils, made her feel like he was going to charge toward her. Instead of backing down, she had no choice but to come clean.

"Okay." Sybil nodded her head. "Yes. I did fuck him," she stated with no shame. "He told me that he thought I was attractive, and I brushed him off, but my curiosity got the best of me. So when he made the first move, I didn't stop him. I knew what I was doing, and I was aware of what could happen if our son found out about this, but I don't want Wyatt to know. I don't want this to destroy our relationship."

"Then you shoulda that about before you slept with his friend, Sybil!"

"So what? Huh? Ya ass gonna tell him? And try to make him pick sides?" She stepped closer to him.

James remained silent.

"I know what I did was wrong, but what happened between me and Jace has nothing to do with us, James. Things have been so great between us. I don't want this to mess up the progress we're making with getting our relationship back on track."

"How the hell am I supposed to move forward knowing what I know? You expect me to look my son in the eye and lie? Every time you and Jace end up in the same room together, the three of us are gonna know what happened between y'all. You and Jace managed to keep that shit under wraps for the entire summer, but me, I can't just act like shit is cool when I know it ain't. That shit is uncomfortable as fuck." James raised his voice.

"So what are you saying?"

"You told me on Friday that you loved me. So now, it's time for you to prove it. If you really love him, you gotta tell Wyatt the truth about you and Jace," he boldly stated. "Wyatt wants us to be together, and I want us to be together, but if you really want this, you gotta come clean, love."

"So before I can get my family back, you want me to tell our son a secret that might cause him to hate me for the rest of his life?" She stared at him. "I don't think so."

"Say what?"

"I love you, James, but I can always get another man. I can't get another son," Sybil harshly stated.

Staring at each other for a moment, she could see the hurt in his eyes. She knew that James wasn't expecting her to say that, but it was the truth. As much as she wanted him back, Sybil wasn't ready to kill the relationship she had with her son. Since he started school, Wyatt had spent more time at the house than he did in his apartment. They had movie night every Friday and dinner every Sunday. The time they spent together meant more to her than a relationship with any man. Nodding his head, James brushed past her again without saying a word. When the door slammed shut, Sybil took a moment to get herself together before joining her friends for breakfast.

After eating a delicious breakfast, Sybil went back to her room, where she prepared to leave. The upbeat mood and positive energy that she had all weekend had faded. The conversation she had with James was in the front of her mind as she washed up and got dressed for the day. Sybil believed that she did the right thing, but the more she thought about it, she started second-guessing herself. Dressed in a black Victoria's Secret sweatshirt and matching pants, she put on her classic chestnut-colored Ugg boots before brushing her long black tresses into a high ponytail. Putting on her sunglasses, Sybil snatched up her duffel bag, room key, and phone, then left the room. Once she was checked out of the hotel, she strolled through the revolving door and hopped in the back seat of her friend's rental car, where she was quiet the entire way to the airport.

After the two-hour flight, the trio got off the plane with their bags in hand. Making their way to the parking lot, Sybil popped the locks to her Lexus, and the ladies tossed their bags in the trunk. While Dominique closed the trunk, she hopped in the back seat while she and Leah got comfortable up front. Bringing the car to life, she pulled out of the lot, carefully maneuvering through the airport traffic to the expressway. Lost in thought, the sound of Leah calling her name snapped her out of it.

"Sybil? What is wrong with you, girl? You've been quiet since we left the hotel?"

"And that's not like you, Tammy-Talk-A-Lot. Spill the beans," Dominique added from the backseat.

"Y'all know I love y'all to pieces, but I really don't wanna talk about this, a'ight?" Sybil kept her eyes on the road. "All I can tell you is that James and I had a fight at the hotel, and we are no longer working rebuilding our relationship."

"Awww, damn!" they shouted in unison.

"I was really rooting for y'all." Leah sighed.

"So was I. The fight must've been about something juicy because James ain't the type of man to give up easily," Dominique spoke up.

"It was." Sybil sighed. "Which is why I don't wanna talk about it. So can we just drop it, please?"

"Okay."

"Fine."

Knowing that her friends weren't going to leave it alone, it only took a couple minutes for them to break the silence.

"Bitch, if you don't give us the tea, we're gonna die," Leah blurted out.

"What I'm about to tell y'all goes no further than this car."

"We promise," they responded in unison.

"James found out that Jace and I were messing around over the summer. He told me that in order for us to move forward, I had to tell Wyatt about it. I told him no, and he left," Sybil explained.

"So that's why ya ass was so happy every time we saw you!" Leah screeched. "You were getting dicked down by the young buck!"

"I thought you spending time with ya son had you glowing and smiling like that. Who would've thought that you were fucking Jace..." Dominique chuckled. "In a way, I can't blame you, Syb. Jace is a handsome thang."

"Yes he is," Leah agreed. "The only thing that makes this bad is that he's Wyatt's best friend."

"I know," Sybil replied. "I don't have any regrets about what I did. I just don't wanna lose my son. I told James that I can get another man. I can't get another son, and I know if I tell him this, he'll never forgive me for it."

"Sybil, you're our girl, so you know we're always gonna tell you the truth. I understand that you don't wanna lose ya son, but you gotta tell him about this. Not to get James back, but for yourself. We want our kids to be honest with us about everything, but we're selective about the things we're honest about with them," Dominique softly spoke.

"You said that you have no regrets about what happened although you knew it was wrong. So be the grown woman that you are and tell that boy the truth. Shit, he might make a confession of his own," Leah added.

"Thanks for the advice, y'all." She gave a small smile. "I don't know when I'm gonna tell him, but I'll tell him soon."

For the rest of the ride, Sybil told her friends about her experience with Jace. When she mentioned that she was ready to buy his ass everything under the sun, they erupted in a fit of laughter. Reliving the memories of her summer romance brought back the feelings she had tucked away. She thought about what attracted her to Jace and discovered that it was his confidence. There wasn't an ounce of fear in him. The way he took control in the bedroom, letting her know that he was not to played with, was sexy as fuck to her. All of the things that attracted her to Jace was the same things she loved about James. The savage love that they gave her was identical. After realizing that James was the man she was chasing all along, she felt stupid for pushing him away. The only man she wanted in her life was James, and she needed to make things right. even if that meant losing her son.

14

After a month and a half of being on line, Wyatt was looking forward to the ceremony his fraternity was holding for the pledges that evening. There were times when he wanted to drop out, but with the help of his line brothers, he managed to hold on. When they first started their journey, it was twelve of them, but only eight remained standing. Everything wasn't meant for everybody, but Wyatt overcame the challenges. Not being able to tell anybody what he was doing was hard for him. He wanted to let the people that were close to him know what was going on with him, but he had to keep his mouth shut. Since his journey was about to come to end, he invited his father and mother to the ceremony to share the special moment with him, even though they weren't on speaking terms.

As his last class of the day came to an end, Wyatt snatched up his backpack and headed out the door. Strolling out the building, he gave a head nod to a few chicks that spoke to him as he headed toward the parking lot. He smirked to himself as one of the chicks winked at him as she passed him. The girls on campus came in all different shapes, sizes, and flavors.

Although he never dated a BBW before, there were a few of them on campus that he had his eye on. With all the temptations the university had to offer, Wyatt remained faithful to Rory. They had been messing around for almost four months, but they still weren't official. With both of them going to school and working, they didn't have much time for each other. It's been a couple of weeks since the last time they had sex and he was fiending for it.

POPPING THE LOCKS TO HIS CAR, HE TOSSED HIS BACKPACK IN the passenger's seat before sliding behind the wheel. As he started the car, Wyatt removed his phone from his pocket and went to his playlist. When Rick Ross's *Hustlin'* came through the speakers, he turned up the volume and pulled out of the parking lot. Nodding his head to the music, he swerved in and out of the midday traffic on the expressway until he got off at his exit. Instead of going to his apartment, he decided to go visit his mom. He couldn't join her and his aunts for Sunday dinner a few nights before because he had to put the finishing touches on a paper he needed to type. Since she returned from Lincoln a couple of weeks ago, there was no doubt that his mom was acting strange. When she told Wyatt about their fight, Sybil said that she messed up, but she never told him how. He went to his father for answers, and all he said was that his mom was selfish and stubborn. He even tried to reach out to Jace to see if he knew what was going with his parents, but he never answered his calls. The last time they spoke was the day before Sybil left for homecoming. Since no one wanted to tell him what was going on, Wyatt decided to leave it alone.

ARRIVING AT HIS MOM'S CRIB A FEW MINUTES LATER, HE smiled when he saw her taking groceries in the house. He didn't understand how women could carry grocery bags in heels, but they made that shit look so easy. Killing the engine, he jumped out the car, stuffing his keys and phone in his pocket. As he closed his car door, Wyatt jogged over to his mom, helping her with the door.

"Let me get those, Ma." He tried to remove the bags from her hands.

"I got these, baby. Grab the rest of the bags for me." Doing as he was told, he grabbed all of the bags out the trunk and slammed it shut. With Sybil holding the screen door open for him, he headed straight for the kitchen. Placing the bags on the counter, he started helping her put the food away.

"I see your getting ready for Thanksgiving."

"Yeah." She chuckled. "I wasn't planning to host Thanksgiving this year, but after ya aunt Leah and Dom talked me into it, I figured what the hell. On top of that, Hazel invited herself and Jace to the dinner. She said she needs to get away from Philly for a few days."

"That's wassup. I haven't seen her and Jace in a minute." Wyatt smiled. "Aye, have you heard from Darrin lately?"

"He texts me every now and then. He wants another chance with me, but I don't want him," she honestly replied.

. . .

"You never told me why y'all stopped talking in the first place." He looked at his mom.

"He couldn't please me... in that special way," Sybil expressed.

He took a few seconds to figure out what she was trying to say.

"Ohhhh! He couldn't handle his business in the bedroom!"

"Right." Sybil laughed.

"Damn, Darrin." He shook his head, putting the last of the food away. "Maybe I should invite Chante to the dinner. She still asks about Jace every time she sees me."

"How did Jace end up with Chante? I thought he was talking to Ivanna."

"He was until she called him another man's name while they were getting down."

"I know you lying!" she screeched.

. . .

"Dead serious, Ma."

"Wow." Sybil grabbed a bottle of water from the fridge.

The kitchen fell quiet for a moment as they went over to the kitchen table and sat down. With both of their minds on different things, Wyatt was about to ask her about his dad, but Sybil beat him to the punch.

"Son, I've been trying to find a way to tell you the reason why me and your dad fell out. No matter how I tell you, it's not gonna make the news any less painful. So, here it goes." She took a deep breath. "Over the summer... Jace and I... had sex... a few times..." Sybil dragged out. "Ya father found out about what happened between us and confronted me about it. I made the choice to not tell you because I didn't wanna mess up our relationship. I pushed ya dad away because having you in my life is more important than anything, but I can't keep this secret from you any longer, Wyatt."

"I can't believe this." He scoffed, getting up from the table. "All this time I thought that you were treating him like a son and he viewed you as his mom, but y'all were actually fucking around for the whole summer! Now I know why that nigga ain't been answering my calls!" Wyatt paced the floor. "How could you do something like this, Ma? And with my right-hand man of all people! Did you think about how this shit was gonna affect me?"

. . .

"I did." Sybil nodded her head. "But that didn't stop me from going through with it."

Placing his hands over his face, he took a moment to calm himself down.

"So what now? Huh? Am I just supposed to forgive you for this and move on?"

"I'm not asking for your forgiveness, Wyatt. The only thing I'm sorry about is that I had this experience with your best friend. Since Jace left, I haven't reached out to him. We ended things the day he left. I don't want him. It was just a fun thing. What happened between us will never happen again. I know it's gonna take you a minute to process this, and if you decide not to talk to me for a while, then I have to deal with that. I didn't do this to hurt you, Wyatt. It was a decision I made. I just don't want this to mess up the bond we worked so hard to build," Sybil expressed sincerely.

"Well, it's too late for that."

Storming out of the house, Wyatt jumped in his car, pulling out the driveway with screeching tires. With his music blasting, he weaved in and out traffic as headed to his off-campus apartment. Parking in a spot, he snatched his backpack off the chair before he secured the locks on his car with the remote as he headed to his apartment. Once he was inside, Wyatt tossed his bag on the couch as he headed over to the fridge. Grabbing the fifth of Henny, he twisted off the top and took a huge swig. With the bottle in his hand, he sauntered over to the couch and sat down. Taking another swig, he removed his phone from his pocket, checking the texts he'd just received. One of the texts was from his dad, telling him that he'd arrived in the A with his sister. The other made him sit up straight.

HAZEL: HEY, BABY. I'LL BE DOWN THERE FOR Thanksgiving. Maybe we can link while I'm down there, and you can give me what I've been missing.

STARING AT THE SCREEN, WYATT'S HEART BEGAN TO BEAT OUT of his chest. He thought that Hazel had got him out of her system, but it was clear she hadn't. It was clear to him why Hazel invited herself to their Thanksgiving dinner. It wasn't so they could enjoy the holiday with him and their family. All she wanted to do was fuck him. With the conversation that he had with his mom still at the front of his mind, Wyatt started to regret storming out on her.

When he met Jace their freshman year, they often made bets on who could get certain girls' numbers. Girls that they felt were a challenge. They each pulled whatever girl they had their eye on, but when Jace pulled a girl they both wanted, Wyatt felt some type of way. Although his homie was willing to stop talking to the girl, he told him it was cool. His first time spending the night at Jace's crib, Hazel didn't hesitate to make her move on him. Denying her advances, he never told Jace what his mom was doing. When Jace invited him to a New Year's Eve party at his crib, Wyatt thought that she was over him because she didn't pay him any attention. After the party, he was too tired to drive home. Falling asleep on the couch, he didn't think that he was going to wake up with his dick in Hazel's mouth. After fucking her on the couch, he felt he got vengeance for Jace stealing his girl. It was only supposed to be a one-time thing, but it turned into something more.

For a year and some change, Hazel was Wyatt's suga mama. Whenever he needed something, she gave him the money for it. Every time they fucked, she would have a gift for him. She brought him everything from expensive watches to the newest sneakers. Hazel made sure he had money for books and everything else he needed. Whenever Wyatt got something new, he lied and told Jace his mom sent it to him. He liked the perks and benefits that came with fucking an older woman, but Hazel started demanding more from him. It was too much for him to handle. Wyatt didn't want a relationship. He just wanted the gifts. After she expressed her feelings for him, he broke things off between them. Every now and then, she would send him texts telling him she missed him along with nude photos of herself. He deleted the messages and moved on like it was nothing, but he couldn't say the same for Hazel.

Placing the phone down the table, he let out an irritated sigh before taking another swig from the bottle. Thinking about his situation and what his mom told him, Wyatt was confused about what to do. He didn't know if he should be honest with mom and put the shit behind them or continue to keep his mouth shut and play victim. Tired of going back and forth about it, he put his issues on the back burner and decided to focus on the ceremony that evening.

After he and his seven-line brothers became official members of the fraternity, Wyatt was proud to be a part of his father's legacy and brotherhood. He was all smiles as they celebrated with their family and friends. When it was over, James took him and his sister out to dinner to celebrate some more. Although he stormed out on his mom, that didn't stop her from showing up to support him. Throughout the night, he tried to stay in good spirits, but he had a feeling his dad already picked up on his vibe. Once they were finished their food and drinks, his dad drove him to the hotel where they were staying. Ready to head to his car, James suggested that Wyatt come up and kick it with him for a minute. Unable to refuse, they made their way inside, taking the elevator to his floor. Entering the room, Jasmine went into the bedroom while he sat down on the couch in the living room. He watched as James removed two Coronas from the fridge. Sitting next to him on the couch, his dad passed him a beer, but he didn't drink it. He just held it. For the first time in his life, he didn't know what to say to his dad. So he let his dad do the talking.

"For this to be one of the happiest moments in ya life, you sure are giving off bad vibes, man." James took a swig of his beer.

"I'm sorry, Dad. I just got a lot on my mind." Wyatt placed his beer on the wooden coffee table.

"What's going on, son?"

"I don't know why she decided to tell me this shit today, but mom told me why y'all stopped talking. She told me about her and Jace, and I stormed out on her." He sighed.

. . .

"You were angry, son. I was furious when Jace and Sybil confessed it to me. I was angrier with Sybil because she's older. She shoulda had more self-control than that, but being as though I was on both sides of this situation, I'm not as mad as I used to be."

"Wait a minute? You mean to tell me that you slept with your best friend's mom?" he asked with wide eyes.

"When I was in my late teens and early twenties, I had a crush on a few of my friends' moms, but I never made a move on them, but their sisters, I ran through them. I always told you that your friends' sisters, moms, and ex-girlfriends are off limits, but sometimes, you throw caution to the wind and cross the line anyway," James answered honestly.

"Did they ever find out?"

"Not that I know of, and if they did, they never mentioned it to me." James shrugged. "And we're still cool."

"But Mom confessed that they slept together, Dad. I feel like I was better off not knowing."

"I guess you can blame me for that."

"What you mean?"

. . .

IT'S HIS SAVAGE LOVE FOR ME

"I TOLD YA MOM IF SHE WANTED US TO MOVE FORWARD WITH our relationship, she had to tell you the truth. She chose to keep the secret and y'all bond, but now that she told you, I guess she really does love me after all." James smirked.

"DAMN. SHE DIDN'T TELL ME ALL THAT." WYATT SHOOK HIS head. "So does that mean y'all gonna pick up where y'all left off?"

"YEAH. I LOVE YA MOM, SON, AND I KNOW THAT SHE SLEPT with Jace, but she didn't make any excuses about it. She owned that shit, and she has no regrets. It's not like she was in a relationship and was cheating with him. Sybil wasn't involved, and she didn't lose her mind like most older women do when they fuck a young dude or a man with good wood. I know that Sybil is loyal, and she knows how to treat a man. I'm willing to leave this shit in the past and get my woman back."

"I DON'T KNOW IF I CAN MOVE PAST THIS. THAT NIGGA betrayed me after he gave me his word that he wasn't going to try anything. I called that nigga my brother, Dad. How the fuck can I just put this shit behind me so easily?" Wyatt became upset.

"THE SAME WAY YOU WOULD WANT SOMEONE TO LOOK PAST what you did," James replied in a stern voice.

"WHAT'S THAT SUPPOSED TO MEAN?"

. . .

"You think I don't know about you and Hazel? You think I don't know that y'all were fucking around for over a year?"

Unable to speak, he looked away from his dad.

"We all got dirt, son. It's how you chose to deal with ya dirt is what makes you who you are. I told you that a man takes responsibility for his actions and doesn't lie to any man. When I confronted Jace about the situation, he looked me in the eye and told me what it was. He didn't back down and he didn't show any fear. So being as though you did the same thing as him, what are you gonna do about your situation? You can't play victim when you're doing the same thing."

No longer in the mood to talk about the situation, Wyatt said bye to his dad before leaving out the room. Taking the elevator to the main floor, he strolled through the lobby, popping the locks to his car. As he revved the engine, his phone began to ring, but he ignored the call. Driving back to his apartment in silence, he thought about the conversation he had with his dad. As he pulled into the lot, Wyatt stayed in his car as he came up with a solution to his problem. He hoped that everyone would be able to respect his decision in the end.

15

As he sat in the passenger's seat of their rental car, Jace stared out of the window as his mom pulled out the lot of the Atlanta airport. Pissed that Hazel made plans for them to have Thanksgiving dinner with Wyatt and his family, he didn't speak to her since they left home. After a stressful month of assignments, exams, and joining a fraternity, all Jace wanted to do was relax in his own house. He didn't feel like being around a lot of people, especially Wyatt and James. He knew that the cat was out of the bag about him and Sybil, and he wasn't ready to face them. He knew that Wyatt had to be pissed by his betrayal and hated he himself for losing one of the best friends he ever had.

Although he didn't regret sleeping with Sybil, Jace wished that he could erase the memories that were permanently in his mind. No matter where he was, his mind would flash back to one of their sex sessions, causing his dick to get hard as a rock. He missed the way she called his name when he was deep inside her and how her ass jiggled when he fucked her from the back. Whenever he smashed one his chicks at school, Jace imagined that he was fucking Sybil. Even though the young chicks could ride his dick as well as Sybil, their pussy wasn't better than hers. When they decided to end their secret romance, he figured that his feelings would instantly fade for her, but they didn't. For the first time in his life, Jace was sprung, and he didn't know how to undo it.

As he continued staring out the window, he felt his mother's eyes on him, but Jace didn't speak. He knew how much his mom hated when he gave her the silent treatment and expected her to break their silence any minute.

"Jace? You haven't said shit to me since we left the house. Can you talk to me please?" Hazel pleaded.

"I don't have nothing to say."

"I thought you would be happy spending Thanksgiving with Sybil, Wyatt, and James. You said you had fun down there over the summer, and Wyatt is ya best friend, unless something happened that I don't know about."

"Nothing happened, Ma." He lied. "I just wanted to stay home."

"Well, I didn't wanna stay home. I wanted to be around some friendly faces and eat some good food. So I need you to try to enjoy yaself since we're gonna be here until Sunday."

"Sunday!"

"Yes."

"I'm not staying here 'til no Sunday. I'm leaving tomorrow night or early Saturday morning."

"Whatever, Jace." Hazel sucked her teeth.

Driving to their hotel, Jace ran his hand over his face when he saw that they were staying in the same hotel he and Sybil spent the night in. After they checked into the hotel, they hopped back in the car and headed to Sybil's crib, where there were a lot of cars parked in her driveway. Seeing the familiar cars brought a smile to his face, but they also made him nervous too. As his mom killed the engine, Jace took a deep breath before getting out of the car while Hazel excitedly jumped out. Joining his mom at the door, he smiled when he saw that it was Jasmine that opened the door. She hugged them both before escorting them to the kitchen where the women were. Everyone greeted them with a cheerful hello while Chante rushed over to him, wrapping her arms around his neck. Sybil greeted them both with hugs before telling him that the men were downstairs in the basement.

Taking his cue to leave, Jace opened up the basement door and slowly walked down the stairs. Everyone's eyes were focused on the TV as James and Glenn played *NBA 2K20*. When Wyatt noticed him, he wasn't expecting the smile he gave him.

"Oh shit! My brother is here." He jumped to his feet, greeting him with extended arms.

"Wassup, man?"

"You tell me, my nigga?" he asked, shocked.

"We'll talk in a minute," Wyatt said before breaking their embrace.

"A'ight."

As he greeted everyone with handshakes, Jace was surprised when James stood to his feet to hug him.

"Aye, you next to get ya ass whooped in *2K20*, lil' homie," James taunted.

"Come on, Mr. JB. You know you ain't no match for me when it comes to this." Jace chuckled.

"Let me get this nigga out the way right quick. Keep that same energy, JC."

"A'ight."

"Let's step outside for a minute, man." Wyatt pointed to the front door.

Following behind him, he closed the door behind once they were outside. As they went into the pool area, he sat down at one of the patio tables while Wyatt made sure the sliding door was all the way closed. Sitting across from him, they both began talking at the same time. When his friend insisted that he go first, Jace sat back and listened.

"Look, man. When my mom told me about what happened between y'all, I wanted to throw away everything. I was thinking about transferring back to Lincoln and everything, but after thinking about the situation some more, I couldn't really stay mad at you when I did the same thing as you."

Looking at him sideways, Jace leaned forward on the table.

"What you mean you did the same thing as me?"

"For a year and some... I slept with your mom," he answered with no shame.

"Please tell me you're lying." Jace dropped his head.

"I wish I was, JC. She was actually my suga mama."

"Suga mama? She bought you shit?"

"And gave me money," Wyatt added. "All the new shit I used to get, ya mom bought it for me."

"Wow!" Jace chuckled. "I can't believe this shit. You kept this shit from me for a year. Why are you telling me this now?"

"To get this shit out in the open and off my chest. Neither one of us was a better friend than the other. I wanna say that we regretted what we did, but I know I don't."

"And I don't either."

"So I decided to put this issue behind us and move on. I figured we could do the same thing. I miss you, bro, and I don't wanna let no shit like this come between us again," Wyatt truthfully stated.

"Neither do I, Dub Beezy." They shook hands. "Can I ask you a question?"

"Wassup?"

"Did you catch some type of feelings for my mom?"

"Nah. Don't get me wrong. I like ya mom. Just not in that way," Wyatt replied. "Don't tell me you caught feelings for mine," he asked with eyes.

Jace didn't answer.

"Don't let my dad hear you say that. He and my mom are back together, and he'll kill a nigga behind her."

"Crazy thing is, so will I," Jace answered in a serious tone.

"Damn! My mom is a dangerous female. She got young and older niggas whipped." He laughed. "I guess that's our punishment when we fuck around with women we know we ain't supposed to have."

Laughing at his friend, they stood to their feet and went back inside through the basement door, where the men were still playing the game. As the men continued to talk shit, Jace and Wyatt gave each other updates on their lives. They were shocked to discover that they were a part of the same fraternity. The men began educating them on the benefits of frat life and the lifetime bond that came with it. Laughing at the stories that were told about their college experiences, Sybil yelled into the basement that dinner was ready.

Jace and Wyatt were the first two at the stairs, and it reminded him of how they would race upstairs to the kitchen for dinner. Joining the ladies in the dining room, everyone was standing behind their chairs. Without hesitation, he stood behind the empty chair that was next Chante while Wyatt stood next to Rory. When the rest of the men came up, they stood next to their women. With James and Sybil at the head of the table, James gave her the go-ahead to speak.

"I wanna say I'm happy that all of you could make it here to have Thanksgiving with us. This is the first time since I've lived in this house that I hosted a holiday dinner, and I'm grateful for the turnout." She smiled. "I'm not gonna go around the room and ask what everyone is thankful for, but I want everyone to take a look around the room for a moment."

Everyone glanced at each other.

"It's times like these that people take for granted the most, and I don't want any of us to take each other for granted either. If any of us in this room has had or have a problem with the other, it ends now. It is considered a past problem and not to be mentioned again. Life is too short to be holding grudges. We need to enjoy our lives being happy and having a good time, a'ight?"

Every murmured in agreement.

"Now that we got that outta the way. Leah, can you please bless the food?"

After the grace, everyone flopped down in their chairs, and the women began fixing plates for their men. As Chante placed his plate in front of him, Jace kissed her cheek, thanking her for making his plate. Once everyone had their plates, they all dug in. The turkey, dressing, mac and cheese, potato salad, and green beans were delicious, and Jace couldn't wait to dig into the apple and sweet potato pies. The good vibes that flowed through the house made him feel better about coming. He wasn't sure if anyone else besides Sybil, Wyatt, and James knew about what happened, but he was glad that no one brought it up. Other than the news about Wyatt and his mom, Jace was glad he had his friend back.

After everyone was filled up on food, desserts, and drinks, the women went into the living room while the men cleared off the table and did the dishes. When they were finished in the kitchen, they went back into the basement, where they turned on the football game. As they watched the game, Jace noticed that Wyatt wasn't with them. Announcing that he was going upstairs to get some more pie, James and Levi asked for more punch before he went upstairs. With the women laughing in the living room, he strolled over to the blinds that covered the sliding door. Moving the blinds, Jace saw Wyatt and Hazel in the pool area. He was holding his mom's wrist, trying to fight her off of him. Although he couldn't hear them, he could tell by their body language that his mom was mad that Wyatt wouldn't give in to her. As a smirk appeared on his face, Jace backed away from the window pleased with what he saw. He was glad that his boy was able to swerve his mom. He just didn't like the fact that his mom was still lusting after his friend.

Grabbing a napkin and two cups, he went over to the kitchen table, cutting himself a huge slice of pie. As he filled the cups with the Bacardi Rum punch, his mom came in, closing the sliding door behind her. When she let out a sigh of frustration, Jace knew that his mom was ready to go.

"Son, I'm full, tired, and tipsy. I'm ready to go back to the hotel. Can you drive me?" Hazel stood next to him.

"A'ight, Mom. Let me run these drinks downstairs right quick."

"I'll be in the car."

Heading back to the basement, Jace gave the drinks to James and Levi, letting them know what he was about to do. He watched a little bit of the game before leaving out the basement. Jogging up the driveway, he jumped behind the wheel, driving to the hotel. He wanted to ask his mom about what was going on between her and Wyatt but decided not to. Just knowing that Wyatt turned Hazel down was enough for him. Arriving at the hotel a few minutes later, Jace stopped in front of the entrance and glanced over at his mom.

"What are you about to do?" she asked with her eyes closed.

"I'm about to go back to Wyatt's and chill there for a minute."

"Okay. I need you to come back and pick me up by nine. I'm going out with the girls tonight. They're gonna try to find me a man." Hazel chuckled.

"Oh really?"

"Yeah. I told them I've been dating younger men for the past few years, and they told me I need a man my own age."

"When you say young, how young are we talking?"

"The youngest I dated was eighteen. Well, I wouldn't say we dated. We had an agreement."

"He gave me what I wanted, and I gave him what he needed." She smirked.

"Mom, get out." Jace shook his head.

Laughing as she got out of the car, Jace waited until his mom was inside before driving away. As he headed back to the house, he chuckled to himself as he recapped the day. What started out as a bad day for him turned out to be one of the best Thanksgivings he ever had. Although he still had lingering feelings for Sybil, Jace decided that it was time for him to be with one woman instead of multiple. He was fucking chicks left and right, comparing their performances to Sybil's. He knew that moving on was going to be difficult, but it needed to be done.

16

With James face between her thighs, Sybil rested her hands on his head as he licked and sucked her pussy. Since he arrived for the Thanksgiving holiday, he'd been waking her up every morning with head and good sex every morning. Although she was a little sore, she wouldn't dare deny sex from him. They didn't get to see each other that often, and Sybil needed all the dick he was willing to give. As he continued licking and sucking her clit, she tried not to moan too loud because she didn't want his daughter to hear them. With her legs shaking uncontrollably, she grabbed a pillow, putting it over her face to muffle her screams as she came. Kissing her inner thighs, he removed the pillow from her face before forcing his tongue in her mouth. Sybil loved the way she tasted. As she sat up in the bed, he laid down flat on his back and she positioned herself on top of him. Once his dick was inside of her, Sybil began to ride him.

Instead of riding on her knees, she placed her feet on the bed and rode his dick on her toes. As she began bouncing up and down on him, Sybil watched James as he cussed, grunted, and groaned. She remembered that he loved when she rode his dick on her toes, and his reaction was still the same. Grabbing her titties, he rubbed her nipples with his thumbs, making her moan. When he closed his eyes, she knew that he was about to explode. So she wasn't surprised when they switched positions. Climbing on top of her, he forced his nine-inch, thick shaft inside her.

"You think you slick. You know I always cum quick when you ride me like that," he whispered in her ear.

"I wanted to see if I could still do it." She giggled, making her pussy tighter.

"Fuuucckkk," he groaned in her ear. "You're trying to be funny."

"Then punish me."

Grabbing her throat, James lifted one of her legs, thrusting deeper inside her. With her eyes trained on his, Sybil became wetter with each stroke. The way he bit his bottom lip turned her on as he squeezed her neck a little tighter. Feeling him deep inside her stomach, she was loving the mixture of pleasure and pain her man was making her feel.

"Fuucckkk, bae! I'm about to cum!"

"Cum all over this dick then," he grunted.

Doing as she was told, James kissed her, causing her to moan in his mouth. A few seconds later, James bit her neck, filling her insides with his cum. Suddenly feeling nauseous, she pushed James off of her, jumped out of bed, and darted to the bathroom. Bending over the toilet, Sybil vomited uncontrollably. When she finally stopped, she rested her head on the porcelain bowl for a moment.

"You a'ight, love?"

"No," she whined. "I don't feel good. I told you that before you started eating me out."

"If I woulda known that my dick was gonna make you sick, I woulda left you alone." He joked. "You haven't been feeling too good since I got here. Is there something you need to tell me?"

"No, James. I probably ate something that didn't agree with me. I'm fine." Sybil slowly stood to her feet, flushing the toilet.

"The last time you told me you were fine, we found out that you were eight weeks pregnant." James glared at her. "When was ya last period?"

"The beginning of October." She walked over to the sink, grabbing a paper towel.

"October? Sybil, it's about to be December."

"And?" Sybil wiped her mouth.

"And I think you need to take a pregnancy test."

"Nigga, what?" She looked at him sideways.

"You heard me."

"Nope. I'll pass on that. There could be another reason why my period is late." She tossed her paper towel in the trash.

Heading back into the bedroom, Sybil turned on her TV before climbing in bed.

"Seriously, Sybil. I want you to take a pregnancy test. For me." James climbed in the bed with her.

"Fine." She sucked her teeth.

"Thank you." He kissed her cheek.

"As soon as I start fucking around with you again, there's a possibility that I could be pregnant." Sybil shook her, flipping through channels with her remote.

"You say that like it's a bad thing."

"James, I'm thirty-five years old, and you're about to be thirty- seven. Our son is grown, and you're about to have a teenage daughter. What the hell are we gonna do with a baby?"

"The same thing we did with Wyatt. What type of question is that?" he asked, confused.

"What I mean is we're older. We're not as young as we used to be. When this baby is Wyatt's age, we're gonna be in our fifties." Sybil pouted.

"So basically, you're telling me that you don't want any more kids?" James became upset.

"Your words. Not mine," she replied nonchalantly. "I told you when you came over here the day after Wyatt's crossover ceremony to use a condom before you pinned me down."

"I don't see what the problem is. It's not like you're gonna be alone in this. I'm gonna be here for you every step of the way, Sybil."

"Yeah, but as what?"

"What you mean?"

"Are we gonna get married, or are we just gonna be shacking up like we did when we were in college?" Sybil glared at him.

He didn't respond.

"See... we shoulda kept taking things slow and really got to know each other again. Instead, I let you fuck me into a relationship that you're not even ready for."

"I am ready to be with you, Sybil. I just wasn't expecting this to happen so quickly."

"You know what I think you did? I think you got back with me outta fear that I would find someone else or go back to Jace," she honestly answered.

"I got back with you because ya ass belongs with me," James roared. "You're *my* bitch, and I don't want any nigga fucking *my* pussy. I know that we didn't really discuss our plans about our future, but I didn't think we had to. We love each other, and that's all that matters. I ain't going nowhere, and neither the fuck are you. If ya ass is pregnant, then you're gonna have to deal with it because you're not getting rid of it," he shouted.

As she watched James storm into the bathroom, Sybil remained in bed with her temperature through the roof. In her feelings and slightly turned on, she put on BET before laying down. As she watched *Martin*, she thought about James and if she was pregnant. Since they decided to get back together, Sybil knew that she was going to be pregnant. She just didn't think it would happen that soon. She wanted to be married before she brought another child into the world, if she did so at all. Although his divorce was finalized the week before, Sybil didn't know if he wanted to be married again or not. That should've been something she asked before they started fucking around.

As her eyes became heavy, she drifted off to sleep, putting her issues on the back burner.

As she began to stir in her sleep, the ringing of her phone woke her up. Still under the covers, Sybil reached over on her nightstand, feeling around for her phone. When she had a good hold on it, she pulled it under the covers and saw it was Leah calling her.

"Hey, Leah," she grumbled.

"Damn, girl. You sound terrible. You straight?"

"I feel like shit, Lee."

"Me and Dom wanted to invite you out for lunch, but maybe we should bring lunch to you."

"I'd appreciate that, sis. Thank you."

"No problem."

"Oh, and can you stop at CVS or something and get me a pregnancy test, please?"

"Pregnancy test!" Leah and Dominique shouted in unison.

"We'll talk about it when y'all get here."

"You damn right we will."

When the call ended, Sybil tossed the covers off of her and slowly walked into the bathroom. Turning on the shower, she waited a few seconds for the water to get hot before stepping inside the stand-in shower. After washing her body from head to toe, Sybil rinsed off before wrapping a towel around her body. Once she was finished in the bathroom, Sybil threw on one of the Lincoln sweatshirts she purchased during homecoming weekend along with a pair of matching sweatpants. Putting on her slippers, Sybil headed downstairs just in time to answer the door for her besties.

"Here, Sybil." Dominique handed her a box of pregnancy tests as soon as she opened the door. "Go into the bathroom and take one now."

Before she could say hello, Sybil was being pushed into the bathroom by her friends. Closing the door, she opened the box, removing on of the tests. Already aware of what to do, she urinated on the stick before cleaning herself and washing her hands. Grabbing a paper towel, she left out the bathroom and headed to the kitchen where they were waiting for her.

"Well?" Leah anxiously asked.

"I didn't look at the test. It's sitting on the sink," Sybil nervously replied. "You know you gotta give it a few minutes."

"How are you feeling?" Dominique asked.

"I don't know. I mean, it's not like we don't have the financial means to take care of a child. I'm just a little nervous about having a child at this age." She joined them at the kitchen table.

"I understand that, and these millennials are something else too. It's like they've been here before." Leah shook her head. "My lil' six-year-old daughter is so damn sassy. I think they switched my baby at the hospital."

"You ain't lying, Lee," Dominique agreed. "My fifteen-year-old son and my thirteen-year-old daughter feel like they don't have to work for anything. They expect everything to be given to them." She sighed. "I need a drink." She stood to her feet, going over to the fridge.

"Oh my goodness," Sybil groaned. "I'm not tryna go through that. I missed Wyatt's teenage years. Am I really gonna have to go through that?"

"Well, whether you're pregnant or not, sis, James has a preteen daughter. You're gonna have to experience the teenage years regardless," Leah pointed out.

"That's right, girl." Dominique came back over to the table with a bottle of wine and three glasses.

"Sybil, you can't get a drink until you check that test." Leah placed her hand over the glass.

"One of y'all go check. I'm too nervous."

Dominique jumped up from the table, quickly heading to the bathroom. Sybil and Leah held hands as they waited for Dominique to return. A few seconds later, she stood in the kitchen entrance with a face like stone.

"No wine for you, mommy-to-be." She beamed.

IT'S HIS SAVAGE LOVE FOR ME

"Oh my God!" Leah screeched. "That's another godchild for us, Dom." She gave her a high five.

Laughing at her friends, Sybil pushed her glass of wine away as Dominique handed them their food from Olive Garden. The stuffed mushrooms and shrimp alfredo looked and smelled delicious. In need of something to drink, she went over to the fridge, grabbed a ginger ale, and returned to the table. As they joked about how James trapped her with a baby, Sybil felt like there was some truth to that. Although he claimed her as his own, she believed that he was scared of losing her to another man. She also felt that her romance with Jace shook him up a little bit. No longer in her feelings, Sybil was starting to feel better about her pregnancy. Despite the reason they got back together, she was happy that they were back together. James was still the man she fell in love with. Just an improved version.

17

"James, I'm not trying to argue with you about this, okay? We agreed that Jazzy could spend the Thanksgiving holiday with you, and I would get her for Christmas. Why is this a problem all of sudden?" Kira huffed over the phone.

"It's not all of sudden, Kira. I've been telling you this for about a week now that Jasmine doesn't wanna spend the holiday with you. She'd rather be with me, her brother, and her friends." James filled his suitcase for clothes.

"Friends? What friends?"

"I have friends down there, and Jasmine has bonded with their kids."

"I knew you were gonna do this."

"Do what, Kira?"

"That you were gonna take our child down there and start a new life without me in it." She became angry.

"I'm not tryna start a new life without you," James protested. "But as long as you're still with ol' boy, Jasmine ain't coming anywhere near you, Kira. I wanna say you got a choice to make, but it really shouldn't be a choice."

The phone was silent for a moment.

"I can't just up and leave this man, James. I don't have a place of my own."

"Well, I suggest that you get one because the longer you stay away from Jasmine, the more she's gonna feel like you don't care about her. Y'all have been good up until this point, and I would hate for y'all to start beefing now."

"You're right." Kira sighed. "When are y'all leaving for Georgia?"

"This evening. Jasmine's bag is packed already."

"She really likes it down there, huh?"

"Yeah." He smiled. "She already has her own room at Sybil's crib. She's gonna let Jazzy decorate it any way she wants."

"Wow. That's nice," Kira replied dryly.

"Why you say it like that?"

"I wanna be angry with her Sybil because you left me for her, but when you tell me stuff like that, I can't. I mean, how can I hate a woman that has welcomed my child into her life and home without a problem?"

"I guess you can't." James chuckled.

"Look, just have Jazzy call me when she gets home from school. I guess you can keep her until I get outta here."

"Cool. Let me know if I can help."

"Okay."

Tossing his phone on the bed, he finished packing his suitcase and zipped it. It was a week before Christmas, and he was looking forward to spending the next couple of weeks with his boo. After the heated argument they had a few days after Thanksgiving, James was a little upset to learn that Sybil wasn't pregnant. She had taken three pregnancy tests before he and Jasmine returned home, and they were all negative. The following day, Sybil told him that her cycle had started and left it alone. Although he was hoping that she was pregnant, James decided to play it safe and let Sybil have her way. If she wanted him to wear condoms, then that was what he was going to do.

Flopping down on the edge of bed, he reached into his

pocket, removing the black velvet box. He opened the box and stared at the emerald-cut, three-carat diamond ring. As a smile appeared on his face, he thought about how he was going to pop the question to Sybil. He thought about proposing at midnight Christmas morning, but he didn't think he could wait that long. He was ready to make Sybil the next Mrs. Bennett. He was already searching for jobs in Georgia as well as condos. Although James wanted them to live together, he figured he would let Sybil have her own space until they were married. He didn't want to move too fast and risk the chance of her pushing him away. The last thing he wanted to do was fuck up his second chance with the woman he loved. Tucking the ring back in his pocket, he stood to his feet, grabbing his suitcase off the bed. On his way out the door, he snatched up his keys, wallet, and phone, then headed downstairs, where he waited for Jasmine to come home.

When his baby girl came home an hour later, James laughed as she dropped her backpack on the floor and darted upstairs to change her clothes. With her suitcase in hand, she came down the stairs, pulled him out of his favorite chair, and headed out the door. Grabbing his suitcase, he locked up the house, popped the locks to his car, and tossed their bags in the trunk. Once they were inside the car, James revved the engine before pulling out of the driveway. As they headed to the expressway, he glanced over at his daughter, who was grinning from ear to ear.

"What you over there smiling about?"

"I'm sooo hype that Ms. Sybil is letting me decorate the room the way I want! I've been looking at different ideas for my room for weeks, and I finally chose one. I can't wait to get started!" She danced. "Ms. Sybil is very nice, Dad, and I love her house. I can see myself having pool parties there and everything."

"I'm glad that you like Sybil, Jazzy, and I'm happy that you're excited about decorating your room." He smiled. "But I don't want you to forget about your mom. She was very disappointed that you weren't spending that holiday with her."

"Dad, you know I love my mom, but now that y'all are divorced, I don't feel right being around other men besides you," Jasmine spoke in a serious tone. "I like that you're with someone that makes you happy, and I'm happy that I get to see my big brother again. Being with you, Wyatt, Ms. Sybil, and all of y'all friends feels like home to me. If I stay with my mom, she's gonna be dating, and I don't wanna meet and be around however many men until she finds her next Mr. Right." She rolled her eyes.

"Well, since you put it like that, I can understand where you're coming from." James glanced over at her. "Your mom said she's cool with you staying with me until she gets a place of her own, but I would like for you to call her a few times a week so y'all can stay connected with each other."

"I can do that."

Giving her a pound, the duo chopped it up the rest of the way to the airport. After finding a parking spot in the crowded lot, they walked hand in hand through the crowded airport until they reached their gate. Boarding the plane, James dozed off to sleep while Jasmine listened to music, staring out the window. When the plane touched down in Atlanta, she woke her father up. Grabbing their bags, he held on tight to his daughter's hand as they picked up their car from the rental place. More than ready to leave, they hopped into the BMW and drove out of the parking lot.

When they arrived at Sybil's crib, Jasmine jumped out the car and ran into the house, leaving him in the parked car. As he jumped out of the car, James smiled when he saw his son pull up. Heading over to his car, he gave his son a hug before Wyatt grabbed the Walmart bags out of the back seat of his car.

"What's all this?" James pointed to the bags.

"Mom wants us to decorate the house and the big ass artificial tree that was delivered last week." Wyatt sighed. "This brings back memories of when we used to do this back home."

"We had fun decorating the house."

"Yeah, but I'm grown now, and Jazz is about to be thirteen.

We're too old to be decorating the house and tree for Christmas," he huffed. "She brought matching pajamas for us to wear tonight and at the Christmas Eve party."

"Son, I know that you feel like you're a grown ass man now, but this is the first year that ya mom is having Christmas at her house. For years, she hasn't celebrated any holiday here. She went to other people's houses for the holidays. So as much as you don't wanna do this, can you get out ya feelings and make the best of this for ya mom?" he asked.

"A'ight, dad." Wyatt sighed. "I forgot that mom spent a lot of time alone until I showed up. So I guess I can make the most of this."

Heading inside, the smell of chocolate chip, sugar, and M&M cookies hit their noses, causing them to head straight to the kitchen. When he saw Sybil, Jasmine, and Rory sitting at the counter, he noticed that something was different about his girl. She was more beautiful than ever. Sauntering over to him, he hugged her tightly, lifting her off her feet.

"Mmmm, I missed you so much," she spoke into his ear.

"I missed you too, boo."

Placing her on the floor, they shared a passionate kiss before they were interrupted by Wyatt clearing his throat.

"I know you better cut that out." Sybil pointed at him. "As many times as I heard you and miss thang over there getting down in my basement."

"Damn, Ms. Sybil." Rory chuckled. "I thought we were better than that."

"He started it." She shrugged. "Did you get all the decorations and stuff for the tree and house?"

"Yup. Hopefully I got enough. This house is big as fuck."

"So where do we start?" Jasmine asked, biting into a cookie.

"The men can start decorating the outside while us girls get started on the tree," Sybil instructed. "But before we do that, I wanna give my baby his first gift." She smiled.

"First gift?" He smirked. "How many did you get me?"

IT'S HIS SAVAGE LOVE FOR ME

"Four, but who's counting?" She chuckled, removing a black bracelet box from the drawer.

"James, these past few months have been a little challenging, but I'm glad to have you back in my life. I know we haven't talked much about our relationship or the direction it's going in. All that matters is that we're together." Sybil smiled. "Merry early Christmas."

Handing him the box, James looked at Wyatt to see if he knew what it was, and he shrugged. As he opened the box, his face frowned when he saw the positive pregnancy test in the inside. Staring at her confused, Sybil just smiled at him.

"Please explain this?" He pointed to the test.

"Okay, the day we had that argument the last time you were here, I took a pregnancy test, and it was positive. I had Dom and Lee take three pregnancy tests for me because I knew you were gonna make me take the tests while you were here."

"So this is real? You're pregnant with my baby?" he asked, shocked.

"Yes, James." She grinned.

"I knew it!"

Picking her up, James spun her around a few times before hugging her.

"Did y'all know about this?" he asked.

"Nah." Wyatt chuckled.

"Not at all." Rory shook her head.

"I did." Jasmine raised her hand. "She told me before we left."

"Good job keeping the secret, Jazzy." Sybil winked at her.

"Well, Sybil, since you gave me my first gift, let me give you yours."

Removing the black velvet box from his pocket, James opened the box, revealing the diamond ring. Sybil's eyes grew wide at the sight of the ring as she waited for him to speak.

"Sybil, the last time I was here, I told you that you weren't going anywhere, and neither am I. I mean that." He slid the ring on her finger. "I'm ready to spend the rest of my life with you. Are you ready to lock me down for life?"

"Hell yeah." She smirked

Kissing his lips passionately, James tightly embraced her as everyone in the kitchen clapped.

"That was the best gangsta ass proposal and acceptance I ever saw." Rory stood to her feet.

"Congrats, y'all." She hugged them both.

"Congrats, Dad and Ms. Sybil. Now that we got the mushy stuff outta the way, can we start decorating the tree now?" Jasmine hopped down off the barstool.

"Yes, we can." Sybil draped an arm around her shoulder, leading her out of the kitchen.

"A baby and a proposal? How about that?" Wyatt chuckled, strolling over to the fridge, grabbing a beer. "Neither one of y'all gave me a heads-up about what y'all had planned."

"You're right. We didn't." James sat down at the kitchen table. "But I'm pretty sure you knew this was gonna happen."

"I did. I lowkey wanted this to happen." Wyatt sat across from him. "I'm happy that you and mom are back together and getting married. I am surprised about the baby though."

"I'm just glad ya mom came to terms about it."

"Now that you proposed to mom, I'm thinking that I should make things official with Rory." He sighed. "We haven't seen each other since Thanksgiving. I miss the fuck outta her. I just don't know if I'm ready to commit."

"Son, if you have feelings for that girl, you need to let her know that because if she starts talking to someone else, it's gonna fuck with you."

Finishing his beer, the men removed the lights and decorations from the bags. As Christmas music played throughout the house, Wyatt grabbed the ladder while his dad gathered the lights and headed outside. With the holiday off to a good start, James and Wyatt laughed and talked shit as they decorated the outside of the house. Everyone was filled with the holiday spirit, and he knew that this was going to be the best Christmas yet.

※

"Mom! Mom! Why don't you let me or Jasmine put the star at the top?" Wyatt shouted.

"Wyatt, I'm fine. I got this." She carefully placed the gold star on top of the tree. "You're so worried about me, you're letting my pies burn. Go take them out of the oven."

Shaking his head, he headed to the kitchen, grabbing the oven mitts. Carefully removing the pies, Wyatt placed them on the counter. He loved his mom's sweet potato and apple pies, and he was ready to dig in. With the house fully decorated, it seemed to put him in a better mood about the holidays. Love, happiness, and cheer flowed throughout the house, and after witnessing his dad's proposal to his mom, it made Wyatt want something special of his own. Throughout the day, he noticed that Rory spent more time on her phone then she did decorating the tree. Knowing that she was texting a nigga, it took all of his strength to remain calm. The thought of her talking and texting another nigga sent his temperature through the roof. Not trying to be on some jealous shit, Wyatt just distanced himself from her.

Hearing the sliding door open, his face got tight when he heard Rory telling someone she was about to be on her way. As soon as she ended the call, he got on her case.

"And where the fuck you think going?" he questioned.

"To go mind my business," Rory answered nonchalantly.

"Don't play with me, Rory?"

"Nigga, I ain't playing with you. You ain't say shit to me all day, and now you heard me say that I'm about to go out, you wanna give me attention. Boy, bye." She dismissed him.

"I've been giving you attention all day. You wouldn't know

that because you've been glued to ya damn phone." He walked over to her.

"Wyatt, I ain't got time for this shit right now." Rory tossed her head back. "You expect me to just keep bussing this pussy open for you whenever you call me without us being a relationship, Wyatt? I know that when we started messing around in the summer, we agreed to be friends with benefits. We know that we love each other, but if you don't love me enough to be with me, then we need to stay how we are," Rory stated sternly.

Grabbing her by the waist, Wyatt forced his tongue in her mouth, kissing her sloppily, which she loved. She moaned in his mouth as his hands found their way to her ass. Breaking their embrace, they stared at each for a moment.

"I know I told you that I wasn't ready for a relationship, but I ain't tryna see you with no one else, Rory. I do love you, and I miss being with you," Wyatt confessed.

"So what does that mean?"

"It means that I want you all to myself. I want us to give this relationship thing a try." He smirked.

"I knew if I acted like there was someone else, you'd come around." She laughed.

"I can't believe you set me up." He tickled her, causing her to squirm.

"Yes, I did." Rory giggled, moving away from him. "Now, that I have one of the gifts on my list, I can roll out of her and go chill with Ivanna for a minute."

"Wait a minute? I just made you my girl and you're still gonna leave me?"

"I made plans with Ivanna a week ago, bae. Since Chante and Jace became official, she's been deep in her feelings, even though she has a man of her own." Rory shook her head. "Let me spend an hour or so with her, then I'll be back so we can make our relationship official." She pulled him by his shirt, kissing his lips.

"A'ight, but if ya ass ain't back here in two hours, I'm coming to get you," Wyatt warned.

"It's 10:15 now. I'll be back before midnight."

Kissing her one more time, Wyatt walked her to the front door and watched her until she was inside her car. When she was out of the driveway, he locked the door, then headed to the living room, where his family was watching Christmas movies. They were in the middle of the classic movie *Home Alone*, and Wyatt divided his attention between the movie and his phone. After an hour of watching movies, his mom and dad told him and Jasmine good night before heading upstairs. Knowing what they were about to do, he shook his head and laughed. He couldn't believe that they were acting like horny teenagers, but he understood why. A long-distance relationship would cause spouses to be all over each other.

Five minutes before midnight, Wyatt received a text from Rory telling him that she was outside. Jumping up from the couch, he told his sister to turn off the TV before she went upstairs and he headed down to the basement. When he opened the door for her, he noticed that she'd changed her clothes. The trench coat and red knee boots she was wearing had Wyatt eyeing her suspiciously. Closing the door behind her, he watched as Rory untied her coat and licked his lips when he saw that she was naked underneath. With his dick ready to bust out of his pajama pants, he was ready to receive some holiday sex from his girl.

18

"Yeeesss, daddy! Fuck this pussy!" Chante shouted, throwing her ass back.

With her hair wrapped around his hand, Jace fucked her hard from the back as she cussed and moaned. Biting his bottom lip, he smacked her ass, making it jiggle more. It had been a month since they fucked each other, and he'd be lying if he said he didn't miss her. Chante was the freak in the sheets that Jace had been looking for, and he couldn't get enough of her. Although they weren't official, he put her before the rest of the bitches in his life. He liked spending time with her, but he loved fucking her more.

"Oooo, Jace. I can't take no more! Can I please cum?" she begged.

"Yeah. Let that shit go, bitch."

On cue, Chante exploded all over his dick as he filled the condom with cum. Kissing her cheek, he released her hair before sliding out of her. Removing the condom, he disposed of it before getting in the hotel bed with Chante. As she laid on his chest, Jace grabbed his phone and began scrolling through his timeline on Facebook. When he saw that Wyatt was on live, he clicked on his video, and they watched the stream. They laughed as they watched the couples dance and sing to Donny Hathaway's *This Christmas*. Even though he declined the verbal invite that Wyatt gave him to come to the Christmas party, Jace lowkey wished he was there. It was always a good time whenever he was at Sybil's, but he couldn't return. It held too many memories for him. Every time he saw the garage that they fucked in before he left and the kitchen table they fucked on the first time they got down, it made him want that back. Since they patched things up, Jace figured that it was best for him to keep his distance.

As they continued to watch the stream, they watched as Dominique turned the music down and Wyatt gathered everyone in the living room so he could talk. When his boy announced that he and Rory were officially a couple, his smirk turned into a wide grin, but when Wyatt made a toast congratulating his mom and dad on their baby and engagement, his grin quickly faded.

"Oh my goodness! That's dope as fuck that Ms. Sybil and Mr. JB are engaged. I knew that they were gonna get married one day, but I never thought it would be this soon," Chante excitedly spoke. "I wish we were there to celebrate with them."

Unable to watch anymore, Jace got up from the bed and headed to the bathroom. Angrily pacing the floor. He tried to calm himself, but he couldn't. He couldn't understand for the life of him how it was so easy for Sybil to move on like the sex and the feelings they had for each other no longer mattered to her. There wasn't a woman, past or present, that could forget about how he made them feel. He had bitches from high school in his inbox begging him for dick still. Although he was happy that James was giving her everything that she deserved, it drove him crazy that Sybil was no longer lusting after him like she was in the summer.

Taking a few minutes to calm down, Jace ran the water for his shower as he washed his face and brushed his teeth. As he stepped in the shower, Chante called his name before knocking.

"Aye, Jace. Ya mom sent you a list of things she wants you to pick up from the market." She peeked her head in the bathroom.

"A'ight." He nodded his head. "Bring ya ass in here so we can fuck one more time before we leave."

Without hesitation, Chante closed the door and sauntered over to him. Once they were inside the stand-in shower, Jace didn't waste any time pinning her against the wall, stuffing his curved dick inside of her. After covering her body with his sperm, they washed each other up, then got out. While Chante stayed in the bathroom, he went back into the room and picked out his drip for the day. Dressed in a pair of black denim True Religion jeans and a Christmas sweater his mom picked out for him, Jace stuffed his feet into a pair of red Timberland boots. Putting on his gold chains and watch, he snatched up his phone and waited for Chante to get dressed. Matching his fly, they made sure they had everything they needed before leaving the hotel room. When they made it to the main floor, they strolled out of the building hand in hand. Popping the locks to his black 2018 Chevy Impala, they hopped inside, and Jace brought the car to life.

After shopping at a crowded Walmart, he parked in front of his mom's crib fifteen minutes later. The new house that they moved into in the beginning of the month was located in Norristown, which was only a few minutes away from Philly. The four-bedroom, three-bathroom home had a large front and backyard with a view of the river. After spending most of his life growing up in the hood, it was going to take Jace a little time to get used to living in the suburbs. As he grabbed the bags out of the trunk of his car, the front door swung open, and his mom yelled for them to come in from the doorway. Kissing Hazel's cheek, they spoke to everyone as he carried the bags to the kitchen. Removing the items from the bags, Chante entered the kitchen, pulling him to the side.

"Jace, you're not gonna believe this shit." she whispered.

"Wassup?"

"Darrin, Ivanna's dad, is here, and he's dating ya mom."

"Get the fuck outta here." He laughed.

"I'm serious. Look." Chante pointed.

Turning around, Jace dropped his head when he saw his mom skinning and grinning from ear to ear. As they made their way over to them, he tried to control his laughter as they approached.

"Jace, this my friend, Darrin. Darrin, this is my son, Jace. He's a junior at Lincoln University and a fraternity man," Hazel bragged.

"Nice to meet you, Darrin." He extended his hand.

"Same here." Jace shook his hand.

"Hey, Mr. Darrin. Nice to see you again."

"Hey, Ms. Chante." He nodded.

"Y'all know each other?" Hazel's eyes shifted back and forth between them.

"Yeah. He's my best friend's dad. He used to date Ms. Sybil. That's how we met Wyatt and Jace," Chante admitted with no shame.

Knowing that Chante was being messy, Jace tapped her leg letting her know to behave. The awkwardness between caused them to remain silent for a moment before Darrin spoke up.

"How is... Sybil doing?" he asked.

"Oh she's great," Chante boasted. "She and Wyatt's dad got back together a few months ago. They're engaged now and expecting a baby." She grinned.

"That's great!" Hazel shouted. "I'ma have to call Sybil later and congratulate her."

Darrin gave a small smile.

"Darrin, baby, how about you go into the living room and watch some TV while I make you something to eat. Chante, you gotta taste this punch I made. It's so good."

"Okay."

As everyone scattered, Jace grabbed a cup and the bottle of Henny and filled his cup to the brim. Taking a huge gulp from the plastic cup, he stayed posted up in the kitchen as more guests arrived. He was all smiles as a few of his favorite cousins came in the kitchen to greet him. When his cousin asked him to step outside with him, Jace knew that it was *puff, puff, give* time. Since he started school, he fell back from smoking, but he couldn't let his cousin smoke alone. On his second cup of Henny, he sipped the strong brown liquor before hitting the blunt. The mixture of being drunk and high along with the conversation they were having about older women had Jace in his feelings. When they finished their smoking session, he remained outside while his cousin went back in the house. In need of some answers, Jace removed his phone from his pocket and called Sybil on Facebook Messenger.

"Hello? Jace?" she answered.

"Yeah. It's me." His words slurred. "I got something to ask you, and I need an honest answer."

"Wassup?"

"How the fuck you just gonna move on with ya life and act like we ain't spend the summer fucking each other's brains out? Ya ass done got engaged on a nigga and about to have a nigga baby and shit. You act like what happened between us don't mean shit to you," Jace angrily expressed.

"Boy, just because I'm engaged and pregnant don't mean that I forgot about that savage love you were giving me," she replied in a low tone. "Yeah, I moved on and so have you, but what happened between us was special to me, Jace. As much as I would love to keep reliving those moments, I can't. You were off limits then, and you're really off limits now. I still have love for you young bul, but what we had is officially over."

"Damn, old head. You really had me thinking my sex was trash or something."

"Jace, you know that's not true." Sybil laughed. "Now, get ya ass off my before you get me into more trouble."

"You know you'll always have a special place in my heart, right?"

"And you'll always have a special place in mine. Goodbye, JC."

When the call ended, he finished off his drink before tucking his phone back in his pocket. Feeling like his cocky and arrogant self again, Jace couldn't stop the grin that appeared on his face. As Sybil's words replayed in his mind, he didn't know if it was the alcohol or her that was making him feel warm on the inside. Even though he and Chante were getting it along well, he knew that he would never come across another woman like Sybil. Knowing that they could never be intimate again made him a little upset, but he knew it was for the best. She had a lot more to lose now than she did before. Thinking about everything that happened, Jace told himself that he would do it all again if the opportunity presented itself. The savage in him would risk it all because, to him, Sybil was worth the trouble.

19

THREE MONTHS LATER...

With her eyes to the ceiling, Sybil laid on the doctor's table as she waited for the doctor to enter the room. When she received a call a few days ago that one of her tests came back abnormal, her doctor suggested that she come in earlier than scheduled for her ultrasound. Upset that her husband was running late for their appointment, Sybil was nervous that the doctor was going to give her bad news about her baby. Ready to get up and leave, she stopped when the nurse entered the room.

"Mrs. Bennett, your husband made it just in time for the ultrasound." She stood to the side, letting him enter.

"Baby, I'm sorry I'm late, but we'll talk about that when we leave." James stood by her side.

. . .

"I'm just glad you're here." She smiled.

"Okay, you guys. Let's get the ultrasound started," the nurse cheerfully spoke.

Holding on to James's hand, Sybil closed her eyes as the nurse put the clear jelly on her stomach. When she heard the nurse gasp, her eyes popped open and focused on the monitor.

"Oh my goodness." She leaned up a little bit. "Is... is that... two babies?"

"Yes, ma'am, and they're in the same placenta," the nurse confirmed.

"What does that mean?" James asked in shock.

"That means we're having identical twins, bae." She smiled.

"Identical twin girls."

"Wow!"

"This explains why one of your tests were abnormal, Mrs. Bennett. You were only tested for a single baby. Other than that, your babies are perfectly healthy."

. . .

"Thank you so much, Nurse Gibson."

"No problem. Let me print out the sonogram, and y'all are free to go."

As James cleaned the jelly off her stomach, he kissed her lips passionately before helping her up. Once they had their sonograms, he helped her off the table, and they strolled out the door. Tossing James her key, Sybil got comfortable on the passenger's side and reclined her chair back while her husband took his place behind the wheel.

"When I first met you when we were kids, I knew you were a special type of woman. Who woulda thought that all these years later that you would get pregnant with twins?" James drove carefully through the streets.

"I know, right?" She smiled. "Twin girls at that. I'm glad that Wyatt is grown so he can help us keep an eye on all these girls."

"Tell me about it. Now that Jasmine is thirteen, I need him to be our eyes and ears in these streets."

They laughed.

"So are you ready to tell me why you were late?" Sybil looked over at him.

IT'S HIS SAVAGE LOVE FOR ME

. . .

"I HAD A JOB INTERVIEW TODAY. STARTING MONDAY, I AM THE new human resource specialist for a technology company in metro Atlanta," James bragged.

"CONGRATULATIONS, BAE! I'M SO HAPPY FOR YOU!"

"THANKS, BOO."

"SO WHAT'S GONNA HAPPEN WITH JAZZY? IT'S TOO LATE IN the school year for her transfer schools."

"SINCE I'M LETTING KIRA STAY IN MY OLD HOUSE, I GUESS SHE can live with her mom until the school year is over. She might not be too happy with that, but it makes sense," James replied. "So now that we know what we're having, are you ready to start decorating the nursery?"

"I SURE AM. I WANNA PAINT THE WALLS A PRETTY YELLOW OR pink color. I already started picking out furniture, but I don't wanna order it until the room is painted."

"I'LL START DOING THAT OVER THE WEEKEND. I'LL GET WYATT and the guys to help me."

ARRIVING AT THEIR HOUSE MINUTES LATER, HE PULLED INTO the driveway, parking the car by the garage before killing the engine. Helping her out of the car, they entered the house, and he helped her up the stairs to their room. As she sat on the edge of the bed, Sybil kicked off her Uggs, then climbed in the bed.

"Aye, boo, I'm about to run to the market to get the things you want. Keep ya phone near you so we can pick out the color paint you want for the nursery." He slid her phone over to her.

"Okay, baby," she answered with heavy eyes.

Kissing her lips, Sybil was already fast asleep before he left out the room. Only sleeping for a couple of hours, she woke, irritated when she heard Leah and Dominique yelling for her to open the door. Slowly getting out of bed, she opened her window, tossing them her keys. Getting back in bed, Sybil turned on her lamp as her besties made their way up the stairs.

"Awww, Sybil. Did we wake you up?" Leah asked, sitting next to her.

"Yeah, but it's cool. If y'all wouldn't have come over, I would've slept the rest of the day away."

"Soooo tell us. Are we having another godson or are we having a goddaughter?" Dominique sat on the bench at the end of her bed.

. . .

"Two identical goddaughters." Sybil grinned.

"Ahhhhh!" they screamed.

"Twin godbabies!"

"Oh my goodness!"

"I know. I'm just as shocked as y'all." She chuckled.

"Between these new babies and my own kids, I'm about to be broke for real." Leah shook her head.

"Did you tell Wyatt yet?" Dominique asked.

"Nah, but I'm sure James will. They already don't let me do anything for myself, but now that I'm having twins, I'm really not gonna be able to do anything," Sybil huffed.

"Girl, I know you didn't expect ya life to change like this. Not only did you get ya son back, but you got ya man back, too. You're married and got twin babies on the way. You went from being lonely in this house to it being filled with life and love." Leah smiled. "I hope you realized how blessed you are."

. . .

"I DO. I COULDN'T HAVE ASKED FOR A BETTER LIFE AND FAMILY than the one I have. I love y'all, and thank y'all for helping me through my mess and not judging me for what I did."

"YOU KNOW WE WOULD NEVER DO THAT, AND YOU KNOW we'll always be here for you." Dominique smiled.

AS THEY WRAPPED THEIR ARMS AROUND HER, THE TRIO embraced each other for a moment. Breaking their embrace, they told Sybil they had to get home and that they would check on her before the week ended. When she heard the front door close, her phone chimed, indicating that she had a message. Noticing that she had a Facebook message, she stared at the screen for a minute. when she saw she had a message from Jace, she debated on whether she should read it or ignore it. When he called her on Christmas, Sybil wasn't expecting him to ask her what he did. She couldn't believe that he actually thought that she was able to get over him that easily. Although she was wrapped up in her husband, there were certain things that made her think of Jace. When she ended their phone call, that was supposed to be the end of their communication, but now that he was reaching out to her again, Sybil didn't know what to do. Listening to her heart instead of her mind, she opened the message.

JACE: IT'S BEEN THREE MONTHS SINCE THE LAST TIME I talked to you, and I can't get you off my mind. I know that we're off limits to each other, but I want you in my life, Sybil. I'm not asking for sex. I just want ya friendship. You're too special to let go.

. . .

IT'S HIS SAVAGE LOVE FOR ME

Smiling at the message, Sybil didn't know if she wanted to respond or leave him read. After everything she almost lost behind him and their romance, it should've been easy to ignore him, but the soft spot she had for him had her ready to give in to him again. Not willing to risk losing her husband and family, Sybil deleted the message and blocked him. It hurt her a little bit to shut him out of her life completely, but it had to be done. By keeping Jace in her life, she was playing with fire. She was already burned once and wasn't trying to get burnt again. The only savage love she craved came from her husband, and that was the only savage love Sybil needed.

THE END

IT'S HIS SAVAGE LOVE FOR ME

The New York City Edition

TINA MARIE

ACKNOWLEDGMENTS

I would first like to thank God for giving me this gift of writing and for providing me with every blessing I have received thus far and will receive in the future.
I want to thank my family, and my fiancé, Jay, for putting up with all the late nights and my crazy moods while I am writing. To my kids: Jashanti, Jaymarni, and Jasheer, I want you to know that I work so hard so you can have it all.
To my Cole Hart Presents team, salute to all of you for keeping on the grind and staying positive. Cole, the fact that you wanted me on your team means more to me than you will ever know. Princess and Anna, I swear you ladies are just amazing, and I love you! Twyla, there is no category for someone like you, any time I need a shoulder, a friend, or a talking to you are there. I know you sick of me but I'mma love you foreverrrrrr! Jammie and Reese, you two truly just make my life complete, and I thank God for giving me friends like you. I want to thank all of my Pen Sisters no matter what company you are in for all of the love, support, and for always helping to push me to my next goal. I appreciate you all!
Ladora, you are the world's best little sister. I love you, and I believe in you always!

Natasha, we have been friends for what seems like forever, and now you're more like family. You could never be replaced in my life. You have seen me at my best and worst and still have my back. Oh, and you have learned to put up with all my moods. LOL. I love you, boo!

Natavia, only in a perfect world would I have thought that my favorite author would be my real-life friend. And even though this isn't a perfect world, I am so happy you became my friend. I value all the talks, laughs, WCC, and advice. Love you soul sister (inside joke).

Coco, I didn't think I could write a dedication to you without crying- I was right. You are a bomb a** little sister. I would go to war for you with anyone. The way you love on my son and have never turned your back on me is everything. You're filled with positivity and joy, and I can't find the words to thank you. I love you!

Sunni there are so many days you have talked me off the ledge and just been a friend I love your whole life. I could never replace you. Your bestseller is right around the corner; I can feel it!

Nisey, Quanisha, and Keke you three have been rocking with me since forever and are the best admins ever. I love how you love me but most of all, how you all have come to love each other. Tina, you may be new to the team, but you are a welcome addition! You ladies don't let me forget a thing and handle all the grunt work so that I can write. XoXo! To my test readers, Kristi, Sweets, and Jammie, there would be no book without you ladies, you all are my blessings! Liz, I couldn't ask for better promoter- one thing I learned in this business is it takes a team, and finding you helped complete my team.

To my Baby. Momma Zatasha, even though we are both crazy Gemini's I still love you boo. Couldn't do this book ish without you!! And to all the Bookies, I appreciate the love and support you show all authors, not just me. It makes a difference having a place where we are respected, celebrated, and offered endless support!

To my friends and family: I appreciate all of the love and support. My cousins, Claire, Dionne, Donna & Tanisha. My friends: Letitia, Natasha, Jennifer, Sharome, Shante, Diana, and Kia. I'm truly grateful for you all, and I love you. To my best friend, there will never be enough letters in the alphabet to thank you for everything, so I won't even try.

To all of my fans, readers, test readers, admins, and anyone who has ever read or purchased my work, shared a link or a book cover, you're all appreciated, and I promise to keep pushing on your behalf to write what you're looking for.

MA'KENNA

I raced down 57th street and frowned as I felt the water splash my stocking covered legs. I clutched the umbrella, praying the rain missed my hair. If it did, my neat bun would be looking like a ball of fur. I checked the time and address on my phone while simultaneously cursing at whoever decided we needed all this fucking rain today. I looked up at the sleek building in front of me and wondered again what Kendric had gotten me involved in. Racing inside the lobby the heat hit me like a welcomed gift, at least until my glasses fogged up. "Ma'am, can I help you with something?" A proper voice asked before I could rush to the elevators. Realizing the voice belonged to someone who worked here, I slowed up some. The doorman frowned as I stood in the lobby, dripping water all over the floor.

"Umm, yes, hello. I'm sorry," I stuttered. My nerves were getting the best of me. I wasn't a fan of unknown situations, and this was for sure one of those times. "I'm here to see Mr. Aleczander," I said trying to sound normal. He stepped behind the marble desk that I hadn't noticed when I rushed inside, not offering an immediate response. I waited impatiently while he pressed a few buttons on a computer screen before finally nodding.

"Take the elevators in front of you to the 30th floor." He promptly went back to his computer when he was done giving his instructions, basically dismissing me. The ride up to the 30th floor gave me time to wonder what my client was going to be like. I was thankful for my homie getting me this little under the table job. But I had to wonder why a man who lived in a condo worth millions of dollars needed a math tutor. As soon as I stepped into the hallway, I heard loud music and smelled weed smoke. Even though I wanted to turn the other way, I thought about my baby girl Sierra. The extra money I made from this job would do so much to help us out. So, I had to push through. I knocked, unsure if anyone would hear me. But the door swung open, like someone was standing there the whole time waiting. A big ass buff dude looked down at me for a minute then stepped back. Looking around I was definitely cursing Kendric's ass out when I left up out of here. This shit was a mess. Niggas everywhere drinking, smoking, and shooting dice. It was like I was at home in the projects or in some ghetto ass club.

"Oh shit, ya'll look, this nigga got us a fucking stripper," some light skin dude with dreads said as he walked closer to me. Two others followed him, causing me to back up. I was trying to find my voice because this shit had to be a fucking joke.

"Son, she is dressed like a teacher, I knew it was going to be a good fucking day," his homeboy damn near sang out. He was grinning like he had won the fucking lottery. I felt a hand on me, and I jumped. This nigga was taking the bun out of my hair. I had nowhere else to back up to, and at this point, it was fuck this job, I was ready to go.

"Don't fucking touch me," I spat as I snatched my hair from him and tried to fix my shit. "I'm not a damn stripper, as a matter of fact, I'm leaving." They were laughing like I was saying something funny, but a few of them had moved some so I had a little space.

"Come on ma, don't be shy. I only bite if you want me to,"

the cocky ass light skin one replied. He winked at me, and I damn near threw up.

"Ayy yo, move the fuck from round her," a voice boomed from behind the crowd. "She's here to see me, and shorty ain't no fucking stripper. You want strippers go down to Hoes and Foes or some shit." These niggas scattered like roaches as I looked up to see who I was going to be working with. "Yo ma, you good?" he asked as he stood in front of me, his deep voice filled with concern.

My eyes followed the tatted hands and arms all the way to his face and the infamous scar he sported on his jaw. It couldn't be. Of all the people I could be working with it just couldn't be Messiah. I must have looked crazy standing there, shaking my head and staring him up and down. I had no words. All I could think of was how dangerous this nigga was, the fights, the stabbings, hell the murder charge he beat, but clearly was guilty of. As famous as he was, Messiah was a menace, a sexy one, but still crazy as fuck.

"Damn, Kendric told me ya ass wasn't going to be star struck. I knew this shit was a fucking mistake," he grumbled. "Let me guess you want to strip for me or be my naughty teacher?" He sounded tired, I guess from all the attention that had to surround him. Or maybe the chaos caused by all these dumb niggas. The look in his eyes was one of frustration, and for a second I felt sorry for him. He laughed, except it didn't sound pleasant. "Wait, I got it. You just want to taste my dick."

"Nigga, you got me fucked up. I am not a groupie or a hoe. I came here for a job. I had no idea who I was working for, and I sure as hell have no interest in sucking your dick. I'm standing here trying to recover from being mauled by ya people, not because I'm star-struck." I crossed my arms as best I could while holding my purse and umbrella. I thought about hitting him with the latter, but he was for sure the kind of nigga who would hit me the fuck back.

"Aight ma, you got that. Let's go handle this business then. I have a busy day." I followed him to the back and the buff nigga who answered the door trailed us as we walked down a long hall. I silently laughed at the irony, if anyone needed security in here it would be me. His spot was amazing, all marble floors and floor to ceiling windows, giving him a view of Manhattan. I bet it was beautiful at night. Finally, we stopped at a closed door, that revealed an office once it was opened. "Ok, before we get started, I just need you to look over these papers and sign."

I nodded and grabbed the NDA. I wasn't surprised at this part, Kendric already told me that my client didn't want anyone to know he was in college or using a tutor. I read the contract page by page before signing and initialing where it was requested. The fact I was being paid five hundred dollars a week for one tutoring session was enough for me to put a smile on my face. The client wasn't ideal, but I would make the best of it. "Here you go," I said as I handed him the papers. His hand touched mine as he picked them up and I swear my pussy jumped. Being in his presence was nerve-wracking as fuck. He nodded to his security guard, who closed the door and left us alone. At least the room was somewhat quiet, even if I felt uneasy being closed in with Messiah.

My eyes followed his movements as he reached into a Gucci book bag and pulled out a Calculus book. I wondered why he was going to college, especially since he wanted it to be a secret. Maybe that was just until he finished. I couldn't judge because I had no idea what it was like to have people constantly in my business. "Ok, let's get started Mr. Aleczander," I said as I sat down in front of him.

※

"MOMMY, ARE WE BAKING COOKIES TONIGHT," SIERRA ASKED as soon as I opened the apartment door, and she ran inside. I was tired as fuck from spending my whole day at the hospital where I did my internship, not to mention I had a four-page paper due the next day and I was only halfway done. It had only been two weeks since I started tutoring Messiah, and it was already wearing me down. All I wanted to do was crawl into my bed and get some sleep. But I hated telling my daughter no, especially since I barely had time to spend with her as it was.

"Ok baby, let mommy change her clothes, and we can bake some cookies before bed." She jumped up in excitement, and I once again felt guilty for barely being around. It felt like my best friend's mom, Miss Vivian, was raising her instead of me. I rushed and showered, throwing on a pair of grey biker shorts and a cropped red tee that said Boss Bitch in grey letters. I pulled my hair back in a ponytail and felt so much better. Finally, I felt somewhat relaxed.

I told Alexa to play *Almost There* from *Princess and the Frog*, and my baby and I started singing and dancing while I mixed the chocolate chips into the batter. Being with Sierra was my happy place. No matter what we were doing it brought me joy. Sometimes I wished I had someone else to share my life with. No matter what other people thought, I did get lonely. But from past experience with men, I knew I was probably going to be alone forever.

"Hi," Sierra squealed, her face buried in my phone. I stayed telling her to stop answering my shit, and she stayed doing it anyway. She sat down on the ottoman in the living room, giggling, holding a whole damn conversation. Shaking my head, I continued humming and moving around the kitchen. I was pretty sure she was talking to my best friend, Cass. She was pretty much the only person who called me.

"Mommy, it's for you," Sierra called out, running towards me with the phone. "It's mister Siah, and he said you can't sing." She laughed like that shit was the funniest thing in the world as my heart dropped seeing Messiah's face on my screen. I snatched the phone and gave Sierra a look. We were going to be revisiting the phone conversation as soon as I got this nigga off my line. She knew not to talk to strangers.

"Can I help you?" I wanted to ask how the fuck he got my phone number, but since he was technically my employer, he would have all my info. It had been two days since I was last in his presence. Two long days of me trying to get him off of my mind. He was intriguing, the way his eyes got darker every time he spoke. How he ran his tongue over the iced-out grill he wore when he was thinking. Everything about him turned me on in ways I didn't even know existed. *Ok, rich and famous rap star with a harem of bitches and a temper*, I reminded myself.

"I didn't know you had a shorty." He said, and I saw his tongue swipe the diamonds in his mouth. His thick NY accent had me losing focus. "How old is she?"

"Almost four, even though I'm sure you're not interested in knowing. We have a business relationship, so again, how can I help you." He chuckled at my attitude as his eyes roamed my body. I wished I was fully dressed. His ass was making me uncomfortable.

"I just need help with this equation for my homework. On God ma, this professor don't like my ass, so I really have to hand this in on time. His bitch ass wants any reason to fail me. I ain't trying to interrupt ya little concert or nothing. Just need five minutes of your time." I rolled my eyes but carried the phone with me as I took the cookies out of the oven and got ready to help him. Messiah was a distraction I could not afford.

2

MESSIAH

I stood in the living room, waiting on her to come. Last week one of my boyss grabbed her ass. The week before, my cousin offered her ten stacks for a blow job. I knew shorty was ready to quit, but I needed her. Shit if I was honest, I liked having her around too. "Son, I don't know what kind of business you got wit lil mama, but you need to stop being stingy with the pussy. I know that shit good as fuck," my boy Micah said as he eyed the front door. I shook my head at him as he popped another pill and chased it with some Henney. Finally, I heard the elevator ding, and I waited in anticipation for her to knock.

"What's good," I asked as I opened the door and looked down at her. Today she had on a red dress. Shit was formal as always. She took this tutoring shit serious. I had a flashback of what she had on the day I Facetimed her. I mean she was cute in these professional outfits, but I loved seeing her in a t-shirt and shorts. Her body was banging, and I could tell it was real. Shit I should know, I had been around enough fake ones.

"Umm, you gonna let me in, or are we just going to stand here," she asked, her caramel-colored eyes wide with uncertainty.

"Shit, my bad ma, I just got done smoking. Come on. You want some water or soda?"

"Naw, I'm good. We have to stay on task today. I got my own schoolwork to do." She always looked so damn serious. I wanted to try and find a way to make shorty smile.

"Yea, I hear you ma." I took out the math book I had come to hate. I wasn't a dumb nigga, but this math shit had me feeling stupid as fuck. I couldn't wait until these next few months were over and I could get this degree and move on with my life. I picked up the freshly rolled blunt and lit up.

"Messiah, why you even doing this college shit? You don't want anyone to know about it, and you clearly are not interested in the shit you studying? And I damn sure know you don't need a degree. I don't get it." My first thought was to tell her to mind her fucking business. That's what I would have told anyone else who asked me that shit. But for some reason, I wanted to tell her.

"Yea I ain't feeling this school shit at all, but it is important to me. My grandmother, she found out last year she has stage four breast cancer. I mean, she's fighting that shit, but you know how that goes. Anyway, she really wants me to get this degree. It's important to her, so here I am, back in school like I'm still a kid. Hating that shit just as much as when I was a lil nigga."

Her eyes filled with tears as she grabbed my hand. "I'm sorry about your grandmother." She only had her hand on mine for a second, and I swear my dick was harder than the marble floor under my feet. I appreciated her though. She wasn't like most of the bitches that I encountered. Even before this rap shit, when I was flooding cocaine throughout the streets of NY bitches still wanted me for two things, money and dick. I never had one show any concern for me, not when I was shot, locked up, nothing.

"Shit, you good ma. Death is a part of life. I done made my peace with the situation." She still gave me a sad look but didn't say anything else. She just lifted her glasses and wiped her eyes.

IT'S HIS SAVAGE LOVE FOR ME

"While we asking questions and all that, when the fuck don't you wear those glasses?"

There was the smile a nigga been waiting on, and that shit was everything. "The hell you mean when do I not wear them? I mean, I guess when I'm in bed or in the shower." She was laughing now and looking at me like I was crazy. But all I was thinking about was her in the bed or in the shower, ass naked. I wonder if she moaned when she was getting hit from the back. "Ummm yeah, that's all though; I can't see shit without them," she finished awkwardly. I realized I was just watching her like a fucking creep.

"Damn, that's fucked up, so if I took them, you just going to be bumping into shit and falling down?" Shorty backed up some like I was going to snatch her glasses off her face so I could find out.

"Basically, yea." We both laughed before she took out her pencil and pad of paper. I guess she was ready to get to work. Shorty was a good ass tutor. Not even twenty minutes later, I understood more about derivatives now than I did all semester. When my cousin told me he had someone who could help me, I was more focused on her being discreet and not some hoe ass groupie. Not on her actual credentials as a tutor. Now I was starting to wonder how smart lil mama really was. In all honestly I felt like she had my professor beat, probably could have taught his hating ass a thing or two.

"What you going to school for, math or some shit?" If she was getting a degree in math maybe Ma'Kenna could handle my money. These white mah'fuckers probably robbing my ass.

"Umm, I am majoring in cognitive psychology and minoring in Bioethics." I narrowed my eyes at her and wondered was she about to be working as some CIA agent or some shit. "It's really just the study of human behavior and making sure that the studies done on humans are ethical." She shrugged and looked down, like she was embarrassed or some shit. Shorty acted like she said she was a home health aide or McDonalds cashier.

"Ayo, lift up ya fucking head. That's dope as fuck, you gonna be like the police of research!" I replied, causing her to give me a shy smile.

"Thanks, most people don't even try to figure out what I'm studying. I could become like the police of research, but I'm going to do my own research, and I just want to make sure it is being done ethically, especially when working with minorities. I hope that something I do someday will help cure a disease or help humankind in some way. But that is later on in my career, like retirement. For now, I just work with psych patients for free until I graduate. But once I finish out this degree, I can get paid." She didn't say it, but I knew she meant get paid and get the fuck out the hood. Kenna was definitely not like other females I been around, shorty was fly as fuck. "Do you have a bathroom I can use," she said as she stood up and smoothed her hand over her dress.

"Yea once you leave out, take a left, and it's three doors down, right before you get to the kitchen." She nodded in thanks and left out. I looked at my phones and sighed. The stupid fucking blogs had tagged me in some story about me whooping a club promoters' ass and facing charges. They didn't even have their facts straight, as always. Yeah, I beat his ass, but I wasn't being charged with shit, and he sure as fuck wasn't talking to no police. There were more comments than one person could scroll through, so I chose to just ignore the shit. Social media always had something to say about a nigga. I felt like I had a camera on my back, watching my every fucking move.

I realized shorty had been gone for a cool little minute, and I wondered if she had gotten lost. I stood and pulled up my True Religion jeans. As soon as I walked down the hall, I knew some shit was off. I heard someone yelling, and I realized it was Ma'Kenna. "Just leave me the fuck alone," she spat hitting this nigga named Darnell in the back of the head. He had shorty against the wall and was trying to force her dress up.

IT'S HIS SAVAGE LOVE FOR ME

"Yo, get the fuck up off of her," I roared as I grabbed him and threw him to the ground. I kicked him in the ribs a few times, all I could see was the fear in shorty's eyes and I hated it. He was about to rape her in the fucking hallway like this shit was normal. "You ok," I asked her as she straightened out her dress and backed away from me. "Come here ma, I got you," I said ignoring a whimpering Darnell who was in a ball on the floor. She didn't come to me. Instead, she ran down the hall to the room we had been working in.

"So, no one was going to step in and help shorty out?" I barked at the niggas just standing there watching the whole fucking thing. Even my security guard Von had a blank face.

"You said we could fuck these hoes that came here. She knew the deal and wants to play like a victim," Darnell managed to get out from his spot on the floor. I took my Timberland clad foot and kicked his ass directly in the face.

"Dumb mah'fucka, she look like she here to fuck? She works for me, she aint fucking nobody in here. As a matter of fact, she ain't coming here again, and Darnell neither are you. Get him the fuck out of here." I motioned for my bodyguards to remove his ass. Before I could go back to my office, Ma'Kenna was damn near running down the hall with her book bag in one hand and her phone in the other.

"Come on ma, don't leave while you're upset and shit." She shook me off and headed for the door. I was faster than her though and beat her there. "Aight cool, let me walk you to your car, at least. Next week you not coming back here, you can meet me at my house." I heard my brother suck in his breath behind me, but not say shit. He had better not either. I barely fucked with him now as it was. He was probably just salty like a bitch since he didn't know where the fuck, I laid my head. My house was my private spot, my sanctuary in a crazy ass world. Dak, my head of security raised his eyebrow to me in a questioning way, but I ignored his ass. I didn't bring people to my crib, but I couldn't keep having shorty come back here. This shit wasn't no place for her.

Ma'Kenna ignored me and left out of the apartment. I followed behind her until we were in the elevator alone. She got that scared ass look on her face, and I knew her fear was about more than just today. For the first time in my life, I wanted to protect a female, and I honestly didn't know what to do with that. "Why are you following me? I ain't got no fucking car for you to walk me to. I take the bus and train to get here. I just want to leave. I will let you know if I will even still be working with you going forward." I reached out to her, but she damn near ran up out the elevator when it stopped at the lobby. "Messiah, just leave me alone."

3
MA'KENNA

I ignored another incoming call from Messiah. After the shit that happened at his condo the other day, I wasn't interested in working with him again, but I was still taking my ass to work today. I made a commitment to him and promised Kendric, so I would see it through. At least until they could replace me. But that didn't mean I had to talk to Messiah on the phone, I wasn't on the clock yet. The crazy part about the whole situation, I was starting to enjoy my time around him. But his friend trying to take some pussy from me, because that was just what they did there, made me want to put as much distance as I could between him and I. He did fuck old boy up for me, that shit was unexpected, and even though his temper was off the chain. I was kind of turned on.

Checking the time, I sighed because at this point, I had no idea where his house was, and I needed to start my journey on the buses if I was going to be on time. I doubt he lived anywhere close to Redfern. Before I could pick up the phone and dial his number, someone was banging on my door. Looking out the peephole, I rolled my eyes and snatched open the door. "What are you doing here," I snapped as Kendric stepped into the room.

"Damn, that's how you talk to ya homie?" I mugged him and flopped back down on the couch.

"What do you want, Kendric? In case you haven't heard I had a fucked-up week, and I don't need you adding to it." Just like I knew he would, Kendric ignored my attitude and laughed. We had been friends for at least fifteen years, so he was used to all of my ups and downs.

"I heard my cousin whooped some nigga's ass for fucking wit you." He smirked like Messiah gave a fuck about me. "He is feeling ya little nerdy ass for real."

"Kendric Hassan Green, get out of my damn apartment. You know ya cousin don't fuck wit me. Not even the way he fuck wit all these groupie hoes that he apparently shares with all his friends. And don't worry, I ain't quitting yet, I will find a replacement first. Speaking of this job you got me involved in, I need to get ready to go."

"Well shit, get ready. I'm here to take you. Ya little ass don't even know where the fuck you going and shit. You was gonna google rapper Messiah's address or something? And trust me, this nigga feeling you, he don't let no one come to his crib." I huffed and went to get dressed. I realized I hadn't had time to wash any of the business clothes I usually wore to work, "fuck," I mumbled accepting the fact that I would have to dress down. At least for today.

I decided on a pair of grey joggers, a red long-sleeved shirt, and red UGG boots. I showered, put on some of my honey vanilla lotion, and sprayed myself with Marigold by Vera Wang. "Yo, you not fucking ready yet," Kendric said, talking shit as he popped his head in my bedroom. I ignored him and finished putting my hair in its usual bun, except this time, it was on top of my head and not at the nape of my neck. I grabbed my black North Face and was ready.

The ride to Messiah's house was longer than I anticipated, and I groaned once I noticed we were all the way in Westbury. Buses didn't even run out here, so I would have to take a taxi to

IT'S HIS SAVAGE LOVE FOR ME

the damn train station, then two buses when I didn't have a ride. And knowing Kendric's hoe ass, I wouldn't have a ride often. Basically, my commute just got longer and more annoying. He was paying me pretty well. I could probably Uber since it was only one day a week. But still, that would probably be a quarter of my pay, and I needed every fucking penny.

We finally pulled up to a gate, and a guard stuck his head out. "Is Mr. Aleczander expecting you?" the security guard questioned, a serious ass look on his face. Kendric nodded and pulled out his wallet. I wondered if he had to pay this motherfucker or something, but instead, he held out his license. "I need to see hers as well," he asked his face blank, no smile in sight. This set up felt different than the playhouse he was running in Manhattan. I fumbled around in my purse and handed over my ID.

He passed our stuff back, and suddenly the gates opened. I have no idea what I expected, but the houses we drove past were for sure mansions. Everything was pristine inside the gated community. Flowers bloomed everywhere, there was grass and trees all over, and I even spotted some fountains. Of course, Messiah's house would be the last one and surrounded by another gate. This time Kendric had a code he entered, and we drove right in. One thing I noticed as we walked to the massive doors was the silence. It was quiet, only the birds chirping and the wind rustling the leaves on the tree. We walked inside, and I saw the same bodyguard from the condo lurking in the background. Then I saw him. He had on a pair of black True Religion sweatpants slightly sagging so I could see his Armani boxers. He had socks on his feet and True Religion slides. But the thing that had me fucked up was the fact he didn't have on a shirt. I couldn't help but stare at his bare chest. The scars mixed in with his tattoos and caused my heart rate to speed up.

"Aight Kenna, I will be back for you at six. Be ready. I ain't no fucking Uber," Kendric said, talking shit. I knew Kendric really didn't mind giving me a ride, so I ignored his antics. He gave me a slight hug, dapped up his cousin, and left right back out.

Just like that, I was left alone with Messiah, a half naked Messiah at that. He was staring at me, his dark eyes not revealing his thoughts. I didn't know what to say, I was uncomfortable just standing there, and I could feel myself shifting from foot to foot. I almost missed the constant party atmosphere of his condo. All the people around made me feel a false sense of security. I didn't really have a lot of experience being alone with men, and from what experience I did, it was all bad. "Umm, do you think maybe we can meet somewhere public from now on? You know, like a Starbucks or a library?"

"Naw shorty, that really won't work for me. I'm famous as fuck. I would never get anything done. Between the fans and the reporters, it would be a fucking mess." He walked closer to me, and I didn't know if I was more anxious or excited. "I ain't gonna fuck wit you ma. I do a lot of wild shit, but I never had to force myself on a female. Come on; we can sit in the dining room." I followed him, my knees weak from the smell of his cologne, and prayed the whole way there that I would be able to focus.

"Ok, I guess that was a stupid request. I mean, I know it was. Sorry, I don't normally do this," I said, gesturing between me and him. He just raised an eyebrow at me in a questioning manner.

"What the fuck you think this is, Ma'Kenna?"

"I just meant, I don't spend a lot of time alone with a man." I was all over the place now. I could feel my face turning red as I looked at the amused look he wore. "Messiah, can you just put on a shirt." His slight smile turned into a laugh. He didn't look like the kind of nigga who laughed much. "I'm sorry, just never mind. Can we start working? I'm sure you have things to do."

"Yea, I'm working on a new album, so I have to head to the studio tonight." He sat down and stared at me. "What's your favorite song?"

"*Sandcastles* by Beyonce," I responded as I got out my notebook and pencils.

"Shorty, I meant your favorite song by me," he said. His gaze watched my every move.

I knew that answer. It was easily *Die for You*. But I didn't want him to know that low key I was a fan. So, I just shrugged. "I never really heard your music," I lied.

※

I HAD NEVER BEEN SO HAPPY FOR A FRIDAY. ALL I WANTED was a bubble bath, a glass of wine, and a good book. I just had to get rid of my bestie, and I would be all set for a quiet night at home. But by the looks of things, she wasn't going anywhere anytime soon. Cass was laying on the end of my bed doing something on her phone while fucking with me. "So, are you going to tell me what he's like? Girl, he looks so sexy on TV. I just know he looks way fucking better in person. He could get all my cookies, anytime anywhere." I shook my head at Cass as I continued folding the never-ending piles of clean clothes.

"He isn't what I expected. He is intense, complicated. I don't know; shit, I barely know him. We work on math equations. But sometimes he asks me questions or reveals little things about himself. He is funny and smart. I mean, aside from the math, he seems to have no problems with whatever he is majoring in. It's just he is also the same as the media portrays him to be. When his friend tried to fuck me in the hallway, he beat him bloody and acted like it was nothing. He is vicious and has no remorse." I sighed, thinking of the hug he insisted on giving me when I was leaving last night. He was taller than me, so he had to lean down to put his muscular arms around me. I had never been held like that, and even though the hug lasted less than a minute, I was weak.

"Umm-hmm, and you like him. Admit it. I have known you almost your whole life. I have never seen you get that look on your face when talking about these other niggas." Cass sat up and was wiggling around like an excited puppy, waiting on the tea I guess, even though there wasn't any to give.

"Even if I did like him, and let's make it clear, I don't! He is

Messiah, that nigga, superstar rapper. I heard he is going to be in a movie next year. He sure as hell ain't taking no single mother from the projects seriously. And anyway, I am not interested. I am focused on school and Sierra and our future."

Cass leaned forward and gave me a serious look. "You know any man would be happy to have a girl like you. You pretty as fuck, smarter than anyone I ever met, and a bomb mother. I'm sure Messiah would be happy to lick ya dirty drawers if you let him." I just shook my head and laughed. My friend was always trying to boost me up. I mean, I was the best mom I could be, even with my fucked-up circumstances, and according to Mensa, I was smart. But I didn't consider myself sexy, or pretty, not even desirable to a man. So, fantasizing about a man that was so far out of my league was a waste of time.

"Enough, you know ain't no nigga's out here checking for me."

"Shit, he doing something because you ain't stopped smiling since I got here. He ate the pussy?" I made a face at her nasty comment. Cass loved sex, and talking about sex.

"I'm happy because I found out today as soon as I graduate, The Mayo Clinic is offering me a full-time position as in their Psych department." I saw the smile fall from my bestie's face.

"Not Hopkins?" I slowly shook my head, no.

"I didn't hear back from them. And don't look sad, Cass. I would be getting Sierra out of the projects. You can come with us if you want. With my salary I will be able to afford a big house, you can have your own room, a walk-in closet. Whatever you want!" I know Cass didn't want me to move, but if I couldn't get a NY job, I had to go where I could.

"Girl what the fuck we gonna do in Minnesota? Do black people even live there?"

"Yes black people live there, and they have the biggest mall in the country! We can shop and not get killed by lil niggas who think they are thugs.

Slowly a grin crept onto her face. "Whatever I want?"

IT'S HIS SAVAGE LOVE FOR ME

"Yep, I will give you the best room in the house. And we still have time before I have to make the decision. Maybe something closer will become available."

"Hopefully, or maybe mister fine, rich ass rapper will lock it down and sweep you off your feet." She stood up and went to my closet. "Now, as for what I want, let's go out and celebrate! I'm not taking no for an answer, just so you know. Now let me find something in here." She continued pushing my clothes around and frowning at everything she touched.

"I really just want to stay inside, relax while I don't have Sierra or work or class." Suddenly a white piece of fabric flew out of the closet, smacking me in the face. I forgot I even owned that dress. I bought it for a trip to Miami I never ended up taking, and it had been sitting around collecting dust all this time. I held it up and admired the way it formed a deep vee in the back. I knew it would show off most of my body. I felt sexy in it for the first time in a long time when I tried it on in the store four years ago. Shit, I wondered if it still fit. Sighing, I tossed it on the bed and gave Cass a pleading look.

"Come on Kenna, you bout to leave me, and all I want is one night out," she whined.

"Fine," I huffed, giving in. "Help me fold these damn clothes so I can at least take a nap."

"YASSS BESTIE YOU LOOKING LIKE A WHOLE FUCKING SNACK," Cass gushed as she made me turn around. I caught a glimpse of myself in the mirror and couldn't believe it was me. The white dress clung to my body like a second skin, causing my booty to pop out. I had a light beat on my face with a subtle pink lipstick. I wand curled my hair, and it framed my face perfectly. On my feet, I rocked a pair of gold strappy heels that made my legs look long and appealing. "How the fuck ya nerdy ass know how to walk in those heels," she asked as I effortlessly made my way towards the door.

"Because I wear heels at work every day," I said, smirking. I may not have dressed up to go out, but I dressed the fuck up for my internship every day. "Where are we going," I asked as I settled in the passenger seat of her Honda.

"Don't worry about it," she sang out as she turned up the music and immediately flew into the night traffic. I didn't drive much since I didn't have a car, but I swear Cass's ass was reckless. Finally, we pulled up to some club called Avenue downtown. I groaned when I saw how long the lines were. We parked in the lot and walked up to the VIP line. I raised an eyebrow, and Cass giggled.

"I got this," she whispered as she gave our names, and the bouncer put sparkly gold VIP bracelets on our wrists. He stepped aside, and we walked in. "This way," Cass directed as she headed to the second floor. I was humble and didn't give a fuck about VIP, but I will admit to being happy I wasn't stuck in the crowd. Just walking through, a bunch of niggas was grabbing at me and shouting out their whack ass pick up lines. I told myself to relax and enjoy. The music was hittin,' now all I needed was a drink.

Before I could make my way to the bar, one of Messiah's newest songs dropped, and the crowd went crazy. "We have NY's very own Messiah in the house tonight. Let's show him some love," the DJ cut in, and I swear these hoes lost their minds. At the mention of his name, I glared at Cass, who shrugged. My eyes started looking everywhere, wondering where he was. Hearing Cass laugh, I immediately focused on some random nigga standing close by.

"Let's get a drink," I said, trying to play it off. We made our way to the bar they had up here. I rarely let loose, my life had been serious for so long, but tonight I was going to turn the fuck up. I didn't even flinch when Cass ordered more than one drink and several shots. We found a table, and I grabbed the first shot.

"Wait, wait, I got to say something," Cass said, holding her shot in the air. "To best friends, to your success and big rich dick," we fell the fuck out laughing and then clinked the glasses and drank. After an hour of pretty much the same thing, my ass was lit. I was normally pretty shy, but those drinks had me out of my seat and twerking in the middle of the floor. I had a feeling my nude thongs were on display. I was going so hard. I felt a hard body behind me and never missed a beat. I glanced back to see a brown skin cutie, his hazel eyes were fixed on my ass, and his arms had snaked around my waist. I was too drunk to care that he was grinding his dick all over me, and his hand was creeping up my leg. When *Bruk it Down by Mr. Vegas* played, Cass and I let the fuck go. We loved to dance to Reggae music.

"Damn girl, your body is sick as fuck. I know you coming home wit me tonight," old boy shouted over the loud music, as I whined my body all over him.

"Naw, nigga she ain't going the fuck home wit you. This dance is over lil homie," I heard Messiah snap from behind me. I didn't even have to look. I listened to his music and interviews so much I recognized who it was off top. But what I couldn't figure out was why he was all in my business. My dance partner backed up, his eyes bucked. I tried to turn around and check Messiah, but my ass was moving too fast, and instead, I fell forward.

His strong arms were grabbing me, and next thing you know I was up against his chest. My heart was beating so fast I thought I was going to pass the fuck out. It had to be the liquor. I tried to step back, but he was holding me tight as hell. "Shorty, the fuck you on? And were ya glasses at?" He was towering above me as always. I loved how much taller he was; I didn't mind looking up at him. Shit, he was so fucking fine I could look at him all night. Even with the scowl on his face.

"My what?" I responded, thinking about the last question.

"Ya glasses? You lose them or some shit."

"Oh, yea, those. No, I didn't wear them. I have in contacts," I replied, confused as to why he seemed so fucking mad. "Are you mad?" I asked, giggling. Shit, I needed a water like now. I just knew I sounded like a fucking drunk.

"Why you got that nigga all in your face like that, touching all over you and shit. Come on, Ma'Kenna. You not even that kind of girl." He shook his head in disappointment. "Why you even drinking like that. And why the fuck you ain't looking out for her," he barked Cass's way. She stood next to me in shock.

"I was, I mean, we were just celebrating her job offer, and the drinking was a bit much. Shit, she was having fun, and I mean she is grown."

"Boss, time to move, too many people in this area." His bodyguard said. I noticed then that everyone had noticed Messiah was mixing with the general population, and even though his security was holding them back, it looked like it was going to be a problem.

"Well, thank you Messiah, you can go. I know you have to go," I said the last part a little lower. I was sad for some reason, thinking about being out of his presence.

"Aight, Dak make a way so we can get back to my area. Keep up," he said to Cass as he damn near carried me to the right until we stopped at a section with armed security. "They are with me," he told the two big ass men guarding the space. They parted like the river Moses and next thing you know I was in his private section. There was still at least a hundred or so people drinking, dancing and popping pills for it to be private. I shook my head, trying to figure out how I got here, just that fast.

"Messiah, why did you bring me over here? I was cool and having a good time." I looked out of the corner of my eye and saw Cass squeal and jump into Kendric's arms when she saw him. Even though we all grew up together, Kendric was like a brother to me. And whatever his hoe ass was with Cass was different, complicated with a side of sex.

"You can't have a good time with me?" he asked, his eyes crinkled as he waited for a response.

IT'S HIS SAVAGE LOVE FOR ME

"I'm your employee," I said carefully, making sure I didn't slip and say tutor.

"You can't be my friend?" He whispered close to my ear as I felt his lips nuzzle my neck. I didn't know what was happening, my whole body was on fire, and my pussy was so wet I knew the juices were leaking down my legs. It had to be the alcohol. Nothing ever made me wet; I wasn't built that way. I remembered my baby father's exact words, *ya pussy is broken, and no man wants a woman like that*.

"I guess," I responded, still off my square, trying to figure out why Messiah had me feeling like someone else.

"You pretty as fuck, friend," he said before turning me around and draping his arms over my shoulders. There was literally a line of females standing next to him, waiting for his attention. I almost felt sorry for him, never being left alone, always having people in his face. At least until I thought about him fucking some of these girls after we left. That shit had me a little sick.

When Die for You started playing, I couldn't help but get hype. Cass and Kendric looked my way. "Oh shit, they playing ya song bestie!" Cass shouted. My body was moving as if it had a mind of its own as I rapped every word.

Suddenly his hands had moved, one was holding a drink, and the other was on my stomach, his arm pulling me closer. I felt how hard his dick was, and I damn near swallowed my tongue. I wanted to run, but instead, I kept dancing on him. "Shorty you so fly, not just your body, but your mind. Just know I will never let you cry. This nigga will die for you." He was rapping the lyrics in my ear, and I knew I was grinning like a fool. When the song stopped, he turned me around to face him. "I thought you never heard my music?"

I felt my face turn red. I hated being so damn light. I shrugged, "I lied," I responded, trying to sound cocky.

"So, I'm ya favorite, huh?" I looked anywhere but at him. He was standing there doing the thing where he ran his tongue over his top grill. All I could think about was him running his tongue over my skin the same way. He leaned down, and I knew he was going to kiss me. Damn, he had me out here like a hoe, and those Long Island iced teas I just drank had me wanting to be one.

"Messiah-" I started to protest, but he cut me off.

"Esai, my name is Esai, don't call me anything else." His gaze was intense, causing me to squirm. Instead of sucking out my tongue, like I was fantasizing, he kissed me on my cheek. "I love that I'm your favorite. That means a lot shorty."

4
MESSIAH

Ever since I saw Ma'Kenna at the club a few weeks ago, I feel like I'm obsessed with shorty. When she cleaned up, she really did her fucking thing. That little white dress she had on had her looking like a model. It took everything in me not to take her home that night and fuck her until she couldn't move. But she deserved better than some random sex at my hoe crib. So instead, I sent her home with her friend, and I left with two professional groupies, like so many other times. Except, it wasn't like every other time, I watched the girls lick, finger fuck and play with each other and all I wanted to do was be in Ma'Kenna's presence.

"Ok, do you understand the extreme value theorem?" she asked me, a questioning look on her face. But my mind wasn't on this school shit. I felt my dick get hard watching Ma'Kenna yawn, then stretch. Her long-sleeved plain cotton shirt rode up some showing me her flat stomach. Every time she was around me, I wanted to rip her clothes off and see what her body looked like underneath, and right now wasn't an exception. Honestly, I didn't care what she had on, she was still sexy as fuck to me. I had my choice of bitches, but it was just something about Kenna that appealed to me.

"You focusing or what Esai? Because it's getting late as fuck, and I still have to make it to pick up my daughter and get home." I gave shorty a slight smile. I loved the way she wouldn't call me anything but Esai ever since I told her to use my government name.

"I mean shit, I'm focused." I bit my bottom lip and tried to tell my dick to go down some. If she saw me bricked the fuck up, she would probably run up out of here. Shorty seemed scared as fuck being around men, at least anytime she wasn't drunk. I noticed how she looked at my bodyguards, or even how cautious she was when we were alone. She would always get this look in her eyes. It was a mix of fear and weariness. I knew she had been through some shit, and I wondered what nigga hurt her.

"Ok, it's time to wrap it up. You are clearly not paying attention, and it's almost ten. If I miss the last uptown bus, I'm going to be pissed." I wondered what shorty was like when she was mad. I bet her angry face was cute as hell. It just hit me that she said bus. I knew a bus didn't really run way the fuck out here.

"Ma, what you mean bus? I thought you took an Uber home or got a ride?"

She looked down at her hands for a second and then back up at me. "Esai, I have to take a Taxi to the Post Ave. stop, then the 35 to Hempstead station and the 31 to Far Rockaway. Once I get home, I have to walk to the babysitter's house a few blocks away and then back home. I'm not sure if you've ever been to Redfern Projects, but it's not my desire to be walking through them at night. From now on, let's just try to finish by seven if we can." She flashed me a smile as she gathered her stuff.

I felt some kind of way that it took her a couple of hours and all that traveling to get to me. All that for something that was less than a thirty-minute drive. "Shit, I feel bad ma. Let my people take you home." I motioned to Travis, who walked over with a huge smile on his face. "Yo, drive Ma'Kenna to grab her daughter, then home. She lives in Redfern. Make sure they get in the apartment safe." I gave him a look, shorty and her little one better get home the same way they left.

"Aight, boss."

"No, no, umm, that is fine. I would rather not. I study on the bus, so I am good." She hopped up, her face flooded with actual terror when she looked at Travis. Before she could run out of the room, I got up and grabbed her by the arm.

"Yo, he fucked wit you or something." I pulled my gun from my waist and put one in the chamber. She was looking at him like he was the devil. Plus, I wasn't feeling the way he was eyeing shorty with a goofy-ass look on his face.

"Wait, no, Messiah he didn't do anything to me. I'm just not comfortable being alone with men I don't know. I'm ok to get myself home, I promise. I was just tired and trying to explain it was a long commute. You can put the gun away," she pleaded, her eyes following my every move.

"Aight ma, let's go. I'm taking you home." I secured my gun back in its regular spot and went to grab my phones from the table. After shooting Travis a warning look, I left the room.

"Boss, you want me to drive," Dak said as he got up from the chair he was sitting in, in the hallway. I hated the way he hovered, but ever since I was shot twice in the back last year, he barely left my side.

"You good here. Travis, you can call it a night. I'm making this run and coming back in. Dak, go find some pussy or something to get into. You're too young to be in the house watching me every night." I could see Ma'Kenna about to protest, but I didn't give her a chance to say shit else. "Don't tell me that you're good. I'm a man, and I ain't about to let you be out here on these buses all night long and shit when you out late because of me. And remember what I told you about calling me Messiah, don't." I had no idea why I didn't want her to use my stage name, it just sounded wrong coming from her.

"Yes daddy," she said sarcastically as I led her outside and to my Range Rover.

"Call me daddy again," I said as I opened her door. Shorty eyes got wide as fuck, and she almost fell inside. "Look at you, falling wit ya glasses on and shit." We both laughed as she sat down, and I closed the door. I got in and made sure I turned on her favorite song.

"You remembered," she said, blushing as she lowly sang along with Beyonce about a love that just sounded fucked up. When the song went off, she turned down the music, which I normally didn't allow. Just because it was Ma'Kenna, I let the shit slide. "You ever met her before?"

"Damn, ma, don't tell me you a part of the Beetribe or whatever ya'll call that shit."

"Nah, I like her music, but I ain't no stalker ass fan or nothing."

"I met her at some award shit once. She was cool." We kicked it the whole way to Far Rockaway, and the ride seemed too short. I wasn't ready to let her go. Once we made it to the babysitter's house, she was grabbing her bags and shit before I could even park good.

"Thanks, Esai, your sweet." She leaned over and kissed me on the cheek.

"Kenna, where the fuck you think you going ma. I'm walking you in to get baby girl and then taking you home. Don't get out this fucking truck til I come over there and get you." She looked confused, but I wasn't repeating myself. After pulling the hood over my head, I picked up the nine I had in my lap and walked to her side. After opening the door and having shorty walk in front of me, I followed her up the porch steps.

"Hey Mama Vivian, I'm sorry I'm so late." She said to the older lady who opened the door. She eyed me up and down suspiciously as I tucked my gun in my hoodie. I was sure I looked like a fucking kidnapper or something. I was just trying to keep my identity low key. "This is my client, Esai, Esai this is Cass's mom Miss Vivian." Ma'Kenna politely introduced us as we stepped inside. Removing my hood, we all jumped from the scream from behind us.

"Oh my God, mom, do you know who that is. I mean, wow, Messiah, are you really standing right here. Can I touch you," a teenage girl was standing behind Miss Vivian, jumping up and down and clutching her chest. She looked like she had seen a ghost, and I was hoping lil mama ain't fall the fuck out.

"The fuck Chelsea. No, you can't touch him," Ma'Kenna said with outrage in her voice. If I didn't know any better, I would think shorty was jealous. Too bad Kenna didn't seem like the type.

"Sorry, Kenna," she replied, looking embarrassed. "I'm just a huge fan, and I didn't know you knew him."

"Hey, Chelsea right? I'm a friend of Ma'Kenna's, why don't you go and grab a pen and a piece of paper and I will give you an autograph. And we can take a picture." She grinned so hard I could see her back teeth before she ran out of the room.

"Well, I wasn't expecting any of that. I'm sorry young man my daughter can get excited easily. Come in the living room. Sierra fell asleep waiting on her mama." I could see a look of guilt and sadness wash over Ma'Kenna's face and that shit had me feeling some kind of way. This was the second time in a row I kept her later than I should have. Shit, our sessions were only supposed to be two hours, but I never let her go sooner than four. I didn't even need as much help as I asked for. I just liked being around her. But that shit was selfish, she had a whole daughter that clearly needed her more than me.

"I'm back," Chelsea cried out as she flew back into the room. After signing a t-shirt for her and flicking it up, it was time to go.

"Ma, you stay trying off the wall shit," I said as she tried to pick her sleeping daughter up. I gently moved her to the side and held Sierra effortlessly in my arms. I wasn't around kids a lot, my boy Ghost had two little girls, and Kendric had a two-year-old son, so that was pretty much all of my experience. I liked kids though. They had an innocence I never got to experience and positive energy that we should all be so lucky to have.

"I like him," Miss Vivian said as I gave her a boyish smile. I heard Ma'Kenna huff from next to me. "That's how a man should behave," Cass's mother continued as she walked us to the door.

Once I got them settled in the truck, Kenna leaned back and closed her eyes. I didn't know if she was sleeping or trying not to cry. I ain't like the thought of either. "You good," I asked. My hand brushed against hers, and I felt her shiver. I wanted to just hold on to her, and that had my head fucked up. I have had girlfriends in the past, but none I really gave a fuck about. I basically threw them the title because it was a good look for my career or because their pussy was A1. I never cared about what they were going through. It had to be because Ma'Kenna was so pure, so timid. I just felt bad for her.

Once we made it to the projects, I parked where she told me. Leaving her and Sierra here was fucking wit me. I grew up in the same environment, and it was the type of place that scarred you for life. Shorty lived on the second floor, and the whole walk there, all you could hear was gunshots, arguing, and police sirens. "Next week Kendric is picking you up and dropping you off. I don't want you out here late and shit all alone." I stepped inside her apartment and smiled. I knew she kept her shit neat. When she would come to my crib, she was always straightening up something on the table or fixing my couch pillows. Shorty had books every fucking were. The living room was filled with bookshelves, and every space was filled with different sized books.

"You can set her on the couch. And I can get myself to you just fine next week. I don't need Kendric disrupting his life for me. I am fully grown and can manage." I set Sierra on the couch and took off her little Nike Air Maxes. "I appreciate you Messiah, I really do," Kenna said as she moved closer to me. "You're a good guy, no matter what the media says." If she only knew half the shit I did, stuff the media had no clue about. Reaching up, I touched her cheek lightly before stepping into the hallway. I stood in the hall until I heard the locks click, and then I walked away.

Leaving Ma'Kenna had my head fucked up. I didn't even want to head back to my crib. I didn't want to be alone. I picked up my phone and called someone to distract me. "Hey baby," she cooed from the speaker in my truck.

"Yo, you in town?" I asked, not wasting time on her bullshit.

"Yes, at my condo downtown."

"Cool, I'm about to slide through," I said and hung up. She wasn't Ma'Kenna, but Nedra would have to do. By the time I made it to my ex's spot, I was ready to smoke, fuck, and lay it on down. I parked in the garage and headed to the elevator, I entered the code for her floor and started to question what I was doing here.

"Sup Messiah," her bodyguard greeted me as I knocked on the door. I nodded, not in the mood for conversation. Instead of greeting me at the door Nedra made me come find her. Stepping into her bedroom, she was laid out across the king-size bed, butt ass naked. Her mahogany skin was covered with some sparkly lotion that was glowing in the moonlight. Any other time I might have gave a fuck, but not now, not since I met Ma'Kenna. I was just here for one thing.

I didn't even bother getting undressed. She didn't need to be getting the wrong idea about her and me. I undid my belt and dropped my jeans and boxers before sitting on the edge of the bed. "I missed you so much Messiah," she whined as I motioned for her to come and handle my man. He was hard as fuck and in need of some attention. "Damn, I missed him too," she said as her lips covered the tip, then she slurped a little. I sat back, enjoying the feeling, eventually tangling my hand in her expensive weave and pushing my dick deeper down her throat. Nedra didn't gag though. Instead, she opened wider and let me fuck her. I was going hard, lifting my body slightly off the bed, chasing the feeling of a good nut.

I had to admit the sex wasn't the reason me and Nedra never

worked out. She was a freak with the best of them, her little bit of fame hadn't changed that about her. She would let me fuck her any way I wanted and still loved me. Her love was so strong I had shorty doing some degrading shit, all in hopes of me still being her man. But as always, Nedra was just someone to do. Her being an up and coming R&B artist on my label was good for headlines. Not so good some of the shit she revealed about me, like the fact I asked her for a threesome with her best friend. I mean shit I never forced her, and I never made any promises after the fact. I didn't even give a fuck when the video was released. My dick and his performance didn't put me to shame. But, it was just another thing that confirmed to the world what a fucked up individual I was. Not that I cared. My shit was still going to sell, whether I respected these bitches or not.

"Come on girl, swallow this shit," I groaned as I felt my nut shoot to the tip of my dick. Like a good girl Nedra sat back on her heels and didn't miss a drop.

"Daddy, how do you want it," She purred as she stood up and bent over in front of me. Her pussy was wet, and she was making a bigger mess in it with her two fingers. I wasn't interested though. My mind was on someone else, even after busting down Nedra's throat.

"Get me something to clean up with, and I'm out." Her face fell as she slowly walked to the master bathroom and came back with a wet rag.

"I thought you came to rekindle things, to fix us." I ignored her as I fixed my clothes and retucked my gun. "Do you hear me Esai?"

I walked over to her fast as fuck and snatched her up. "The fuck I told you about calling me that." My voice was cold, and so was the look on my face. This was the real me, someone that wasn't capable of love or of being with a woman as sweet as Ma'Kenna even if she was interested in me.

"Not to do it," Nedra managed to get out.

"Then don't fucking do it," I gritted as I dropped her back to the ground. "I came because I needed my dick sucked, nothing more, nothing less. I'm out."

※

IT WAS HARD NOT SEEING MA'KENNA; SHE WAS GETTING TO me. The only thing that kept me away this week was the fact I had a trip out to Cali for some promotional shit. Radio interviews for my upcoming album. I picked up the glass of Hennesey and waited for the plane to land. "Boss, which house you going to," Dak said once we stepped off the jet.

"I will meet you at the crib in Westbury, I got some shit to handle." I brushed off the questions and went to get in my truck that Travis had pulled around. I know they liked for me to keep security with me at all times, my publicists, my label, hell, even my mama. But I was a hood nigga, and I liked to do shit my own way. I left JFK and headed right to the projects. I parked and looked around, happy for the rainy ass day. I didn't need to be seen. I was hoping to be in and out. Once I got to the second floor, I knocked on Apartment B and waited. I should have called, saw if she was even home.

The door opened, and Ma'Kenna stood there, her mouth opened in an O shape. "What's good ma?" I never even thought of a reason for me to be standing on her doorstep.

"Esai, what are you doing here?" She looked confused but cute as fuck. I let my eyes rake over her body. She only had on a pair of Nike Pro shorts and a matching sports bra. Her hair was pulled up on the top of her head in some messy bun type shit.

"The fuck you opening the door in that shit for?" Were ya clothes at?" I backed her in her house, my hand gripping her side. As soon as I felt her silky skin, I was ready to throw her in the back of my truck and take her with me.

"Hi," a tiny voice said, and I looked up to see her daughter standing in the kitchen holding a popsicle. I dropped my hand from her mother and crouched down to her level. She was wearing colorful striped tights and a purple tee shirt. Her hair was in three ponytails with matching bows. Her smile was cute, and she didn't have all of her teeth in, so there were a few gaps in the front.

"Hey, lil mama what's up."

"I'm Sierra, not lil mama. Mommy, he is funny," she said, grinning up at her mother. "I remember you, Siah. You called mommy's phone."

"Yes I did. You have a good memory. You going to share your popsicles with me."

"Yes, I love to share. Mommy, Siah wants a popsicle. Can he have an orange one too? It's my favorite." Ma'Kenna was still standing there like she was trying to figure something out.

"It's Monday, right?" She sounded perplexed. "No, of course it's Monday. I went to class, then the hospital, and now I'm home—no tutoring session. So, I just don't get it. Did I forget something? Am I being fired?" She whispered the last part, mindful that her daughter was clinging to her every word.

"My bad shorty, I just got back in town, and I need some extra help. I should have called. I was just in the area, so I figured if I could pick you up now, it could save us some time. I will pay you extra. I get that it's your day off, and I know you busy as fuck. It shouldn't even take a long time."

"I'm sorry, but as you can see, I have my daughter, I'm sorry, but I really can't help tonight." I could see she was torn. I hated that she needed the money that bad. "If you have the work with you, I can try and help, or you can call me. You don't have to pay me extra. I mean seriously, you pay me enough for a few hours a week."

"You can bring Sierra with you. It's not a big deal. I don't have any toys, but she can watch TV or eat cookies." I felt like I was begging her. I didn't even need any damn help. I just wanted to see her.

"Umm ok, I guess we could. Let me get dressed and clean her

up. You can sit down if you want. You look tired as fuck." She wasn't lying, I was in some club in L.A. all night, and now that I was back in NY, the time zone change was fucking wit me. I damn near fell asleep on her couch until Sierra bounced into the room. She smelled like baby lotion and was now rocking some pink and white footie pajamas.

"Are you sleeping," she asked as she sat down next to me, holding a doll. I nodded, opening one of my eyes.

"It's not bedtime yet," she said, giggling. "Guess what, Siah? I'm having a birthday party on Saturday. It's at Chuck E Cheese. Do you want to come?" I sat up and saw her watching me. "Please, Siah," she added, giving me the same pouty face her mother made all the time.

"Aight lil mama, I will be there. But don't tell mommy, it's a surprise."

5

MA'KENNA

I hurried and got ready as fast as I could. Having Messiah in my space had me nervous as fuck. It was just something about him that had me fantasizing about a lot of shit I could never have. Ok breathe, I told myself as I glanced at the mirror one more time. I didn't put on anything fancy, just a pair of black and Gold Nike tights and a matching top. I walked in the living room to see Sierra talking Messiah's ear off about an episode of Peppa Pig. He listened and nodded in all the right places. "Ok, let's go; it's getting late." I grabbed a small bag I had packed for Sierra with a few toys, a change of clothes, and some snacks.

"What kind of homework you need help on," I asked on the way to his house. I swore he had nothing due for math. But maybe I missed something on his syllabus.

"It's a paper for this literature class I'm taking. It's required and shit." I side-eyed him, and I had to wonder since when the nigga who wrote songs needed help writing anything. He never elaborated, just kept driving, the radio on low. We pulled into his community, and for once, I didn't have to dig out my ID. The toy cop looked intimidated by Messiah. I wasn't really surprised, he had that effect on people.

"Wow, mommy look," Sierra pointed at the house as we got

IT'S HIS SAVAGE LOVE FOR ME

up and walked to the door. "It's so big," she said in awe. I hated that she was so smart for her age. Most three-year-olds still had baby minds, but not my daughter. She was always on point, and if you asked me knew too damn much. As soon as we walked through the door, she kicked off her rain boots as she ran around the marble foyer singing and stopping to jump every few minutes.

"Sierra," I snapped, "you know better. We don't run inside of people's houses. Now get over here." Her face fell as she apologized and walked over to stand next to me.

"Yo, you better leave my little friend alone," Messiah said as he led us deeper into the house. I had never been back here, and I had no idea where we were going. "We can work here so she can be entertained." He opened double doors to reveal a huge movie room, complete with a popcorn machine, snack bar, and comfortable oversized couches and chairs. "Here you can find something for her to watch, get whatever ya'll want, and I will be back. I'm going to change and get my laptop."

I sat down and tried to figure out the remotes he gave me. By the time he made it back, Sierra was happily eating popcorn and M&M's and watching *Wreck-it Ralph*. We worked on his paper for a few hours, and just like I suspected, he didn't really need me to help. "You could have done this on your own," I fussed as he attached it to his e-mail and sent it to his professor.

"I wanted to make sure it was approved from the best." I gave him a yea fucking right look. He got up and found a thick grey throw blanket from somewhere and covered a sleeping Sierra.

"How many kids do you have," I asked?

"Shit, none. A few bitches tried to pin some kids on me, but I'm careful as fuck."

"You're good with kids. You don't want any?" I was curious, Esai was a mystery, and I really wanted to know all I could about him. I knew it was all for nothing, no nigga ever took me seriously, and he wasn't about to become the exception.

"I'm not against having kids. I just never found a girl to have them with."

"Shit, I know you've had girlfriends. What about Nedra? You and her seemed pretty tight."

He moved closer to me, and the smell of his cologne had my pussy jumping. "On some real shit ma, I don't want to have kids with some random ass girl. I have had girlfriends over the years, but none of them meant shit to me. All the women in my life are with me for their own reasons. Either they want my money, my dick, or to be attached to my name. None of them ever loved me for me, shit they don't even try to get to know me. I was with that chick Tia for two years. I bet she ain't even know what the fuck I liked to eat, or my favortie color. That ain't no situation to be bringing a kid into."

He sounded sad. I guess being famous definitely had its drawbacks. "Green right," his head snapped back to look at me. "It's your favorite color."

"How did you know?"

"You wear a lot of green. Even if your shirt is red or blue, it usually has green in there somewhere. I can't really tell you your favorite food since we haven't eaten together. Esai, never settle. No matter how much money or shine you have, a woman should always care about you first."

"Yo, you a real one ma." I stood up so we could go. I didn't want him to think I was another girl trying to be down on his team.

"Kenna on some real shit ma, I'm tired as fuck, and I wouldn't even feel good to be out on the road wit ya'll like that. You mind staying the night? I have a lot of extra bedrooms in here. I just need to catch a nap or some shit. I'm about to crash."

I felt my stomach do mini flips, thinking about staying at his house. I would have normally felt some kind of way about being in a house with some man overnight, but Esai made me feel comfortable. "Umm ok, no problem, I have to be home early though, I have class at eight."

IT'S HIS SAVAGE LOVE FOR ME

I GOT OUT OF THE TRUCK AND WENT TO GRAB SIERRA FROM the back, except Messiah beat me to it. "I got her, the fuck I look like making you carry her. She heavy as fuck. I swear I told you that the last time." I just shrugged, it was way too early to argue with any nigga, definitely not this one. Esai wasn't all there and I didn't want to be the one to set him the fuck off. I trailed behind carrying me and Sierra's stuff. Staying the night at his house was probably not smart on my end. It felt like I was mixing business with pleasure, which was always a no no. The next time he asked me for extra help I was going to tell him no.

"Come on ma, walk in front of me," he demanded. He placed his hand on the small of my back and led me in front. He was doing the most, his bodyguard was behind me, so I was pretty sure I was safe. I swear he was confusing, he didn't seem like the chivalrous type, but he always showed me a different side to him. If we met under different circumstances, maybe I would have tried him.

"What's good baby mama," a voice said, startling me out of my thoughts. Seeing Isaac leaning against the building with a smirk on his face, I rolled my eyes. His gaze went to Messiah. "Sup my nigga."

"Sup Iz, I didn't know this was your shorty and lil one." Messiah kept his hand on my back the whole time he spoke to Isaac. I had no idea how he knew him, but since he was using his street name, I was sure it was on some hood shit.

Isaac waved his hand towards us. "Nothing like that my man. I don't even fuck with the little one. Her mother's pussy was trash, so I moved on. I wouldn't waste your time on them though; you will be disappointed." I felt my heart drop into my stomach. I was in no way surprised by the shit that Isaac was saying. I was just ashamed that he was saying it in front of Messiah.

"The fuck you say nigga?" Messiah was handing me Sierra

and pushing us behind him before I could react. "Don't fucking get quiet now, pussy ass nigga."

"Son, the fuck you mad at me for? That bitch pussy is broken, dry as a cheap rough towel. Her body is garbage, too scrawny for me. She ain't even got an ass. I fucked it a few times, and she got pregnant. Thought she could trap me, but fuck that, I never said I wanted any kids, and I sure as fuck didn't want her. So, if you enjoy whack pussy and snotty-nosed kids, have at it." Before the last word was out of his mouth Messiah had punched him in the face. He fell back, but Siah wasn't finished.

"Don't you ever fucking talk about either one of them again." Isaac was bloody now, crumpled on the ground holding his side. Even though it was only six in the morning, somehow a crowd of people had formed to watch the show.

"Damn ain't that Messiah; he's always into some shit." I saw people with their phones out recording and taking pictures.

"Siah, stop, it's not worth it," I pleaded as he pulled his gun out. I looked to Dak for help, and he finally pulled him back. "Please, Messiah, I don't want you in trouble on my behalf." I knew I was crying by now. I hated Isaac and should have felt so much satisfaction at him being beaten half to death. But how could I be mad? My pussy was trash, I couldn't satisfy him.

"Come on," Messiah said after he kicked Isaac once more. He put his arm around me, and we walked inside my apartment. "Yo go put her down and come holla at me," he demanded. I moved slow, making my way to her room and putting Sierra in the bed, then covering her up. I knew I had to face him, but at this point, I would have been happy never to see him again. I stepped out of the room to see him pacing in the hallway, waiting.

"The fuck you crying for? I know you too smart to still be hung up on that asshole."

"What, no. I don't care about him. I'm crying because what he said was true," I looked at the floor instead of at him. I had never been so embarrassed, so ashamed of myself. "I mean not

IT'S HIS SAVAGE LOVE FOR ME

all of what he said. I never had Sierra to trap him, but he was right about my pussy. I can't fuck. I don't react like a woman should. Please, I don't want to say anymore. It's not something I like talking about. But it's why I don't date, why I will never have a man or a husband. I just thank God I was able to have a child. Sierra is my blessing, and all I really have in life."

He stopped walking back and forth and pulled me into his arms. I felt my tears hitting his hard chest and I felt so stupid. I would have done anything to take this day back. I saw how he looked at me sometimes like I was someone he would at least fuck. All that would be over now. "I don't believe that ma, that's shit niggas wit whack ass dick say. So, what if you didn't sexually satisfy him. You gave him a sweet ass little girl. What kind of grown man doesn't even take care of his kid. You need to stop walking around here acting like something is wrong wit you. I promise you it ain't."

I stepped back and shook my head. "I have to get ready to go. Thank you for trying to make me feel better. I usually don't cry over it. I guess I just didn't want you to know." I turned to go into my room, hoping he would take the hint and leave. Instead, he followed right behind me. "Esai, what?" I damn near yelled.

"Yo you cute when you mad," he said smirking. "Sit down for a minute," he said as he ran his hands over his waves. Slowly I sat on the edge of the bed. He pulled me into him, so my back was to his chest. "Shorty, how old were you when you got pregnant?"

"I was seventeen. Isaac was my first, and clearly my last. I never thought I would be bad at sex or that I would hate sex." I laughed a little to try and hide how nervous I was. I felt his big hand slide across my exposed belly, and I shivered. I felt his lips on my neck, and I stiffened.

"Kenna, relax ma, I ain't going to hurt you." He kissed me again, gently, like he was afraid I would break. I felt something I never felt before. My body was on fire. "I bet ya pussy is wet right now," he murmured close to my ear, and I felt his hand go lower until it was at the edge of my tights. I wanted to stop him, but the closer he got to my treasure, the better it felt. I jumped a little when his finger brushed over my clit. His other hand slid under my shirt and cupped my breast.

"Mhmmm," I moaned, not knowing what was happening. I wanted something more, and I was opening my legs wider, trying to find it. "Fuck," I yelled as he slipped a finger inside of me.

"I knew you got wet for a real nigga. This pussy wasn't made for him. It was made for me. I don't want you to hold back Ma'Kenna. Let that shit go, cum all over my fingers. I want to feel that shit." Every word he said turned me on even more, and as soon as he pinched my nipple, I felt my body contract. The pleasure he just gave me was like nothing I ever experienced. My panties and tights were soaked.

I felt the sudden urge to curl in a ball and sleep that was how good that shit was. I didn't know if he expected to fuck or not. I could feel how hard his dick was behind me. "Come on ma, go shower, you got class. Now stop walking around here thinking something is wrong with you, fuck that nigga. Next time I see him, I'm handling his ass." He got up and bent down, so his face was close to mine. "Don't let no other nigga touch this pussy," he whispered before kissing me.

6

MESSIAH

Touching Ma'Kenna the way I did a few days ago was a mistake. I couldn't get shorty off my mind. I felt like a fiend the way I kept thinking about her body. I still had two days until I saw her again, but it seemed like it was too fucking long.

"Mr. Aleczander, would you like breakfast?" My housekeeper asked as she lightly knocked on the door of my bedroom.

"If I wanted it, I would have asked," I barked. She turned and went back to whatever she was doing. My attitude today wasn't the best, so that was a smart fucking choice. I sent a text to Ma'Kenna just to see what she was on.

Me: You good?

Kenna: Yes. You ok? How did the paper go?

Me: Shit, I ain't even check. I know it's straight since you helped me with it. What you doing?

Kenna: At my internship until four. What are you doing?

It took me a minute to respond. I wasn't used to being careful with my words. I usually just said whatever the fuck I thought. But I knew I couldn't move like that with Ma'Kenna. She was sensitive, she had been through a fucked up relationship. I was sure I only knew the half of the shit that nigga Iz put her through.

Kenna: You must be fucking, that's why you not answering my question. LOL.

Me: Sitting here, wishing I was fucking you. You got my dick harder than a fucking rock. I can just imagine how pretty that pussy looks. I just want to watch you play with it, see you squirt.

The bubble showing she was sending a message popped up and then disappeared. See, I should have lied, told her I was working on a song or watching TV. I just reacted off of her. For some reason, I didn't want her thinking I was with another female.

Kenna: I don't really know what to say to that.

Me: You ain't got to say shit ma. I want to see you tonight, you gonna come through the studio? No funny shit, I just want your opinion on a song.

Kenna: I guess I could just this once. Send me the info, and I will stop by after work.

I texted her the address and the number to a car company in the city. If I found out she was on the train or bus, I was fucking her little ass up. I was still tired, but I rolled a blunt and started my day. I picked up my phone and dialed my cousin. "Where the fuck you at?" I asked as soon as he answered.

"Shit in my crib still sleep nigga, you know the life I live. What you want this early?"

"I don't give a fuck about all that shit, wake up. I'm on my way to you." I hung up on him, not giving a fuck about him cursing me out on the other line.

I smoked and showered, throwing on jeans and a Versace hoodie with a pair of wheat Timbs. I placed my custom Jesus piece around my neck and made sure to grab both of my guns. I didn't leave home without them because all this money didn't change a nigga. I was still about my shit.

Dak drove me, so I sat back and started answering e-mails, no matter how much lil niggas in the streets thought this rapping shit was just about rapping. It was like any other business, filled with contracts, politics, and a heavy ass grind. I still remember what I had to go through when I signed with my first label. I had to leave the fucking CEO, and his lawyer slumped because I wasn't about to let anyone fucking play me with a whack ass contract.

"I ain't gonna be in here long, so don't go no fucking where." I hopped out and made my way to the door. As soon as it opened, KJ was there running around, knocking shit down. "Lil nigga, what you doing," I asked as I scooped him up and threw him in the air.

"Terrorizing my fucking house," Kendric's baby mom said as she gave me a hug and shook her head at her son. "Let me go tell ya big head ass cousin you here." I played with KJ a few minutes more until his sleepy ass daddy came downstairs.

"See, to fucking early." He threw himself on the couch and glared at me.

"Nigga, I ain't scared of you. Need to start getting ya ass up and helping with KJ. Latia looking like she ready to dip out on both of ya'll. Get a nanny or some shit, give her a break, it ain't like you don't got the bread."

"Latia straight, she don't need no fucking cheerleader. If she want a break she better speak the fuck up." See this was the shit I was talking about. Kendric had a baby with this girl, maybe liked her a little, cared about her, what the fuck ever he had going on. At the end of the day, he had no respect for her. He fucked every female moving and didn't give a fuck if Latia felt some way about it or if she needed help at home with their son. Now I was far from the best nigga, and I played females like a piano. Talked shit in their face, and fucked and moved on like it was nothing. But I wasn't bringing no kid into that shit. Any girl I have a baby wit, got to have my respect before she gets pregnant and after. I just shook my head at his dumb ass and changed the subject. I was going to start coming to scoop KJ up. Maybe he could hang out with Sierra, and Latia could get a break.

"The fuck you ain't tell me that nigga Iz, is Ma'Kenna baby daddy?" That woke him all the way the fuck up. He sat up excited or some shit like I was here for his entertainment. Nigga was messing around making dumb ass faces and shit.

"Why would I nigga, she's your tutor, not ya girl." He grinned like he knew some shit I didn't, and it was a fucking joke. I thought about the way this nigga dicked down every female he ever met and felt my blood boil.

"Yo, Latia, come grab KJ," I yelled, ready to beat her man's ass. She came and got her son right away and gave me a strange look before leaving the room. "Let me ask you something Kendric, you fucked shorty." I moved to the edge of the couch, just waiting for him to say he smashed Ma'Kenna.

This nigga started laughing, like bent over the couch, crying and shit. I pulled out my nine and laid it on my lap. He was testing my patience on a day I didn't really fucking have any. "Oh fuck, nigga you serious ain't you. I knew you were feeling Kenna little nerdy ass. No, I ain't fuck her, you ain't got to shoot me cuz. You were really gonna shoot me?"

I just stared at his ass. "I have never known you to have female friends, so yea I had to ask."

"Nah, it really ain't like that. I grew up with Ma'Kenna, like from the sandbox type shit. You don't remember Redfern projects was home when I was young. It was always me, her and Cass. I would never smash Kenna for so many reasons. First of all, that's little sis. Shit wouldn't even feel right. Second of all I used to smash Cass. I mean shit, it was more than that. She was the one that got away," he said, whispering the last part. I swear I never knew he gave a fuck about any female, but when he said Cass's name, his voice changed up.

"So who fucking with Ma'Kenna now? She got a man?" She said she didn't date, that nigga's didn't fuck wit her like that. But I saw how these dudes look at her. She just wasn't aware.

Kendric sat back, his face serious now. I watched darkness enter his eyes, and that shit caused me to tense up. He drug his hand down his face. "Shit with Ma'Kenna is complicated. Yea, Iz is Sierra's pops. He don't fuck wit her though. Nigga was twenty when he started fucking Ma'Kenna, and she was sixteen. Broke her virginity like a savage and then wondered why she wasn't into having sex with him. He broke her down, physically and emotionally."

"Hold the fuck on, he put his hands on her?"

Kendric sighed, "I ain't supposed to know all this shit. Cass would tell me stuff that Kenna trusted only her with. If she knew, she would never forgive Cass, and that shit can't happen. Ma'Kenna doesn't have anyone else. Her mom is alive but not interested in her. None of her cousins or aunties fuck with her. Kenna is smart. I mean you know she is smart but like genius status. So growing up mother fuckers always had a lot of hate for her, even her ole girl. But Cass and her family showed her love, Vivian was like a mom to her, never treated her funny because she was different."

Hearing all this shit had me fucked up. I grew up rough, but my mom and grandmother loved my bad ass. We ain't always have the shit we needed, but knowing I had someone that loved me softened the blow. "Ok got it, you not supposed to know. Keep fucking talking. I mean, I'm killing that nigga regardless. But I want to know how much he damaged shorty."

"The fuck you need to know for? That's my friend Esai. You not about to fuck her and set her to the side like you do the rest of these bitches. I know her, if she let's you get that close, she is feeling you, she gives a fuck about you. I can't let you break her heart. I won't. Keep this shit professional and move the fuck on." He was snapping, and I had to tell myself not to go off on my cousin. He was looking out for Kenna, and my reputation wasn't the best. Shit, I know I wanted to fuck her, but then what, was I trying to make her my girlfriend? I had never taken that shit seriously, and I had never stopped freaking random hoes when I was in a so-called relationship. I knew he was right. I needed to leave Ma'Kenna alone before I broke her heart.

"I hear you. You right. I just want to take care of that nigga.

That's why I'm asking. I'm trying to be a friend to shorty. Not fuck her."

"I hope you not capping son. Anyway, Iz ass wasn't straight beating on Kenna. But he was basically raping her. He would force her to have sex, she wouldn't react how he wanted, but he still managed to get off. Personally, I feel like he enjoyed the fact he was causing her pain, but that is just based on shit other bitches he fucked be saying. He didn't start putting hands on her until after she got pregnant with Sierra. I feel like he knocked her up on purpose. It was a control tactic. She had a rough pregnancy, alone most of the time. He was fucking other bitches, and she was home, sick as fuck. I remember me and Cass would be checking on her every other day. Shit even Latia was making her soup and trying to get her to eat, bringing her ginger ale and cookies.

I guess he tried to make her give him head, and she stopped and had to go throw up, so he beat her ass. After that, anytime he couldn't get pussy when he wanted it, he started slapping her around and shit. I never addressed it with Kenna, even when I saw the bruises. But I made sure that nigga Isaac left her alone. As for her fucking with someone else, she isn't. She is single, and seems like she wants to keep it that way. Long story short, Ma'Kenna is scared of men. She isn't comfortable around them, especially alone."

For the first time ever my heart ached. I wanted to head to the hospital and snatch shorty up. Take her and Sierra home with me and tell her I wasn't ever letting shit else happen to her. I had never felt this need to protect someone the way I did with Ma'Kenna. "Good looking," I said as I stood up. "Get me an address on Iz by tonight." I threw five g's on the table and bounced.

IT'S HIS SAVAGE LOVE FOR ME

I WENT TO TARGET IN JERSEY, HOPING TO AVOID THE CROWDS. I wanted to get Sierra some shit for her birthday. I didn't know what four-year-olds liked, but I was sure someone who worked up in there could help. I could have had my assistant cop baby girl stuff, but that felt like some lame shit. Something you would do for people you really didn't give a fuck about. All the little pink shit in the girls' aisle made my head hurt, but eventually, I found some dolls, a dollhouse, a car, and some accessories. I knew lil mama liked that British Pig, so I grabbed some of those toys and then made my way to electronics. Shit, I ain't even know if little kids could even play video games. They were hella smart these days, so I grabbed a Wii, some games, and an iPad. I hoped Maria's ass knew how to wrap all this shit.

I dropped off the stuff at home and threw my housekeeper some money to get the toys wrapped by the weekend. Instead of letting the car service pick up Ma'Kenna, I was just going to get her myself. I didn't want her to feel uncomfortable with some random ass nigga. I parked the truck and decided to take one of my cars. Hopping in my Bugatti Veyron, I peeled out under Dak's disapproving stare.

I sped through the NY streets, damn near getting pulled over a few times. A part of me hoped I was going to catch up wit Iz around the way, but if not, there was always later. I knew shorty would be home by the time I made it to the crib by the time I pulled up. I pulled up in front of her building but stayed in the car. I could see all the little nigga's looking, ready for a come up, when in reality they was ready to get they head split. I picked up the phone and called Kenna. "Yo, I'm out front. You ready?" I asked as I rolled down my window and set the barrel of my gun outside.

"You said to call the car company at seven. It's only five. I mean I'm dressed. Just give me a few more minutes so I can do something with my hair."

"It's ya world shorty, take ya time." I hung up, my eyes on my surroundings. I didn't give a fuck about being out this way. But I hated this shit for Kenna and Sierra. It wasn't even any place safe for baby girl to play. The ground was littered with crack pipes and used condoms. There were crackheads sitting on all the benches, and corner boys posted up on every doorway. Yea this wasn't it. I sat back and smoked until I saw Ma'Kenna walk outside. It was like shorty didn't even fucking know how banging her body was.

She had on some tight ass ripped blue jeans and a green off the shoulder sweater. Her hair was pulled into a slicked up ponytail and she had her glasses on. She rocked a small pair of studs in her ears and a pair of small ass wheat Timbs. Her feet was small as fuck. It looked like she stole her baby shoes. Her whole outfit was simple, but she was still every fucking thing. I stepped out of the car, and she smiled as soon as she noticed me. "Ayy yo, come fuck wit me since you finally stopped dressing like somebody grandma and shit." This nappy head nigga said, walking her way.

"She good homeboy," I said as I walked over to her and put my arm around her shoulders. She looked so uncomfortable when he was talking to her that shit made me mad as fuck. "Get in," I instructed as I opened the door and watched her slide inside.

"Damn, you don't even be giving me a chance to see if I like these nigga's. You are worse than Kendric. Always in my business and shit. He could have been the man for me. What if I wanted him?" She crossed her arms and fake pouted.

"You know you ain't want that busta ass nigga," I said, and we both laughed. "On some real shit though, can't no nigga holla at you when I'm around. He better find you on Facebook and send a secret message or some shit."

"Nigga you mean a DM? I know you got a Facebook, shit I follow you, and I'm sure these thirsty ass hoes be blowing ya DM up."

"Shit you be sending me messages? I might have to check it some day."

"Umm naw playa, not me. I like your music. I never said I liked you." She rolled her eyes at me but was still smiling and shit.

"You like the way I make you cum," I said, squeezing her fat pussy through the jeans she had on. The way she blushed confirmed what I already knew. "You do know I aint the one behind the Facebook, IG or Twitter right? I have people for that. Real niggas don't be on social media like a bitch all day." I drove off, removing the gun from my lap once we hit the expressway.

"You wouldn't have to ride around like that if you would just stay the fuck out the projects. Nigga's always hate on the ones who made it out. Then you roll up in there wit ya jewlery, Rolex, and this car. It's like you want a nigga to rob you."

"Ma I ain't scared of no ma'fucka out here. We all breathe the same and bleed the same. If you in the PJ's then that's where the fuck I'm at. I ain't like these other nigga's, walking around wit fear in my heart. I came from the gutta, I know what I'm doing. I aint ever letting shit happen to you so you aint gotta worry."

"If you say so and it aint me I'm worried about." She looked unsure as fuck and I thought it was cute she was worried about me. Last female who worried about my ass was my grandmother. "Why you pick me up now? You had to go in early? Are you sure you can bring people in the studio wit you?"

"We bout to go eat so you can get to know my favorite food. And hell yea I can have people in the studio, I own the fucking place." I drove until we made it to Sammy's Fish box in City Island. It was a nice chill spot, one I could come to and not worry about a bunch of people harassing me. The owners had no problem giving me a private table whenever and the food wasn't bad either.

"That's cool, I didn't eat dinner, or lunch," she said shaking her head.

"You better stop doing that shit," I replied hating that she was always so busy. "Where baby girl at? We have to bring her wit us next time."

"With Cass tonight, they having girls night. That's her God baby and she spoils her rotten, always painting her toes and watching Frozen over and over again. Sierra stole my damn friend," she whined.

I pulled into a parking spot and laughed at shorties antics, "aww don't worry I will be your friend."

※

I PULLED INTO THE PARKING LOT AT THE STUDIO AND SAT there for a minute. Ma'Kenna was knocked out sleeping in the passenger side of the car. I didn't even want to wake her up, she looked peaceful. Just like the night she stayed at my house, she had a nigga sneaking in her room like a fucking creep and watching her sleep. I reached out my hand and lightly touched her face, I traced the small line of freckles she had running from the corner of her eye going down. "Mmmm," she moaned in her sleep and my shit was on brick. "Esai," muttered in her sleep as I leaned over and kissed her neck. I knew she loved that shit, it was her spot. I wondered what other places she liked being kissed.

A loud ass knock on my car window caused us both to jump up. "Bitch ass nigga, you gonna sit out here all night," my boy Ghost said from the other side of the door.

"Nigga fuck you, lucky I aint shoot ya lite bright ass," I snapped back.

"Damn, I'm sorry I fell asleep. You should have woke me up, I know you got to go handle ya work. I'm sure making music isn't easy." No one had ever said no shit like that to me before. This shit was hard work, but I guess it looked like it wasn't to most.

"If you are tired I can take you back home, you can go to my house if you want and sleep."

"I'm good, that nap got me feeling new. Plus I'm interested in

IT'S HIS SAVAGE LOVE FOR ME

seeing you lay down a track. Is that how ya'll say it?" She giggled and I just shook my head.

"Cool," I said as I got out and opened her door. My boy was standing at the door snickering, his nosey ass watching my every move. I felt Ma'Kenna tense up next to me. "That's my people, he just acting silly as fuck. You don't have to worry about him.

"Isn't he a producer," she said as we walked inside.

"Yea, you recognize him. Hard to forget his pale ass," I joked, and she laughed a little.

I frowned when I walked in and noticed the small group of people hanging out. Even though it was my brother and cousin and their women I was pissed. I hated that hanging out in the studio shit, and they knew it. No one else was supposed to be here but our boy Micah, and that was only because we had a track to work on together.

"Shorty you good?" I asked watching her as she looked around. I knew she recognized these nigga's from the condo. Tebo was the one who tried to drop ten stacks on her. But I just wanted her to know as long as she was with me, she was straight.

"Yea, where do you want me to sit?" I formally introduced her to everyone and had her sit as close to the booth as I could. I was barely able to focus on what I was doing because I had my eyes on her, after the shit that happened at the condo, I was trying to be careful wit shorty. My cousin Tebo made her a drink and Kenna started talking to his girl Quita and my sister in law Erica.

"Shit you ready or you gonna just sit there and watch ole girl all fucking night," Ghost barked from the sound board.

"Nigga fuck you," I shot back. I got through the first two songs and stepped out while he played them back. Walking up behind Ma'Kenna I buried my face in her neck and held on to her. She smelled good as fuck, like some fruity shit. "Sup," I said in her ear.

"Your songs sound good, maybe I will find a new favorite one," she said, smiling up at me.

"I got you." I kissed shorty on the cheek even though I wanted to tongue her down. I could see everyone watching me, surprised, but not bold enough to say shit. I was feeling Kenna and I didn't care who knew about it.

"Aight Ghost drop the new beat you sent me." Ma'Kenna inspired me and when I started rapping the words to Motivation it was effortless. She stopped what she was doing and kept her attention on me, she was cute as fuck sitting there with her mouth slightly opened, bobbing her head a little. It felt like it was only me and her in the room, but when I finished everyone got hype.

"Nigga, that shit was fucking fire," Micah said and everyone agreed. I wasn't really pressed about what those nigga's thought though. I watched Ma'Kenna as she mouthed to me, *new favorite*. Shorty was so different from these other hoes. I noticed Quita trying to hand Ma'Kenna a pill, but she shook her head no. I already knew baby girl wasn't on that type of time. I guess the girls didn't like that answer because the next thing I knew Erica was slipping the pill in her drink.

That bitch didn't even notice I came up out the booth until I snatched her by the back of her neck. "The fuck wrong wit you retarded ass?" I shouted as I choked her.

"Nigga get ya hands off my girl," my brother Banks shouted, but it wasn't stopping shit. He better go talk to his damn self because I didn't give a fuck.

"So even though shorty told ya'll hoes she aint want no pill, you turn the fuck around and slip it in her drink? She doesn't get down like that, she aint no fucking bird, and from now on when you see her don't even fucking speak." I dropped Erica to the ground and stepped over her like the trash she was. Just like I thought her man didn't do shit but watch, all bark and no bite ass nigga. He was soft since he came out of our mama's womb.

Quita was looking on, her eyes wide in shock like she wasn't in on this shit. "Bitch you included in this fucking public service announcement. I should knock ya head off." She jumped back, almost knocking Tebo to the ground.

"Son come on. You are acting like she so fucking special. Since when you go hard for these hoes. That pill might have loosened her up, you know you like ya bitches down for whatever." Tebo stepped to me like he had a death wish. Before I could spilt his shit to the white meat the door opened and Kendric walked in.

"Yo, I've been calling ya ass, I got that for you."

"Before I get up out of here, this aint no hoe, she aint like these bitches I be bussing down so you need to respect her. This shit is a wrap for tonight, I got some urgent shit to handle."

"Come on Siah, we supposed to be finishing up this track," Micah whined. I ignored him, he was on my time, he needed to collab with me, not the other way around.

"Kenna, some urgent shit came up ma, Kendric about to take you home." Her face looked worried until I bent down and kissed her soft lips. "I will be good, I'm going to text you later." She slowly nodded and left. Everyone else slowly followed behind like some lost souls, except Ghost.

"Nigga we good for the night," I said as I checked my guns.

"Shit whatever you on I'm on." He followed me to my car. We rode to my crib in silence. It didn't take long for me to switch cars and head back out.

"I thought you was done with this murder shit. That you have your temper in check?"

I wasn't sure if I wanted to tell Ghost why I was about to send Iz to his maker. He was the only nigga I trusted out here, even more than my brother. We literally came out the mud together.

"It's because of her aint it?" He asked then shook his head like he answered his own fucking question. "She's the one. I just hope you don't fuck it up."

"Nigga, the fuck you know she the one. You were around us

for ten damn minutes. Hell, she aint my girl, we aint even fucking. She is my tutor."

I parked down the street from the decrepit house in Queens. I knew the address well. This house had been a traphouse since I was a lil nigga. He was in the spot all alone, an easy target, almost too easy. "But we here about to off some nigga behind her," Ghost replied. He chuckled as we got out and crept to the back. I tried not to think about what he said. This nigga Iz wasn't shit. Anybody would have murdered him just because. I gave the coded, crack head knock and waited for this nigga to answer.

I didn't bother hiding my face, I wanted him to know who and why. "Nigga really? You still on that shit with my baby moms?" He had the nerve to say like I was bothering him. I put my gun to his head, and he stopped talking. "All this for her," he asked, now his words sounded shaky and he had tears in his eyes.

My response left him lying in a pool of blood.

7

MA'KENNA

"Girl, you did not tell me ya new nigga was coming to the party," Cass hissed in my ear. I looked at her in confusion. Turning my head, I was just in time to see Messiah walking in with a bunch of balloons. Dak and another buff ass nigga following behind him with gifts, way more than one little girl needed. What the hell was he doing here?

"Yay, you came," Sierra called out as she ran up and hugged Messiah. I racked my brain for a time when she asked him to make an appearance at her birthday party and couldn't find one. He scooped her up and held on to her like it was natural to him. "Wow are all of those presents for me," Sierra said using her version of whispering. Shit I was wondering the same thing.

"Yea they are all yours," he said as he walked closer to me. I could hear all the preschool moms behind me talking. Some were amazed that the rapper Messiah was here, others were busy talking about the ways they would suck and fuck him if they got the chance. Damn I was still standing here, like these hoes had no idea who he was to me. That could have been my fucking man. I looked at a few screwing up my face and causing Cass to giggle.

"Damn bestie did you give him the pussy? Because it sure seems like his ass is whipped and you're jealous." I felt myself blush as I remembered the way he had me screaming his name just from his touch. "Oh hell, I was just joking," Cass said staring in my face. "But damn, that's a good fucking look."

"Cass, I didn't have sex with him, you should know better. Now come on so I can start the party." I wanted to grab Messiah and ask him what the fuck he was doing here. We had only spoken a few times since the whole studio fiasco, and he even cancelled his tutoring session this week. Said he had a meeting that couldn't be rescheduled, so I just helped him with a few things over Facetime. I thought about the way his dick looked in his grey sweats that day. I was thankful for it being a virtual lesson.

"Sup ma, what are you over here thinking about?" he asked, smirking like he could read my mind.

"Messiah, what are you doing here?" I asked as I started gathering all the colorful plastic

cards the kids used to play the games.

"It's my friend's special day, I wasn't missing it." He set Sierra down who looked at him like he was going to disappear if she left.

"Sierra go play with your friends baby," I coaxed as I handed each little girl a game card. I watched for a second as she ran off, her two long French braids bouncing on her back. Turning my attention back to Messiah, I admired how sexy he was. Even if I wasn't one of those girls who had orgasm's, or squirted on demand, I still knew a fine ass man. Catching myself I stopped admiring him and grilled him instead. "But how did you even know when or where?"

"Sierra invited me, you are overthinking this Kenna. I'm here because I want to be. Just relax, you stress too fucking much." He was in front of me now causing parts of my body to throb, parts that I didn't even know existed until I met him. "I know how to help you loosen up," he said close to my ear. Before he stood up he brushed his lips across my cheek, and I swore my whole body woke the fuck up.

"Girl if you don't give him the pussy," Cass mumbled from behind me, causing me to choke on my gum. "Why the fuck he bring her," she said much louder this time. I followed the direction of her gaze and saw Kendric, KJ and Latia walk through the door. Well, I guess I just found out how Messiah knew where the party was.

"Cass, you the one who don't want to fuck wit him. He would drop Latia in a heartbeat if you gave him some play. It aint her fault she met him in the middle of yall messy situationship." Cass was my best friend, and I had her back, but I wasn't about to let her be on no dumb shit. She was mad at the wrong person in this situation. Better blame herself or friendly dick Kendric. Latia was an innocent party.

"Ma'am we really need to get ready to bring out the food soon," the hostess said, interrupting my thoughts. She looked at her watch like she was being funny than back at me. "Remember you did not get the package with an unlimited room, you only have a total of two hours with the tables. This includes times for food and cake." She stood there rolling her eyes like I was inconveniencing her, bitch this ya job. I felt like telling her I was smart as fuck, so I could clearly tell time.

"Yo, the fuck you rushing her party for?" Messiah barked at the hostess. Her name was Risha. She went from having an attitude to being patient, sweet and starstruck.

"Oh wow, hi Messiah. I didn't know you would be here today. I was just explaining to her," she made sure to stop and give me a fucked-up look. "That she did not pay for the upgraded package and her time is running short. Do you have kids? I can clear some space if you need us too. I am the manager." I wanted to punch her until those racoon looking eyelashes flew off her face, her wide ass smile too.

The look on his face wasn't the best and I feel like Risha didn't catch the warning. The pizza was brought out and she began half haphazardly throwing each slice down on the table. Her eyes never left Messiah's as she waited for a response. "Bitch are you fucking kidding me? Go get ya fucking manager, now," he boomed causing her to stumble backwards. Messiah's hand went towards his pocket and I said a silent prayer he wasn't going to shoot this girl. Instead, he pulled out a Gucci wallet. I saw him slide an American Express card from one of the slots and hand it towards the girl. "She wants the best package you got in this place, and I mean the best. When my shorty leaves up out of here, she better have a permanent smile on her face. Pick this fucking pizza up and bring us some fresh shit, and don't forget the manager I requested and a new hostess."

"Esai, the two hours was fine," I tried to tell him, but he cut me off before I could continue.

"Ma'Kenna don't push me." I just shrugged and backed off. Once the franchise manager came over and apologized numerous times and assigned Ashley as our hostess the rest of the party went smooth. Chuck E Cheese went all the fuck out for Sierra and her friends. She had slushies, chicken and pizza, nachos and enough cotton candy to keep her up for the next two days.

"That nigga do not play about you Kenna," Cass teased as she helped me organize the goodie bags. I was tired at this point and ready to go home and relax. I really didn't want to do presents here and I was trying to think of a way to skip to the cake.

"Ok mom, dad, it's time to do the presents," Ashley's bubbly ass said causing every nosey person nearby to stop and look. Instead of denying that he was Sierra's dad, Esai grabbed her up and got into position. The crowd of people that had been staring at him the whole time tried to get closer, but his bodyguards pushed them back. I was barely paying attention to my babies excited squeals as I watched people snap pictures of us. It was creepy, I didn't even know these people, and I wondered where the photos would end up.

"You good," he asked as Ashley put the candles on the cake. He draped his arm over my shoulders and brought me into his chest. It was comfortable, I never had no shit like this. Even though I didn't know what this was. I caught Kendric mugging Messiah and wondered what that was about. I was going to make sure I asked him later on. I was so caught up in the feeling of being in Esai's arms that I forgot to respond.

"Kenna," he said, getting my attention.

"My bad, I was just enjoying the moment. I'm good. Why is Kendric looking at us like that?" He looked down at me and I felt like he wasn't going to say shit.

"Kendric don't want me to fuck wit you. He thinks I'm going to treat you like the rest of these hoes."

"Are you?" I asked and held my breath waiting on what he had to say.

"Mommy, mommy, mommy," Sierra screamed, jumping up and down in front of me. "Can I go home with KJ, pleaseeeee. Auntie Tia said we can have a slumber party." Seeing my daughter broke me out of my trance. What the fuck was I even doing, this was a bad look for her all the way around. This nigga was my boss, not my man. I stepped out of his arms and ran my hand over Sierra's braids.

"Let's thank all your guests for coming and then we can make sure it's ok." I could feel his eyes on me the whole time I wrapped the party up. Once a hyped-up Sierra was on her way home with Kendric and his family I sighed in relief.

Messiah was still standing there like he aint have shit else to do. "Thank you for coming, you really made her day. And as for the party, if you want you can dock my pay to cover the cost." I held out my hand, and he looked at me crazy as fuck. I had decided to try and keep shit professional with him.

"Dak, ya'll load all this stuff in the truck." He barked at his people.

"No, it's fine, Cass is waiting to take me home. We are about to load up her car," I said the last part with a hint of doubt. I was trying to figure out how all this shit was fitting in her Honda Civic.

"Cass, right?" he asked looking at my friend. "I got this from here, you can head on out. Thanks for looking out for Ma'Kenna." This bitch had the nerve to grin, give us both a little wave and head for the door. Not before mouthing *get that dick*.

I didn't say much the whole ride from Brooklyn back to my house. I kept glancing at Messiah, he seemed so unbothered as he smoked a blunt, and drove. A blacked-out Tahoe followed with his guards and all my daughters presents. Once we pulled up and they unloaded everything inside, I had to admit I was happy I didn't have to carry all that shit. Although if Messiah didn't clear out half the toy store, it wouldn't have been that much to begin with.

I didn't argue when he walked me to the door, one hand on my back, the other on his gun. His bad boy behavior turned me on, even if I wasn't going to do shit about it. "You always walk bitches to their door," I couldn't help but ask.

He stared at me for a second before running his tongue over his grill. "Shorty, I'm sure you know the answer to that. Before you keep running ya mouth, stop putting yourself in that category. If you were just some bitch, I would have left you home alone, with a face full of nut a long time ago." I just shook my head, his mouth was foul as fuck, and I knew he meant every word.

"Aight, ya'll good," he said dismissing Dak and the other nigga he had with him. I was glad he didn't have creepy Travis this time. He made my skin crawl, and I would never want him to know where I laid my head. Instead of leaving me in my apartment he locked the door and took off his boots. "Why you still standing there?" he questioned after sitting on my couch, like this was his shit.

"Don't you have somewhere to be?" My ass was nervous, and

IT'S HIS SAVAGE LOVE FOR ME

I wished for a moment I never let my baby go to Kendric's house. Because being here alone with Esai had me shook.

"I'm where I need to be," he responded. His usually blank eyes were filled with lust as he looked me up and down.

"Umm ok, well I'm going to jump in the shower. I have kid germs all over me. The remote is on the side table, if you want to watch something until I get back." I never waited to see what he was doing. Instead, I ran to my room. I grabbed my towel and something to throw on after I washed my ass. The whole time I was in the shower all I could think about was him in the other room. I rinsed my body one final time and got out. I air dried while brushing my teeth, lotioned my skin and threw on the pink pajama shorts and matching spaghetti strap top. For some reason I made sure I grabbed a pair of pink lace panties. It wasn't like he was going to see my panties, but it just felt right.

I walked into the living room, but he wasn't there. "Messiah," I called out.

"Shorty, a nigga tired as fuck, come get in the bed." I slowly walked in my room and saw him in my bed. I swear my eyes must have bucked as they roamed his cut-up body. This nigga only had on a pair of boxers and as my eyes wandered lower, I started to turn back around. His dick was huge, I felt myself blush and my heart rate speed up.

"I can sleep on the couch, if you need a nap or whatever," I stuttered.

He got up and came to grab me. "Why would you sleep on the couch. I want you here wit me." I watched his full lips move and barely understood what he was saying. This nigga was not good for me, had me out here acting silly as fuck. "You scared," he whispered as he looked down at me.

"Yes," I whispered.

"I got you," he responded as he leaned down and kissed me. Once his tongue touched mine, I felt my knees get weak. I knew what came next, and it had always been unpleasant, in the past. But everything felt different this time, my body was craving his touch. "Relax," he demanded as I felt myself being led back to the bed. He took my clothes off and I knew I should stop him. This was the opposite of being professional. This was going to be messy, and once he realized I couldn't fuck he was probably going to fire me. As soon as my body hit the bed, I scrunched my eyes closed. It was stupid since he took off my glasses and I could barely see anyway. But it made me feel better. Blindly I felt for the blanket so I could cover my body, but he snatched them from my hands.

"Open your eyes," he demanded. Slowly I opened my eyes and watched as he kissed my collar bone, then the top of my breasts and slowly made his way down my body stopping at my rib cage. "You like that," he asked, but I couldn't respond. My head was spinning, and like they had a mind of their own my legs fell opened to the side. I could feel the night air on my pussy, causing my clit to get hard. "Damn," he said as he sat back and looked. "Kenna, you sexy as fuck ma. Your pussy looks so perfect, I always want to see you like this, wet just for me." I didn't know how to respond or if I should be doing something, so I just laid there.

"Ma'Kenna, I want you to play with your pussy." My eyes flew to his and I felt myself turning red. When I was alone sometimes, I would watch a video and rub on my pussy, but never in front of someone. The look on my face didn't deter him. He grabbed hand and guided it towards my slit. I couldn't believe he had me doing this shit. After a few minutes I was enjoying the feeling too much to be embarrassed about the situation.

"Damn girl, ya shit is leaking. Rub on your clit, I want to see you cum." He was watching me with such intensity it turned me on. When I felt my body jerk, he bit his lip then started kissing my thighs. When I felt his breath on my nub I jumped. "I know ya shit would taste sweet," he said before I felt his tongue touch my clit. I cried out and arched my body. I felt like someone else was in control. When he demanded I cum again and stuck his fingers inside of me, I did what he asked. My hand made my way to the top of his head, holding him in place so I could enjoy the feeling. Finally, he let up and my body went limp, I wanted to curl up like a newborn. I wondered why he had that effect on me.

His body covered mine and I tensed up. This was the worst part, but Esai had made me feel so good, he deserved to at least try and get something out of it. He stopped to suck my breasts and I felt my body react. "Don't be scared," he coaxed as he led my hand to his dick. It was so hard I was afraid to touch it. Before I could think about what I was doing his mouth was on mine. "Taste yourself," he whispered before his tongue invaded my mouth. My hand was sliding up and down his dick and I swear it got bigger.

"You want to feel me," he asked, his tone was serious. From past experience I knew it didn't really matter what I wanted. He waited for me to answer. "If you don't want this Ma'Kenna we aint got to do shit else."

"I want to," I heard myself say. It was like I was watching all the shit I was saying in doing from across the room. I felt the tears slide down my cheek when I felt him at my entrance. I knew that two things were going to happen, I was going to be in a lot of pain and two he was going to be disappointed. Oddly enough the second one made me feel worse than the thought of the pain. As much as I didn't want to admit it, I liked Esai, really liked him. I had barely known him a few months and he had somehow become special to me.

"Shorty, why you crying," he said, pulling away from me and gently wiping my tears. "I promise you, I aint that other nigga. I'm going to go slow." I shook my head as I looked towards the wall, I was ashamed. I felt so inexperienced, and at twenty-two that was fucked up. I felt him slowly enter me and I tensed up. It felt like I was being split in half, but for some reason it still felt good. "God damn girl, this shit is tight as fuck."

Messiah took his time with me like he promised and by the end of the night I was begging for more. As soon as he put that big dick all the way inside and touched my womb I was cumming. By the third time I could barely keep my back arched, I was so fucking tired. I held on until I felt him nut and then I collapsed. The last thing I remember was Messiah wrapping his arms around me.

8

MESSIAH

The bass from the loud music in the club had the floor vibrating under my feet. Ma'Kenna bent over in front of me and popped her ass to the music, the pink dress she had on was barely covering her black silk panties. She looked back and gave me a shy smile. It had been a month since the first time we had sex and shorty was coming out of her shell. I was spending more time in the projects than I was at my own spots. I just wanted to be up under Kenna every night I could, it was more than just sex. But I wouldn't allow myself to think about that part. The part where she cooked for me or I played with Sierra while she did her homework. It felt too much like settling down, felt like something I wasn't ready for.

I felt my temper rise as I watched all these niggas with their eyes glued to her body. I had never been jealous behind a bitch, but there was always a first time. "Shorty, come here," I said as I stood up and dragged her to the corner so we could have some privacy. If this wasn't an event for my label I would have just left. The tiny dress she had on caused my dick to swell as soon as she got close. "Yo, why you showing these niggas my body and shit," I whispered as she backed up into me.

"Sorry daddy," she said sarcastically. I didn't give a fuck if she meant it or not, hearing her call me daddy had me horny as fuck.

"Come ride this dick," I said as I sat down and pulled her on my lap. She hid her face in my neck and shook her head no. But I already had her panties to the side and my dick head against her clit.

"Ohhh," she managed to get out as I grabbed her ass and pulled her down on my dick. After she adjusted to my size she started grinding her body against me. Her pussy was still tight like a virgin and took me the fuck out every time. "Esai," she moaned as she moved faster, slamming her pussy down on my dick.

"Fuck girl, let me feel you cum. You know I love that shit." I caught her lips in mine and bit down lightly. As soon as ai felt her muscles clench my dick I bust inside of her. Laying my head back against the leather couch.

"Damn Messiah let me go clean myself up," she said trying to stand. She was looking around nervous as hell like someone was watching. Shit they probably were, but I didn't give a fuck. This was my pussy, I was sliding in those guts anytime, anywhere.

"Come right back, I don't want you just wandering around by yourself. Matter of fact, give me a kiss shorty." She rolled her eyes, then smiled. I tangled my hand in her hair as she leaned in and gave me a kiss. Slowly I let my tongue tease hers until I could hear her moan. Letting go she looked dazed as she turned and headed towards the restroom. I started to follow her but that was some stalker, in love type shit and that wasn't me. Instead, I went back to the table me and Ghost had for the night.

"She got you open like a bitch," he said before I could even sit down good. His wife Kina laughed but shook her head in agreement.

"You aint had to say all of that G, damn. But I have to admit I never seen you act like that with these other females. There must be something special about her."

"Kina, shut the fuck up, I was special." Nedra interrupted as she came into my area uninvited.

"I got ya bitch," Kina said as she tried to get up, Ghost was holding her back and that was all that was saving Nedra. I don't even know why Nedra was starting shit with a real one. She had seen Kina whoop a few bitches over the years and she never lost. Honestly if she was losing I think Ghost would take off on the hoe. He loved his wife, literally cherished the ground she walked on and never let anyone get the best of her.

"Esai, I need to speak to you," she snapped, her hands on her hips like I gave a fuck. "In private," she said, rolling her eyes like the spoiled bitch she was.

"Mane, the fuck you want. I'm high and I just finished bussing inside my shorty, so I sure as fuck aint about to get up."

"Fine Esai."

"Bitch my name is Messiah. I aint about to keep telling you the same shit," I barked on her. I saw tears pool in her eyes, but I could care less. Even when I was with her we wasn't on that fucking level.

"This is what I want. How could you do this to me?" She was blubbering by now causing a fucking scene. I glanced at the cell phone she had thrust in my face to see pictures of me, Ma'Kenna and Sierra. "When they posted you at the little girls birthday party, I thought it was some charity shit. Now they are saying this is your daughter!" At this point I was ready for her to go. She was standing here doing all this extra shit for nothing.

"First off, don't be fucking screaming at me. If she's my daughter or isn't has nothing to fucking do with you." Nedra acted like we were married or some shit, and I had cheated on her. I noticed Ma'Kenna standing at the edge of the section, I guess she was waiting on this bitch to leave. "The fuck you doing over there," I asked motioning for her to come inside the velvet ropes. She looked at Nedra first before coming to sit next to me. I picked her up and slid her on my lap. I placed a kiss on her neck and felt her relax some. "The fuck you was standing there looking at her for? Know your fucking place, wherever I'm at."

"Really Messiah? You want her over me? Is it because she gave you a kid? I would have had a baby if you wanted. You never fucking asked!" Nedra must have been drunk or on crack. Something, because the way she was acting wasn't cute at all. I could see reps from the company looking her way and the ever-lurking paparazzi watching, camera's ready. By morning this whole encounter would be splashed all over some news channel in the morning.

I ran my hand over my waves trying to remain calm. Too many eyes were on me to knock her head off the way I wanted to. "Nedra, I'm warning you, just move the fuck along ma. I don't want you. Shit never worked between us. You doing this shit for nothing."

"Bitch, what are you smiling about? You think he gives a fuck about you? I guess you're special because he fucked you in a club. Girl we all did that shit. His dick is for every fucking body. Did he tell you about the three some with me and my best friend? Just wait until it comes to that, he is going to be bored fucking you. That's going to be one of his requirements. I hope you don't fall in love because this nigga don't love back." I nodded to Dak, who came over and dragged her out of the area. Shorty was yelling all kinds of shit as they escorted her out of the building.

"I'm glad I met Ghost first, nigga your dick is toxic," Kina said laughing. Normally I would have found that shit funny, but I could tell Kenna was upset.

"Shorty you ready?" She nodded so I got up. "I'm out," I said dapping Ghost up and hugging Kina. Ma'Kenna waved and we headed to the back entrance and got in my truck.

"You staying with me?" I asked, even though I wasn't really asking. I wasn't taking her ass home. She shrugged and looked out the window. "Kenna, I don't like when you got shit on your mind and don't just say wats up."

She looked at me, her eyes sad. "Are you upset about the

pictures, the accusations? I know how you feel about having kids, plus Sierra isn't your kid. So, I'm sure you wouldn't want someone telling the world she is yours. I never thought shit like that would happen when we all go out together, but I am not stupid. So, I should have known better."

"So that's what you over there looking all sad for? I know how those mah'fuckers are. Nothing in my life is private, if I didn't want to be seen with you and Sierra, believe me we would have remained inside. That shit doesn't bother me at all, if I did have a kid I would wish her to be as sweet and smart as Sierra. As always you overthinking shit."

※

"DAMN SHORTY, YOU HAVING TROUBLE WALKING," I TEASED the next morning. She turned to give me the evil eye as she went to handle her hygiene. I had to stop fucking her so much, had her walking around looking all crazy and shit.

"We're gonna go eat after we pick up Sierra," I said once we left my house. Kenna had her hair pulled back, her glasses on and was rocking a red t-shirt, with some black tights. She was literally the prettiest girl I had ever seen, even when she was dressed down. I watched her the whole ride to Miss Vivian's crib, dreading the fact I had to go out of town the next two weeks for some promotional shows. I would have asked her to come, but I knew she had school and that shit was important to her.

"Be right back," she said once I parked. I smirked, because she knew better. We both went inside, her rolling her eyes and pouting. "I was just running in to grab her, you didn't have to come."

"Hey Chelsea," I said to my lil mini fan, ignoring Kenna's wanting to be independent shit. She still squealed every time she saw me, but at least she stopped screaming. I noticed today she had another girl her age over.

"Hey Messiah, this is my friend Alicia." She introduced the other girl. I just nodded. "See, I told you Kenna was seeing him," she told her friend with a smug ass look on her face.

"Girl she aint seeing him, she is fucking him. Big difference. And also, something a lot of women have done." She popped her gum and sucked her teeth with an attitude. "Didn't you read the post from Nedra's IG last night. Kenna is one of many, and everyone agrees."

"Yo, how old are you? You got a nasty fucking mouth," I barked. Before I could tell her ass off Ma'Kenna grabbed my arm and led me to the door.

"Not in front of Sierra," she begged, and I saw baby girl looking up at me, her face filled with confusion. I picked her up and gave Chelsea's little hoe ass friend a warning look.

"Let's go," I said grabbing Ma'Kenna's hand so we could leave.

"Si Si, you missed us?" I said as I buckled her in the booster seat that was now a permanent fixture in my truck.

"Yes I did, and I want pancakes with sprinkles and whip cream for breakfast please," she grinned after she made her demands. Me and her mother laughed as we made our way to IHOP. The meal was quiet except for Sierra chatting about everything she saw. Ma'Kenna barely ate her breakfast, just picked over the eggs and French toast. That wasn't like her, I knew her well enough to know by now she loved French Toast. Maybe she was just tired, she was up all night.

"You guys coming to the crib?" I asked when we left. She shook her head no. "Cool," I responded, trying not to sound disappointed.

I wanted to ask Ma'Kenna what the fuck was wrong wit her, but I didn't want to be snapping in front of Sierra. I wasn't a fan of people who kept up bullshit in front of little kids, especially ones I cared about. "Tell Messiah thank you for breakfast," she coached Sierra as I parked in front of her building.

"Thank you Siah," she said and gave me her little cute smile.

"Anytime baby girl. I'm going out of town for a few weeks, you gonna be good for mommy?" Ma'Kenna's head shot up when I said I was going out of town. I hoped she missed me.

"I can try." She said and fell out laughing as we walked to their door.

"You better try hard, or get ya lil behind whooped," her mom said frowning. As soon as we got inside Sierra ran to her room so she could play. She really was well behaved, Kenna barely had to say shit to her.

"Aight Messiah, I'm about to lay down, I'm exhausted."

"So, you telling me that shit for what? Like you want me to leave or something? Whats ya fucking problem, you sat through breakfast face all turned up. Didn't even eat your food. If you got some shit you need to get off your chest do that." I knew my tone was harsh, I could see how she was looking at me like I was about to jump on her. "You better yell the fuck back if you feel some kind of way. I would neve do shit to you so stop looking all fucking scared. But I also aint about to play no games with you.

"I really don't feel good. But, if you have to know I don't think I should fuck wit you like that no more. This was a mistake, people think I'm one of the many women you pass around wit your friends. I have to remember that in ten years Sierra will be a teenager and I don't want her coming across some shit that basically said I was one of your hoes."

"Ma, is that what you think? You just some girl I fuck right along with a bunch of other bitches? I aint fucked no one sense I started sleeping wit you." It was the truth, I wasn't even interested in another girl at this point. Although sometimes I missed getting my shit slobbed on. I wasn't saying I was about to be some faithful ass nigga to shorty. We wasn't even on no official shit, but I sure as fuck wasn't dogging her out, the way she was making it seem.

"Ma, I can't let you leave me alone, I feel good when I'm around you. My life is filled with superficial shit, mostly everyone around me is fake. But when I'm with you and Sierra I can be myself. That shit is real. If you want me to tell the media you my tutor I will. It aint some shit I want to do, but you worth it."

"No, I can't allow you to do that. I am not that selfish, maybe we can just be more discreet. And I think it's best if Sierra stays with a babysitter when we hang out. I have really done a lot of dumb shit where you are concerned. Stuff that is out of my character, I should know better than to have a random nigga around my daughter."

"That's some fucked up shit ma, now I'm some random nigga? What if I was trying to be your man? You not even giving me a fucking chance." I was hurt when she said she didn't want me around Sierra. I damn near felt like she was my kid, I loved hearing her tell stories about school and her friends. She would even get me to play with her dolls. I felt some kind of way when I didn't talk to or see Sierra. She had become my baby girl just that fast.

"Messiah," she began. But I stepped closer to her and roughly grabbed her chin.

"The fuck you call me?"

"Ya name, now you gonna let me speak or not, Esai!" She was mad, I could see it in the way her eyes flashed. Good, I would rather she be pissed at me than scared of me. "Sierra loves you, she told my neighbor the other day you were her father. Of course, I corrected her, but the issue is, she is getting attached. You talking about, maybe you were trying to be my man, but the fact remains, you're not. So where does that leave her when you get bored and move on to the next one?"

I was still stuck on the fact that Sierra was telling people I was her dad. That shit had my chest swelled up, I felt honored that she looked at me that way. "Just give me some time Ma'Kenna, I promise I'm going to make shit right." I pulled out some money and shoved it in her hand. "Yo hold this for you and Si Si, I have some shows in Florida and I won't be back for a few weeks. I want y'all to be straight."

"I don't want it," she said and tried to give it back.

"I don't give a fuck." I kissed her on the cheek and stepped back. "Sierra," I called, and she came running into the room. "Come give me a hug, I have to go. I will call you tomorrow after school. Remember what I said, be good until I come home."

She gave me a hug and a sad smile. "Come home fast." She touched my chain that always seemed to fascinate her before going back to her toys.

※

I SAT LOOKING FROM THE OVERSIZED ASS LAWYER AND THE REP from my record company to my Rolex. Time was against me today; I had a hard dick and a naked bitch waiting to suck him up in the other room. Not to mention that my tutoring session with Ma'Kenna was tonight. Shit she was going to have to come here just for today. Nothing was going to affect the little time I be getting in with shorty. Ever since I got some of her pussy, she had me fucked up. It wasn't just the fact that she had good pussy, it was damn near brand new. It learned all of its pleasure from me, her shit was made for me. Her pussy aside I enjoyed being around shorty, she made a nigga happy. Had me on some new shit, and even if I wasn't sure about settling down, I knew Ma'Kenna meant more to me than any bitch in the past. Just the fact I hadn't seen her in two weeks, combined with the conversation we had before I left, had me feeling on edge. I came straight from a show in Miami last night, and home to this bullshit.

"Look, those are my terms for the new contract. Either add them in or I go sign somewhere else, it's simple. Now I've spent way too much time on this shit today, so meeting over." I stood up and both men looked bewildered. I was giving them two weeks to decide. I had offers from every major label in the rap game and I had no issue with picking the fuck up and leaving.

"Ok Mister Aleczander, thank you for your time," big and wide stuttered as he gathered the papers from the table.

"Dak, I need you to go and get Ma'Kenna in an hour and bring her back." He nodded his head acknowledging my request

I only had two hours before Ma'Kenna had to be here, I picked up the phone hoping to catch shorty before she headed out. "Hello," she answered, sounding like she was out of breath.

"Yo, what the fuck you over there doing?" I swear if she was fucking some other nigga I was murking both their asses. I hadn't been gone that long and that shit she was saying about not fucking wit me no more was bullshit.

"I just walked up the stairs to my apartment, the elevator is broken as always. The fuck you thought I was doing Esai?" I loved when she snapped back at me, turned me on even more. I thought about all the ways I could bend her over and punish her little ass.

"Yo, I had a meeting at the spot in Manhattan today and that shit went long as fuck. I need you to do the session over here today. I'm going to send Dak to come and scoop you up."

"Esai, if you're busy we can just cancel for today it's no big deal."

"Shorty don't make me come over there. I miss ya ass, I aint seen you in two fucking weeks. Be ready in an hour." I ended the call not giving her room to argue with me. I went to the kitchen and grabbed a water only to see Juicy walking around in a pair of thongs and nothing else. A part of me felt some kind of way for having this bitch up in my shit, especially since I was going to fuck wit her. It felt like I was cheating, except I was single.

"These bitches act like other people aint up in here. Got her whole pussy out in the kitchen like we don't eat in this bitch," Ghost said, turning his nose up at shorty.

"You just made you can't get none," Juicy clapped back rolling her neck. Shorty was a true hood rat.

"Bitch, I don't want none, passed around, plastic looking hoe. I wouldn't piss in your fucking mouth." Juicy looked at me like I was supposed to stick up for her or some shit. When I didn't

IT'S HIS SAVAGE LOVE FOR ME

bust a fucking grape behind her she stomped back to the bedroom where I told that hoe to wait anyway.

"You really about to do this shit man?"

"Do what nigga? Bust down Juicy throat? Hell yea."

"I mean, fuck with this bitch and you got Ma'Kenna. You willing to lose her over some hoe who had their stomach injected into their ass?"

"Nigga it aint that deep, I promise. It aint like I'm marrying this hoe, I aint even feeding her. She gonna top me off and be on her way."

"Aight homie, don't fucking call me crying when this shit goes bad." I ignored his comment even though it replayed in my mind a few times as I made my way closer to the room I used for random bitches.

"Damn daddy, you look so fucking sexy," Juicy commented as she began dancing around the room. My dick stood straight up as I sat on the bed watching the show. I slightly pulled my jeans down and pulled my dick out. She made her ass clap and stuck a finger in her pussy, playing around in the wetness. I had pre-cum dripping down my shaft and I was ready to feel her wet mouth on my shit. I waved her over, but she bent over more, giving me a full view of her pussy. I watched as she fucked herself using two fingers until finally she squirted all over.

"Damn," I mumbled as she crawled across the floor, stopping in front of the bed. I immediately grabbed her lace front and guided her to my throbbing dick. As soon as she started slurping I leaned back and enjoyed the feeling. Instead of picturing Juicy, my mind was invaded with images of Ma'Kenna. I could see her plump lips wrapped around the head of my dick. I pictured her playing with herself, I loved the way she made these cute little faces when she was ready to cum.

"Oh," I heard someone say and my eyes flew open. Ma'Kenna was standing at the door, her mouth open and tears streaming down her cheek. "Umm sorry," she stuttered as she turned to leave the room. That's when I noticed Travis standing behind her, a smirk on his face.

"You are sorry bitch, shit wait your fucking turn, you messing up his nut." Juicy was talking shit from the floor, her mouth still close to my dick. I mushed her ass in the face causing her to stumble.

"Shut up and get the fuck out of here." I pulled up my pants and ran towards the hallway. "Kenna," I yelled but she kept moving to the front of the condo. "Shorty come on, let me holla at you for a minute." She stopped for a second and seeing the hurt on her face heart my fucking soul. Ghost was right, I should have left Juicy where she was at, or passed her to a friend.

"Messiah, I should have knocked first. We can reschedule today's session since you are busy, no problem." Her lips quivered on the last word.

"Come on ma, I'm sorry, I swear I am. I don't even know why I did that shit. It just wasn't something I wanted you doing." I tried to pull her into my arms, but she jumped back. Not giving a fuck I forced her into my arms and let her cry on my chest.

My eyes fell on Travis who still had a smile on his face. Why the fuck was he even here when I asked Dak to pick shorty up. I checked the time and realized it was before the time Ma'Kenna was supposed to be here. "Nigga, you picked her up," I asked letting Kenna go.

"Yes I did boss. Is there a problem?" He asked, an attitude in his voice.

"Oh, you a fucking funny ass nigga," I walked up on him and bust him across the face with a bottle of Ace of Spades. "You on some funny shit right," I started choking his thick ass, the rage I felt was no match for anything he was sending my way. I felt someone grab my arm and I turned around and grabbed them hard. It took me a minute to realize I had snatched Ma'Kenna up and shoved her against the wall. "Fuck."

Her eyes got wide with fear and she ran out the front door, before I could catch her.

9

MA'KENNA

Pulling the covers tighter around my body, I looked at the TV, whatever was playing was watching me. But for some reason I felt the need to at least stare in that direction. Today I had done something I would never do, I missed school and my internship. I just didn't have the strength to do people or get out of bed today. I didn't know who I was angrier at, myself for falling in love with Messiah. Especially knowing the kind of nigga, he was, or him for breaking my fucking heart. It was ten times worse because he literally just talked to me about not fucking with other women since he slept with me. I guess that was a lie. Shit I don't even know why he bothered lying. I was going against all my best judgement and fucking a nigga who was never going to take me seriously. Shit I knew better. I watched as my phone rang, Messiah had been calling me every hour, on the hour since Thursday but I refused to answer.

I saw Cass's name flash against my screen again and I decided to answer her. Sierra was
staying with Miss Vivian until I felt better so I had to answer just in case there was an emergency. "Hello," I said low into the phone. My head and stomach hurt, I could barely talk because I wanted to throw up so bad.

"You sound like shit, you need to go and see a doctor."

"Wow, nice to talk to you too," I clapped back. I knew I sounded like shit, I didn't need a

reminder. "Give me a minute," I said, interrupting whatever she was saying. I ran to the bathroom and threw up the little bit of food I had today. After rinsing my mouth out I crawled back in the bed. "Ok, I'm here."

"Girl, this nigga sent so much shit to the job today it's all over Jenna's desk. Nigga had roses, chocolates, a card and a bag from Gucci. I don't know what he did, but his ass is sorry sorry." I sighed but didn't respond. I didn't want to get into details with my best friend, shit with anybody for that matter about me and Messiah's situation. I just told Cass I wasn't fucking with him anymore, that we had an argument. She asked for details and I told her to mind her business. "I'm coming over there after work," she said before hanging up. Cass was an RN at the same hospital I did my internship at. I wondered why her fast ass even worked, she always had some nigga paying her bills. Kendric being one of them. Rolling over I decided to get some sleep before her ass showed up.

I woke up to someone ringing my bell, I knew it was too early for Cass to be here, unless she took a half a day. Plus, she had a key. I wouldn't put it past her to leave and rush right over, since she loved anything that looked like drama. "Who is it," I barked into the intercom. I prayed it wasn't Messiah, if it was he would have to stand out there all fucking day, he wasn't getting in.

"It's Kendric," he responded. I sighed but buzzed him in. Maybe he wasn't here because of the shit I had going on with his cousin. I opened the apartment door, and he was staring at me with a strange look on his face. "What did he do?"

"He aint do shit, I'm not feeling well. How can I help you? Or better yet, what the fuck do you want?" Throwing up twenty times a day didn't help my already foul mood.

"Kenna, I already know he did something, or he wouldn't

have called me over here to check on you. So, you can either tell me or I can guess." The door flew open as if on queue and Cass rolled her eyes at Kendric as she struggled to get inside with my flowers, a bear and several bags.

"Kendric, leave," she snapped as she set the stuff down and made her way over to me. She hugged me and I did my best not to cry, I didn't need them knowing how stupid I was.

"See, I told that nigga to leave you alone. He aint shit when it comes to women. I warned both of y'all about this shit. I knew he was going to fucking hurt you," he yelled. Kendric was walking back and forth in front of me like a crazy person. "Let me guess, you gave up the pussy, he fucked you and then he moved on to another bitch." I started to sob when he said that shit because it was true. I should have never even taken this job once I saw who I was working with.

"I know you aint fucking talking. Is this a speech from one aint shit ass nigga, about another. You fuck anything walking, apparently get their asses pregnant too. Then you want to come in here on like you're so much better than the rest of these niggas. Fuck you Kendric, she is your friend and doesn't need, an I told you so lecture. She needs a fucking friend."

"My bad Kenna, I just didn't want this for you," he said. His voice sounded sad and I knew he was mad for me and not at me. "As for your confused ass, keep my baby mama name out ya fucking mouth. And that means those little slick ass comments too. She may not be you, but she gave me my son and holds me down, all while I be out here cheating on her ass. If anything, she deserves better, not me. In reality all I deserve is a bitch like you." He hugged me and watched him walk to the door. "I'm out."

We both stood there with our mouths opened looking fucked up. "Did this nigga just, call me a bitch. Wow." She was surprised for a totally different reason than me. I honestly never thought he would see what a good thing he had in Latia. And Cass, never thought he would turn on her. "Ok well, umm I brought you something and I don't want you to while out on me. But I think you need it." She reached in the Duane Ried bag and pulled out a pregnancy test. I felt the world spin and my knees get weak.

I silently counted the days from my last period, after forty-five I lost count and realized I was two months late. *Shit.* "Ok, I guess it can't hurt to take it." I reluctantly grabbed the test and walked to the bathroom. I was so dizzy off this nigga, I never told him to put on a condom, or to pull out. "God, I can barely afford the child I have. I know this is my fault, but please look out for your girl. Amen." I prayed as I peed and berated myself at the same time. For me to be so smart, I was so fucking stupid. Five minutes later I opened the door, with tears in my eyes. "I'm pregnant."

"Damn girl you about to be straight. You are not even going to have to move to whack ass Minnesota now." For some reason as my life crumbled around me, my best friend was more excited than I had seen her in years. "Ok, so this is the plan, don't tell him shit until you're six months. That way he can't force you into an abortion. He's going to want a DNA test so be prepared for that. He will probably have some high price lawyer contact you, and we will be ready with a list of wants and needs for the baby." She was rubbing her hands together like she just caught a fucking lick.

"Cass, you need to leave. I aint doing none of that shit. That's not me, first of all it aint right. I wouldn't do that shit to someone I didn't give a fuck about let alone a nigga I fell in love with. I love you, but you have to change your way of thinking. Because I promise that shit you on brings nothing but bad karma. I am telling him. Not today, but soon."

"I'm sorry Kenna. Your right, I know I have to do better, I just been hurt so many times it's always fuck these niggas. But you love him," she squealed, sitting me on the couch next to her. "That nigga love you too Kenna, I can tell. I know he did something fucked up. But I think you should give him another chance. Hear him out. It can't hurt." I just closed my eyes, my mind was swirling with all the ways my life was going to change with a new baby on the way.

※

"Mommy, I miss Siah. Can you please call him," Sierra begged as I slowly made her a peanut butter and jelly sandwich. I was too sick to do much else, this was going to be the pregnancy from hell.

"Not today baby. When he isn't busy he will call." I felt bad for lying to my baby, and on Messiah. He had called me so much I turned my phone off most of the time. He made sure to ask could he speak to Sierra and told me how much he missed her. I didn't know if I believed him. At this point everything he said was suspect as hell.

"Mommy, he is calling now." She said happily pointing to my phone. Shit, I must have left it on after I scheduled an appointment with my OBGYN. Sighing I slid my finger across the green bar.

"Hello Messiah," I said trying to keep my voice regular.

"Yo, shorty you had me worried as hell. I know I fucked up, but I need to see you, make sure y'all are good. You haven't answered me in days. Let me talk to Sierra." My traitor, daughter damn near snatched the phone from me once she heard her name. I hadn't even noticed that she was that close. She got to my level by perching on the counter, something she knew I didn't allow.

"Siah, can you come and see me? I miss you. And can I have a cheeseburger? Mommy is giving me peanut butter and jelly again. I don't want a sandwich." I rolled my eyes at her little begging ass. She was seconds away from getting a spanking. "Because she is sick, she said when she feels better she will cook for me." I choked on the water I was sipping and grabbed for the phone.

"Tell Mister Siah good night. You are going to eat your sandwich and apple slices and get ready for bed." I waited to snatch the phone completely until she said goodbye in her little sad voice. I wasn't moved, her ass was getting spoiled being around Messiah. He never told her no and shit like this was the result.

"The fuck you doing her like that? And why you aint tell me you've been sick?" He paused for a minute like I was about to explain myself, but I wasn't "I'm coming over there, and you better answer the door. If not I'm still finding a way the fuck inside, even if I have to find the office manager and splatter his brains on the concreter. I promise Ma'Kenna, I will be seeing you tonight."

I groaned as he hung up. This nigga was a fucking menace to society, I had no idea that savage shit turned me on. He had me wondering if I had a type. Would the next nigga I fell for act just like him? There was no point in trying to leave, I didn't have the energy anyway. So instead, I sat on the couch, trying to stay awake long enough for Sierra to finish her food, and him to invade my space. I must have fallen asleep anyway, because I was startled when I heard a knock on the apartment door. No telling how his ass got past the outside door. "Coming," I managed to get out as I forced my body to cooperate to stand up.

I opened the door and felt lost as I looked up at him. He was so fucking fine, his Yankees cap was pulled low over his eyes and he had let his facial hair grow out some. If anything, he looked crazier than usual, but I had already determined that shit turned me on. "What's good ma," he said as he stepped inside uninvited. "Si Si," he called to my daughter as she ran towards him and fell in his arms. I swear she was such a drama queen. "I got your burger," he said, pulling a happy meal from behind his back. I wanted to smack the shit out of him. It was like he didn't listen to shit I had to say, it was bad enough with Sierra, but I couldn't imagine adding another child into the mix.

"Yay, thank you," she called out and ran back to the table with her food. She gave me a look, you know the one that says fuck you, I got my way. I swear as soon as I felt better I was tearing her ass up.

"Seriously, I told you and her no. What the fuck." I felt dizzy all of the sudden, so I stopped talking shit and just stood still. I was trying everything to not get sick, the saliva was building in the back of my mouth and just looking at the man who tore my heart in half made my stomach hurt worse. "Give me a minute," I got out as I raced to the bathroom. I threw up, again and again until I was just straight dry heaving.

"You alright ma," he sounded worried, but I kept telling myself not to be fooled by his concern.

"I told you, mommy is sick," Sierra said from the doorway. Her worried look mirrored his and made me burst out crying. I couldn't do this, a baby and a four-year-old all alone. I still had my finals and my internship. I was already living hand to mouth. How was I going to make this work?

"I see baby girl. Go finish eating and I will come and get you ready for bed." Sierra left to do as she was told, leaving us alone. "Can you stand up," he asked, and I shook my head yes. Slowly I got up and brushed my teeth and rinsed my mouth out. "Come on let's get you in the bed." He helped me to my room since I was weak as fuck. It was just from lack of nutrition. Everything that went in my body came right the fuck back out.

"I have to tell you something," I said as he tucked the covers around me. "I'm pregnant." I gestured towards the positive test on the bedside table. His hand went still, and his eyes got darker as he looked. I sat up as fast as I could so I could reassure him, he didn't have to do shit for me or the baby. "Listen, I know it's a fucked-up situation. I swear I just wasn't thinking and I'm sure you weren't either. I, we, I mean I don't want you to feel obligated. I can keep the baby and raise it alone. I mean as you can see I'm already pretty much trained to be a single mother. Or if you want, I can get an abortion." It hurt my heart to say that shit, I never would want to kill my fucking baby. But I had to remember it wasn't just mine, he should at the very least have an opinion of some sort.

"I have to constantly remind myself that you only used to fucking wit some sucka ass niggas. But let me remind you, I aint one of them. First of all, you not getting no fucking abortion. That's my seed, I would never do no shit like that." He dropped his hand to my still flat stomach and rubbed slowly. I hated to admit it, but the shit felt good. "Kenna, I'm a grown ass man. I don't randomly fuck women with no condom on. You are the first and most likely will be the last. I Knew the chance I was taking. And I didn't mind the thought of having a baby with you. I fucks wit you the long way. More than you know. I know shit is bad between us and I know I caused that. But I would never leave you to take care of our kid alone."

He sat with me until I was damn near asleep, then I guess he went to put Sierra down. He was good with her, he was going to be a good father. I felt a little better now that I told him. Hearing he wanted our baby helped too. After a while he came back in the room, he was on the phone arguing with someone. It sounded business related so I tried not to listen. He ended the call and took off his jeans and shirt before getting in the bed with me. "I aint hear on no funny shit ma, I just want to stay and make sure you straight."

"I'm good, you can't stay here every night just to check on me. Remember I told you to stay out of the projects."

"Ok, move in with me then. I don't want you and the kids living here." I rolled my eyes, he was starting the dumb shit rather quickly.

"That would be a no, I can figure out my own shit. And I don't want my kids being raised seeing firsthand how you treat women. Or seeing a bunch of women." I lifted my glasses and rubbed my eyes. He was stressing me more than I already was. "Look Messiah, I'm barely a minute pregnant. We can work out visitation once the baby gets here. I'm not asking for anything more than if you want to be a part of his or her life, be consistent."

"Well, if you aint moving, I guess my ass gonna just be up in the projects. Come here and let me rub your belly, I could tell you liked that shit earlier." Closing my eyes for a minute I prayed for strength to resist any temptation he put my way. "I missed you Kenna. I swear to God I didn't mean to hurt you. Losing you was the worst fucking feeling."

"Why did you do it then? Didn't I satisfy you?" I could hear the insecurity in my voice, and I hated it.

"Come on Ma'Kenna, you can't tell you more than enough for me," he said in a strained voice. I could feel how hard his dick was on my ass and my pussy was soaked. "I love fucking you, the way you feel, how you leave those scratch marks on my back. You do more than satisfy me, you complete me." I felt his lips on my neck and I shivered. "I just didn't want you doing that." He hesitated before he continued. "Look, I know about the shit your baby dad did to you. I didn't want to ask you to suck my dick and nut all over your face. That's some shit you do wit hoes, not with a woman you want to wife. Especially not someone who has been through some shit, like you."

I felt violated, I didn't want people to know what I had been through with Isaac. "You didn't even ask, maybe I would have tried for you. Like you always around here saying, you aint him. My feelings for you aint the same. I would have done a lot for you Esai. You had my heart."

"Shorty you got mine, I just didn't know how to handle that shit."

"It was more than that," I said thinking back to how he threw me up against the wall when he was fighting Travis. I went through a lot with my baby father, and yea the sexual experience fucked me up. But him putting his hands on me traumatized my ass. It had me scared of ever being in a situation like that again.

"Ma'Kenna look at me ma," he waited until I was facing him. It was hard to meet his eyes. I was suddenly back in that moment and was scared. "If you don't know shit else, please know I would never hurt you. I would never put my hands on you. I didn't know that was you and I acted in the heat of the moment. I was mad as fuck because I know that nigga Travis did that shit on purpose. I saw the way he was looking at you. I never even told that nigga to pick you up. I told Dak to do it." He stopped and wiped the one tear that was about to fall from my eye. "I'm here to keep you safe, not hurt you.

"Fuck all that ma, I want you to give me another chance. You having my lil one, I want us to work out. I never had to beg a female to be with me in my life, but Kenna, I'm begging you." He kissed my jaw, then the corner of my lip, then he kissed me. I never responded to him, I didn't want him to try with me just because of a baby. Even I deserved better than that.

10

MASSIAH

"Mama," I called as I walked into the split level I bought my mother and grandmother to live in. I offered something bigger, but they fell in love with this place and the neighborhood. The house sat in a cul-de-sac and was in a gated community, one that was filled with other older people. Everyone had golf carts and shit, it was like in the movies.

"Boy what you in here shouting for," my grandmother said as she rounded the corner. Seeing her hurt my heart, the cancer and chemotherapy had caused her to lose so much weight, she didn't look the same. I prayed so many nights begging God to keep her with us, but it felt futile. I doubted he was even listening to me, with the amount of fucked up things I had done, I was sure I cancelled out most of my blessings. Well, at least that's what I thought until Ma'Kenna told me she was pregnant. My baby would be the biggest blessing.

"I see you gave me my dying wish. I'm so proud of you," she said gazing at the diploma
my mother had hung on the living room wall. "I thought that math class was going to take you out," she said laughing. Afterward she held onto the side of the couch to catch her breath.

"Come sit down. Always doing too much. See what happens

when you tease your favorite grandson." I helped her to the couch, and she took a seat. Handing her a bottle of water from the bar, she slowly sipped it. "As for the math, yea it was taking me the fuck out ma, real talk. But someone came to save me. Kendric hooked me up with a tutor and she got ya boy right."

She stopped and stared at me funny for a minute. "Did she now, tell me more about her. I'm interested in how she got you right. There has been something different about you lately. Your spirit has been calm, I just thought it was because I was near the end. But now I see it has something to do with this tutor."

"Ma, stop saying it's the end. You got too much to live for. I aint letting you die, you have the best doctors, the best care. We're going to beat cancer. Besides, don't you want to live to see your great grandchildren?"

"That sounds like you have a plan. I've been wanting a great grandbaby to spoil. I thought you were never going to have one. Not that I'm mad, lord remember that last thing you brought around. Nesta, she was horrific. That chile would have given you a defective baby for sure." I was laughing at my grandmother's antics, she hated every female I ever dated. Always said they were only after one thing. I thought that was shit you told your grand daughters, not your grandsons.

"You have great grandkids," my mother said as she walked in the room, with my brother trailing behind her. My grandmother grunted but didn't respond.

"Exactly Ma, you never ask to get my kids." I looked at him funny. I swear Banks was slow. I wanted to ask my mom sometimes if she smoked dope when she was pregnant with him.

"Because those aint ya damn kids. Lord this one is special. Those babies are fathered by a pink man. You got a little pink dick I forgot about," she said causing me to laugh. "Shit, I aint playing. Want me to waste my last energy on the milk man's babies. Dumb nigga, please get a DNA test, and try and do that shit before I die."

"Mom," my mother hissed at her. But my big Ma didn't give a

fuck about any of that shit. She said what she said and didn't apologize. That was probably why I acted the way I did. "Anyway, what do we owe this visit." My mom said as she walked over to me and kissed me on my cheek.

"He came to tell me about someone special." My grandmother said snitching. I mean I wanted her to know Ma'Kenna was pregnant, but not necessarily everyone else. It was early to be telling my family, but I didn't take the fact that my grandmother's days were limited. And the way Paparazzi stalked me, shit would be on someone's site or post sooner than later.

"I came to tell you the shorty I've been messing with is pregnant. You know how shit goes in my life, so better you hear it from me now than the blogs tomorrow."

"What? I haven't even met this girl. Banks, did you know he was seeing someone?" My mother was giving me and my brother a dirty look. I remained unfazed, I loved her, but I didn't owe anyone an explanation on my personal life.

"Son, I hope you don't mean that tutor bitch. Doesn't she already have a kid and live in the projects? You know she is just trying to get a check. Everybody on me to get a test on my fucking kids, I hope you get a few on this one. I heard shorty is a hoe." I jumped up and hit this nigga in the mouth causing blood to splatter my mother's glass table.

"If you weren't my brother I would end ya ass right here. Don't speak on her again."

"Oh my God, stop Esai. You can never just have a civilized conversation. Now is it true she already has a child? That does seem suspicious." I shook my head at her and focused on my grandmother's reaction.

She looked up at me with a smile. "Can I meet her?"

※

I TRIED TO TALK MY GRANDMOTHER INTO WAITING A FEW weeks before she came to meet Ma'Kenna but she wasn't trying to hear that shit. So here I was exactly two days later waiting on her and my mom to come over. Ma'Kenna had a doctor's appointment and would make it after they left. "Hey baby," my mom greeted me as Maria led her and my grandmother into the living room.

"Sup," I said as I went back to what I was doing. I was trying to hook up this Nintendo shit to the TV for Sierra. Her and Kenna had been staying with me for a few days. A gang war was going on in Redfern and she finally broke down and came to stay at the house. But only until she found a better place. She said she was saving her money to move so it wasn't a big deal. I was hoping she wouldn't find shit, because I didn't want her to leave. The moment she walked out of the condo that day I knew I loved her. When she cut me off, I was walking around fucked up. Drinking, smoking and crying to an amused Ghost seemed like all I did.

"Siah, can I have an orange," Sierra said from behind me.

"Sure, tell Miss Maria, to peek it and cut it up the way you like it." I looked up to see her still standing there holding her baby doll and looking at my mother and grandmother.

"Well, who are you pretty girl," my grandmother said with a smile. My mother had a slight frown but said hello. Leaving my project behind I walked over to Sierra who immediately held out her arms to be picked up. She buried her head in my shoulder and peeked through her lowered eyes at our company.

"This is Sierra, Sierra this is my grandmother and my mom. Can you say hi?" She waved shyly and then clung on to my neck. I sat down and texted Maria about her snack.

"Well son, looks like she has you playing daddy already," my mother said.

"Yo, I don't know where this animosity came from, but save ya dumb shit. This as much my kid as the one her mother is carrying. And you sure as fuck won't be coming up in here, which is her home by the way and giving off fucked up vibes.

Straight up, you can step." I pointed to the door in case my mother forgot how she came in.

"Son, who are you talking to," she gasped like she didn't know what kind of nigga I already was. I heard the front door open and knew Ma'Kenna was here. I stood up, so I could do introductions again. But as soon as I saw her face I didn't bother. I set Sierra down to the ground. "Go find Maria and have your snack, then it's nap time." She must have sensed something was wrong because she went to do what I said with no discussion. If my housekeeper minded being a part time Nanny these days she didn't show it. I knew Sierra was in great hands with her.

"Ma, mom, this is Ma'Kenna. Kenna, this is my mother and grandmother."

"Nice to meet you," she said, only that shit didn't sound right.

"It's nice to meet you too baby. You look like you're tired, would you like to sit down," my grandmother offered, patting the space next to her.

"So are you the girl that's claiming to be pregnant," my mother said causing me and my grandmother to look at her like she was fucking crazy.

"Actually, I'm the girl who was pregnant." She turned and ran towards the stairs. I just stood there trying to figure out what the fuck happened.

"Esai, you need to go and take care of her, she needs you right now. Let her know there will be other babies." My grandmother stood up and came to give me a hug. "I like her for you, I can see the love between the two of you. Don't let anyone come in between you two." She gave my mother a harsh look and waved her hands at her. "Well don't just sit there wit ya rude ass. It's time to go. Just time for me and past time for you. So, come on." I walked them out and then went up to my bedroom. Ma'Kenna was sitting on the edge of the bed, crying hysterically.

"Shorty, what happened?" I asked sitting down next to her and taking her in my arms.

"I started spotting this morning, but I didn't think it was a big deal. But when I went for my check up I was bleeding more, like my period was coming on. They said I lost the baby. I wasn't very far along, so I most likely didn't even notice it today once I started cramping and bleeding. I know this solves our problems, but I just feel so sad." Hearing she lost my baby had me feeling fucked up. Hearing the way she was crying hurt in a different way.

"First of all, this baby was never a fucking problem. Shit I'm sad as fuck too. It's ok for you to be sad, shit I'm sad. That was a part of me and you, I loved that baby." She cried some into my chest and I just held her until she stopped. "You need something," I asked, not knowing if she was in pain still.

"I'm good. And thank you, I mean for everything. Letting us stay here, helping out while I was pregnant. Even with everything we've been through I can say this, you have a good heart." She got up and went to the closet. I watched as she started removing her clothes and placing them on the bed. Those frumpy ass suits she used to wear when she first started working for me. I was confused, I actually had to think about what I was going to say.

"Why the fuck you taking your shit out the closet?"

"I mean, the baby is gone now, me and Sierra can go home." She shrugged like it wasn't nothing. But I could see how broken down she was. They weren't lying when they said loving someone changed you. Any other bitch I wouldn't have noticed shit about her.

"Shorty, why you think I want y'all to leave. Matter of fact put that shit back in the closet. You not leaving me again. I was never letting you leave me, pregnant or not. This your home now and I'm ya nigga. I asked you to give me another chance, you can't just do that?" She shook her head like she was clearing her head from a fog. I didn't even give a fuck about that shit, she was mine. And if she didn't want the beast to come out in me, she had to get on board.

"I'm scared. And honestly I don't think you will ever be ready to settle down, to be with one woman." I could hear the truth in her voice, and it made me feel like shit. I really fucked up a good thing. But I wasn't about to give up, either.

"You know what, that's fair for you to say that. I broke your trust. You want to know why I won't be fucking up again? Because I love you, nothing is more important than that. I love how you smell, how you smile, the way you look with your glasses on, like a sexy ass schoolgirl. Don't you see how content I am with you and Sierra? Money and fame could never buy some real shit. And what we have is real, ma. I thought I was going to die when you stopped fucking wit me. Shit I was paying you for tutoring sessions after I already graduated. That was how bad I wanted to be in your presence. Stop doing that shit where you over analyze everything. Just come tell a nigga that you love him too."

I stepped in her space and looked down on her. "I love you," she whispered, like she was scared to tell me again.

"And I love you. Nothing else matters. You want another baby, or ten I got you. Whatever you want I got you." I kissed her and held her tighter. Shorty was it for me, and even if I had to tie her up in this big ass house, she was going to be mine forever.

EPILOGUE
TWO YEARS LATER

MESSIAH

I looked over at Ma'Kenna as Sierra bounced around in my lap. My shorty was bad as fuck even with the round belly she had in front of her. She was rocking the shit out of an all black dress by Versace with a slit up the side. I reached out and touched her hand and she smiled up at me. "Are you nervous," she asked. Shit I was, but not for the reason she was thinking.

"Not really. I always get nominated for a bunch of these awards. Sometimes I win, I go up and give a speech. Not really much to it." She smiled and squeezed my hand anyway. Normally I didn't know if I was walking away with an award or not, but this year they asked me to perform, then accept rap album of the year, so I had a heads up. That was why I planned it for today. My shorty deserved for the world to know how much I loved her.

The handler for BET motioned from the side of the stage that it was time for me to come back. "Sierra, daddy has to go backstage now." She pouted as I slid her back into her seat.

"Daddy I want to come too, I think you need me," she tried to whisper, but it came out loud as fuck. Everyone around us smiled at her, some laughing. Sierra never let our lives get boring. I had adoption papers drawn up the day Ma'Kenna finally agreed to move in with me. I knew what I wanted, and I wanted to show Kenna I was serious about both of them. She was a package deal, and that was ok with me. Honestly Sierra was the best part.

I performed Motivation, the song I wrote a few years ago for Ma'Kenna and the crowd sang along, hoes screamed dumb shit like always. I swear some of them didn't give fuck that I had a pregnant girl, they would do anything to fuck with me. Wiping my face with the white towel my manager handed me, I stepped to the podium. I thanked Daisy, the singer who announced my award category and ultimately the winner.

"I wanted to start by thanking God, without him I wouldn't be here, wouldn't have any talent to even make this music. My record label, the fans, BET and all the radio stations and DJ's who are playing and promoting my music. Ghost, this music shit wouldn't be a hit without your beats, and my life wouldn't be the same without a friend like you." I was sweating now, the clock was counting down and I knew it was now or never. I found her watching me, her face filled with love and pride.

"And last but not least I have to thank my family. My daughter Sierra, for being the best part of me, my jr. who will be here any day now and their mother, Ma'Kenna. Shorty come up here right quick." Sierra damn near blew the surprise she was so hype about me asking her mom to get married. Luckily she held it together and walked next to her mother, stopping every few seconds to wave at the camera's. The star life came natural to Sierra. Ma'Kenna still hated the media and all the events, but my baby girl soaked all that shit in. She was already boujee as hell, I had to admit it was easy to spoil her. I kept telling myself some day I would be stricter, buy her less toys and shit. But so far it hasn't happened.

Ma'Kenna stopped to stand next to me but I stood and faced her. "Kenna, the first day I saw you I knew you were special. You were the first girl to see the real me, to love me and to show me what true happiness was. I thank you for being a strong, intelligent black woman, an amazing mother and my motivation. I just want to know will you give me the honor of being my wife," I dropped to my knee and held out the two karat princess cut diamond ring. She stood there crying, and I thought for a minute she was going to say no.

"Yes," she finally got out as she threw her arms around me. "It's the savage love for me," she whispered as the crowd cheered around us.

THE END

Made in United States
Orlando, FL
25 March 2025